MOUNTAIN MADE

Center Point
Large Print

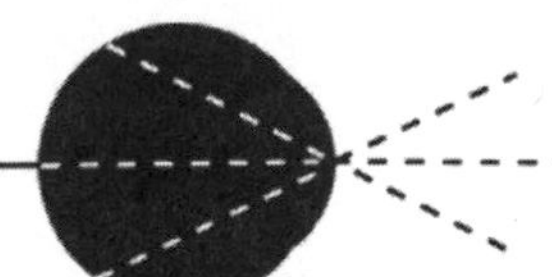

This Large Print Book carries the Seal of Approval of N.A.V.H.

Mountain Made

A Western Story

Max Brand®

Center Point Large Print
Thorndike, Maine

This Center Point Large Print edition
is published in the year 2014 in conjuction with
Golden West Literary Agency.

The text of this Large Print edition is unabridged.
In other aspects, this book may vary
from the original edition.
Printed in the United States of America
on permanent paper.
Set in 16-point Times New Roman type.

ISBN: 978-1-62899-345-5 (hardcover)
ISBN: 978-1-62899-352-3 (paperback)

Library of Congress Cataloging-in-Publication Data

Brand, Max, 1892–1944.
Mountain made : a western story / Max Brand. — Center Point Large Print edition.
pages ; cm
Summary: "Beaten and disfigured by Jack Rutledge, Winsor Glanvil recovers in the mountain den of a she-wolf and her cub. When spring comes, he leaves the den to exact revenge on Rutledge, accompanied by the wolves he has befriended"—Provided by publisher.
ISBN 978-1-62899-345-5 (hardcover : alk. paper)
ISBN 978-1-62899-352-3 (pbk. : alk. paper)
1. Large type books. I. Title.
PS3511.A87M596 2014
813′.52—dc23

2014028581

Mountain Made

Chapter One

Nothing, of course, was at all too good for the wife of Hector Glanvil. He himself drove fifty miles across the mountains to get the best doctor on the range. This was young Mahan, who, coming freshly out of a medical school and a hospital, had made his fame by saving Ham Perkins's little boy from the deadly grip of diphtheria and curing the perennial rheumatism of Joe Chalmers. He became, in the course of a single fortnight, a byword and a prophet among a sparse but widespread population of cattlemen, lumberjacks, miners, hardy sons of toil, with fists as resistless as the heel of a high boot, with oaths more wonderful than those of a conjurer, but, withal, possessing the power of faith. They believed in young Dr. Mahan. They even brought their favorite cutting horses to him in scorn of the veterinaries, and he did his best.

He said to Hector Glanvil: "Man, man, how can I take a day off to drive up to your ranch, and then a day to take care of your wife, and then another day to come back . . . three days when I'm so crowded with work?"

Hector Glanvil laid a hand upon the shoulder of the young doctor. Hector himself was young, but he was a hero, and heroes seem to be of no particular age. When they are young, they seem old. When they are old, they seem young. So it was with Hector. His presence was like that of a great rock face when the fierce brightness of morning is striking upon it, or like a shining silver spruce on the crest of a hill.

So this Hector Glanvil laid his hand upon the shoulder of the doctor and said: "You're tired . . . you're coming up with me to rest . . . you better go pack your bag."

The doctor looked up to the thick shoulders, and up to the noble throat, and up to the glorious face of Hector Glanvil. All the little needs and duties of his life fell away from his consciousness and left him free to serve this man. He felt that Hector Glanvil was a spring of youth in which he would bathe and be renewed in body and soul. So he packed his bag and tumbled into the buckboard.

They began to rush through the mountains as fast as high-blooded horseflesh could whip the buckboard along.

"I suppose it will be a boy?" said the doctor.

"It will be a boy," said Hector calmly, and thereby made it an inescapable fact.

"And the name?" said the doctor.

"The name is Winsor Terence Glanvil."

"A considerable name," said the doctor lightly.

Hector was never jovial. He said with perfect calm: "He will be a considerable man."

The doctor, after all, was only human. He would

have given a great deal if it had been a girl, simply to disprove what Hector had prophesied, but fortune was against him. A boy baby was born the next day. He had hardly opened his eyes when he caught the finger of the nurse in one tiny fist and the finger of the doctor in the other.

"I suppose," said the doctor, "that he will be a ruler of women and of men."

"I suppose," said Hector, who had been watching everything, "that he will."

"Why are you so thoughtful?" asked the doctor afterward. "There you have eight pounds of babyhood and as flawless a little body as I ever saw enter the world . . . he will grow into a glorious manhood!" And he could not help looking up into the bright, calm face of Hector Glanvil.

"Mary's eyes are blue and her hair is gold," said Hector. "My eyes are blue, also, and my hair is brown . . . but Winsor's eyes are brown and his hair is black."

The doctor would have been just a little embarrassed in the presence of any other man.

"Somewhere in the past," said the doctor, "your family or her family has had black hair and brown eyes."

"My great-grandfather and her great-great-grandfather," said Hector instantly.

"You've studied the family trees, I see."

"Naturally. One would study the descent of a good horse, I suppose? And this is my son. What

Mary and I give him is very little, but each of us has a past. This, however, is very odd."

"Why so?"

"I don't mean, you understand, that I think characters are transmitted through a lapse of half a century or more. But my great-grandfather, Terence Glanvil, was a famous beau in his day . . . he was one of those men who make women smile and tremble by merely glancing at them. Mary's great-great-grandfather, Hugh Marston, who had brown eyes and black hair, also, could do the same thing with men. He was a cruel devil. He could pick up a man with a gesture, you might say, and crush the heart out of him. He shot straight by instinct, you might say, and his sword turned into a living thing in his hand." After this, Hector Glanvil paused. He said a little later: "The important thing about both of them was that they used their power."

To this the doctor did not feel like replying. For even a great soul like Hector Glanvil does not care to be questioned about its inner suspicions.

The next day two fresh horses whirled Dr. Mahan out of the mountains and back to his headquarters; he said good bye to Hector Glanvil as to a young god, but he was never to see that young god again. Poor Hector had barely reached his ranch to hear that a forest fire was heading his way. All his timber lands were imperiled. He went out and fought the flames for ten days with all his men and had almost won when a gale leaped out of the north and sent a smooth-sliding arm of the fire around Hector Glanvil and gathered him to the breast of the advancing flames.

There was nothing left for Mary Glanvil except the broad estates of her husband and the son he had left behind. But neither was enough. She waited on earth for two years until Winsor was a strong, hearty infant. Then she closed her eyes and died.

A cousin of Hector Glanvil, a young man called Philip, of the Glanvil name, came out of the East to manage the estate. He gambled away part of it in his first year. In his next two years he speculated to make up for the losses he had inflicted on the estate. In the fourth year of his management he fought desperately to avoid the inevitable. And at the end of his fifth year he turned to the last resort of a confused man. He shot himself through the head.

There was nothing left—absolutely nothing. Mary was the last of the Marstons. Philip was the last of the Glanvils. The joint heir of both those lines and all the long glories of their past histories had not a penny to his name and not a relative to furnish him with means. He was mysteriously shuffled about and in the general direction of an orphan asylum. But children hate orphan asylums. They hate institutions of any kind—as though they understand that in such a place the delicate flower of childhood is cropped at once, half opened, and only the naked stem of existence remains.

Winsor Terence Glanvil was brought to the door of the asylum, so to speak, and then he disappeared. There was a feeble search for him by people who really did not care. Before they finished searching, Winsor was five hundred miles or more to the south. He had simply gone down to the railroad station and crawled onto the rods beneath a coach. He almost died of fatigue and exposure, but, when he crawled out from his unpleasant place the next day, he was in a new and very different land.

There was a broad valley with mountains piled about it, blue and red and purple mountains carved out of uncarvable rock as hard as diamonds, and one solitary peak at the end of the valley living in a golden mist of sunshine. Below the mountains time had made a carefully leveled plain and sent a lazy brown river running through the midst. There was water enough to have turned all the valley into a lovely garden, but the men who lived there did not care for such arduous labors. Only random spots of greenery edged the river. Here—there—and again farther up the valley, there were three little towns with shining white walls and red roofs and clustering trees.

Winsor climbed back under the train. At noon he was in one of those towns. A brakeman fished him out and held him at arm's length, dangling.

"Where did you drop from?" he asked.

"I just happened along," said Winsor, and, although he was more than half choked, he smiled at the strong man.

The brakeman beheld that smile and felt the iron in his heart melt away, and a spreading spot of warm compassion passed over his soul. He carried Winsor home to his wife.

His wife dropped the boy into a bathtub, tugged clean stockings over his legs, and combed his tangled hair. She put a white shirt on him and looked over her work. Straightway she ran out to her husband, gasping with astonishment.

"He looks like a young prince," she said. "He says his name is Winsor Terence Glanvil. That has a big sound to it."

"Sounds ain't dollars," said her spouse. "But we'll keep the poor kid till we find out where he belongs."

That afternoon, the brakeman's wife dressed up Winsor and tied a flowing bow tie under his chin and took him out on the street. She strolled with him where beauty would be admired—in the Mexican quarter—and, when she brought him out, his pockets were stuffed with candy and trinkets. For everywhere that he looked with those big eyes and that quiet little smile, fat *señoras* and slender young *señoritas* hurried out to see him and squat down before him and laugh and murmur with pleasure over him. Then she took him into the hilly section of the town where the big houses of the well-to-do stood. In ten minutes a carriage drew up to the sidewalk and a withered lady leaned out to say: "Is that your little boy?"

The little boy looked at the withered lady and wrinkled his nose in distaste. But he looked at the fine horses and the silver-mounted harness and the shining body of the carriage and changed his mind. He gave her his best smile and saw her flush and saw her eyes melt.

Afterward there was much talk that resolved itself into: "But what can you do for him, my dear woman?"

So Winsor Terence Glanvil was taken into the carriage and the brakeman's wife, dim of eye and faltering of step, went off down the street. Winsor was glad to see her go, for he was not too young to know that to be raised by her was to be raised to a life of toil, and he was not too young to know that he would never care to toil.

CHAPTER TWO

There is no reason why Sabina Curtis should be given a place here, for the simple reason that in the mind of young Winsor Glanvil she occupied no place at all except that of a source of supplies. Her chief pleasure in life was to have this beautiful boy near her.

And the chief torment of Winsor Glanvil was to be near Sabina Curtis. But after one year of tutoring at home, her care for Winsor and his future made her send him away to a school in the East. After that, he had to see her only during the summer and at the Christmas vacation, and even these visits were not unbroken, for there were always plenty of invitations for Winsor. Not from the other boys at the school, however. He was never popular among them. He did not care for their sports and their games. He did not mingle with them except covertly to roll dice or play cards, for he had all the instinct of the born gambler.

But when mothers came to the school to see their boys, they never failed to notice Winsor Glanvil. His face attracted them; his name attracted them. They always insisted on meeting him, for he had an unobtrusive way of making himself noticed. And when he met them, his manner was so quiet, so easy, so gentle, so smooth, his attitude was so respectful, his big brown eyes so admiringly attentive, and his smile so instant and so involuntary, as they thought, that they could not resist him.

"He's nothing but a sissy," their sons told them.

"There's something to that boy," they would answer. "He has a mind of his own. Besides, poor child, he has had misfortunes enough to break his spirit. No mother . . . no father . . . at his age!"

So Winsor was asked here and there in the summer and in the winter, also. The only sports he learned were those in which a girl could accompany him. He paid not the slightest attention to football, baseball, the track, or crew, those four idols of the college boy's life and his four dreams of greatness. Nothing could have persuaded him to risk his head and his shins in a hockey game. Polo was a bore to Winsor, and boxing was simply brutal. But he learned to swim like a fish; he handled a tennis racket like a master, and he was acceptable in any golf foursome.

These were sociable sports in which the ladies could join. Perhaps the feminine heart was greatly impressed by spectacular deeds upon the gridiron and the track, but he did not care to impress them greatly in the beginning. Not at all. He wished merely to have an opportunity for a quiet little talk now and then—such as one may have between sets at tennis, or walking after a golf ball, or riding knee to knee through the park, or walking at the edge of the surf, or dancing over a polished floor. As for the rough sports—what are they worth?

Only once did he go in for brutal exertions. In the summer before his last year at the school he met a pretty little blonde girl whose brother was captain of the next year's football team. She was full of fire and of scorn. And she told Winsor Glanvil with the brutal frankness of youth that she would never care a whit for any boy who did not have the courage to risk his neck at football.

She was just pretty enough and rich enough to make Winsor take her a little seriously. He spent his spare moments that summer learning how to kick and handle a football. And in the fall he startled the school by coming out for the squad.

It was impossible to keep him out of the backfield. He was so green that he hardly knew in what direction to run, but, when he started correctly, it was like trying to catch an eel. He was sixteen, then, and stood his full height, which was five feet and ten inches. And he weighed a hundred and fifty pounds, which was within ten of his ultimate size. He looked too delicate, too slender, too girlishly smooth for rough work, but he had that surprising, inexpressible strength of a light thing put strongly together. He could twist through a mass of fighting linesmen as though his body were covered with grease. He could clip off tackle so fast that the tacklers saw only a blur of speed.

And when he started around end, the entire opposition grew cold with dread. Besides, because he hated to be hurt, he learned how to avoid a tackler in the open field, and to see him sift through a whole team of eager enemies was enough to thrill the heart of the most expert college coach. And college coaches watched him work and their hearts ached to have him. But when the big game of the school season was over, he sat one evening in a corner with the pretty blonde. After all, he decided, he had made a ridiculous effort for the sake of one with a nose so short as hers. As for her rich father, she had too many brothers to divide the spoils.

So he said: "Football is a stupid game . . . I shall never play it again."

"Oh, Winsor," she cried, "but it will make you a great man in college!"

"I'd rather be comfortable than great," said Winsor. "Good bye."

He lived up to his word. No persuasion could make him try for the college team; for four years he played through his courses, dabbled at the social sports, and, just after he had received his diploma, he got word from Sabina Curtis that she was very sick. He took the first train West, filled with immense hopes. Not that the money of Sabina was enough to give him all that he wanted. But it was enough to enable him to move where great fortunes grow on every tree. So he sat by her deathbed and heard her say that her fortune had been turned into an annuity and that he would not have a penny after her death except her big house and the movables that were in it.

He looked coldly down upon her. “I wish you had warned me a year ago,” he said. “I could have become engaged to the Warner girl last fall, you know.”

“Winsor, Winsor,” murmured the sick woman, straining her dull eyes toward him. “Do you care for nothing in the world except money?”

“Money is nothing to me,” he told her. “But comfort is. I’m not equipped to make a living, you know. You never insisted on that, Aunt Sabina.”

She sighed, and a cloud formed on her brow. “Winsor, do you really care nothing about me and the deep, deep love I have felt for you, dear,” she asked him in an agitated voice.

“Of course I do . . . tremendously,” said Winsor.

He spoke so coldly that it went through and through her heart. And she looked up to him, startled into clear-seeing, for a moment. But when her glance met those big, gentle, brown eyes fixed upon her with what seemed a melting tenderness, all her suspicions vanished.

“Ah, Winsor,” she said to him, “I have loved you as a mother loves her son.”

He leaned above her, wondering if her will was really made out already.

“You have been more than a mother,” he said.

"Do you speak from your heart?" said the poor woman, yearning up to him, and raising her weak hands toward his face.

She was an ugly picture, and Winsor Glanvil hated ugliness in any form. He could not help turning from all that was repulsive to the eye. Now he steeled himself. He called up into his voice a little tremulous fiber of sound that, he had discovered, is peculiarly effective with every woman, old or young.

"Dear Aunt Sabina," he said. "I cannot talk . . . I am too sad. . . ."

He was able to leave a little after that, and a few minutes later she died. Within the hour he had learned the price that he could get for the house and the land and all that was within the old mansion—$50,000.

"But you ought not to sell," said the lawyer when approached later. "Consider those books in the library. To duplicate them would cost you fifty thousand dollars alone . . . I mean their bindings done afresh without any of the charm and the allusions that these old books have."

"I am a Glanvil, not a Curtis," said Winsor. "I desire to sell everything at once, and I hope that you will arrange for it."

The lawyer swallowed certain hot words that had formed in the deep of his throat and went away to do as he was ordered. Yet he could not refrain from a touch of irony when he handed

Winsor Glanvil a check for $48,500 a few days later.

"You have done amazingly well with yourself, Glanvil," he said. "Fourteen years ago you were without a penny in the world. Here, at the age of twenty-one, you have equipped yourself with a fine education, fifty thousand dollars in cash, and no regrets, I presume?"

Glanvil knew perfectly well what the other was driving at, but he merely lighted a cigarette and mocked the lawyer with a smile through the mist of blue-brown smoke.

"I am only an amateur so far," he said with equal irony to the man of the law. "I hope to do better later on."

"Ah, well," said the lawyer. "I rather doubt that. I think you were born with the professional touch, young man. But," he added when he reached the door, "I suppose that you have plans for increasing the fifty thousand greatly before long?"

The one thing that Glanvil had always lacked to make him a successful gambler, he felt, was a large bank roll. Now he nodded with the utmost complacency. "Of course," he said.

The lawyer broke into loud and very rude laughter and left the house; Glanvil walked out after him. He had a fortune in his pocket, a laugh on his lips, and not a single regret, as the lawyer had suggested, in his heart. For the past never bothered Glanvil. Nothing but the future lay before him.

Chapter Three

Now four swift years passed over the head of Winsor Terence Glanvil. It is, as a rule, a sign of peace when the annals of a country are a blank, but these were not blank years with young Glanvil. But since the events wrote not a line into his face, it is permissible to omit the record of what actually happened.

We leap across the four years that had carried Mr. Glanvil around the globe but brought him back, after so much wandering, to his native West. To follow his trail we leave the railroad and advance to a little town in the mountains from which rough roads lead here and there to mines near the timberline. We come to a little unpainted shack of two stories, dignified with the name of hotel, and in the hotel we go to the best front room. There sits Winsor Glanvil. He has before him the mirror—not of the room, but from his own leather toilet case—he has a lighted lamp upon either side of him—and he is busy manicuring his nails with the care of a precisian, with the speed of an artist. What has become of the varied interests of Winsor Glanvil? Where is the tidy fortune with which he started out upon his wanderings in search of an easy life? There is nothing left—nothing except the toilet case and the big, roomy suitcase that could contain a whole trunk full of odds and ends. That is all that he has accumulated—physically. In the brain there are gathered all manner of talents that do not show outwardly, for in his face we look in vain for a single trace of the passing of time. There is not a line about his mouth nor near the corner of his eyes; there is not a shadow; there is not the slightest crease between his eyes. His face is as untouched as that of an infant.

Such was the Winsor Terence Glanvil who rose in answer to a knock at his door. He opened to a dark-faced man well advanced in middle age, dapper and trim as a youth.

"It is true!" he cried. "It is true, after all! It is the immortal *Monsieur* Glanvil himself!"

"You are Paul Santelle," said Glanvil, and drew him through the door. He went on, without emotion: "Why are you here?"

"You are not overfilled with friendliness, my dear Glanvil. Your eye does not light when you see me. You do not wring my hand."

He did not say this with the slightest sharpness of irony, but smiling in perfect good nature.

"As you know," said Glanvil, "I detest action and love repose. Besides, I am really curious as to what can have brought you here."

"Can you imagine nothing?"

"One can imagine a thousand things on the smallest grounds. But as I said before, I hate effort. Please do not force me to imagine to deduce . . . to analyze like Poe's detective."

"What is that?"

A thunder of hoof beats, a rush of shouting voices—then came the sound of doors slamming, a deep, throbbing tumult through the street.

"Go to the window and look at the picture if you wish," said Glanvil. "I prefer to sit still. I suppose there's another gold strike. In the meantime, you cannot doubt my hospitality. I offer you my best chair."

Santelle nodded at the window. "They are going mad, as usual," he announced. "This must be something real. In a day or two I suppose we'll have a few more of these incipient millionaires in town. I hope so."

"You are doing business here, then?" asked Glanvil.

"Yes."

"I am sorry to hear it."

"*Tush,* man. I would not cramp you for room. There is enough food here to supply a dozen even of such hawks as you and I. The field is so open that, when I first came, it was possible to work bad dice on them. They didn't want to win, I swear. They wanted the thrill of losing their money as fast as they could, and that was all." He laughed softly, contentedly. "I have been here seven days . . . I have made a shade over seven thousand, working only an hour or two a day."

Glanvil was not impressed. “That,” he said, “is wages. When are you to make your profit?”

Santelle stared at him, but then nodded in good-natured agreement. “You, of course, are the plunger, the star taker,” he said. “Remember that I have seen you at Nice and in Buenos Aires. In fact, you have always been so successful that I wonder why the devil it is that you have to keep at the work?”

Glanvil regarded him with a perfect equanimity. He said, with the calm of one who reserves lies for important occasions and believes in the truth for nearly all the affairs of everyday life: “My total possessions are in this room. I have fifteen hundred in cash. The rest you can see.”

Santelle shook his head. “I understand,” he said. “You have invested in some Mexican revolution? Is it that?”

“It is not that.”

“What, then? Man, man, I have seen you take in so many thousands in a single night. . . .”

“Why should I lie to you?” murmured Glanvil. “As a matter of fact, my dear friend, there is only the one answer. I occasionally meet with a gambler cleverer than I am. His tricks are better . . . he cheats with more skill. And there goes my money. You understand? But of course you do.”

“It amazes me,” declared Santelle with warmth. “I swear to you. Glanvil, I believed there were not three men in the world capable of . . .”

"Nonsense," answered Winsor Glanvil. "You are flattering me now."

"But even discounting the cards," said Santelle. "Ten thousand pardons if I'm too curious."

"Not at all," answered Glanvil. "I am fond of talking . . . particularly about myself. And at this very moment I am in the humor for chatting. Say what you please and dip the bucket until I feel like cutting the rope."

"Very well, Glanvil. Suppose that you left the cards to one side, and abandoned all gambling whatsoever, still you have remaining 'that one talent which is death to hide'. I really cannot comprehend why you have not connected yourself with some great fortune."

Over this, Glanvil paused for a moment. "We seem to be more intimate than I thought," he said.

"I was in Venice when you and Costello . . ."

Glanvil raised his hand. "That is quite enough," he said.

"You admit that I have reason to be astonished. The lovely countess, everyone said, was only too eager to give away her fortune and herself to Mister Glanvil."

"There is one hideous drawback that handicaps me hopelessly, as it seems, as a fortune hunter."

"What is that?"

"I am infernally particular as to the lady who is to share the name of Glanvil."

It might have been considered an atrocious

stroke of egotism except for the smile of the speaker.

"It is an old name, I have heard," said Santelle with much interest.

"Immensely old. It goes back past the Conquest a dizzy distance. I am foolish about it."

"But the family of the countess . . ."

"Was old, also. But she had a voice like a chorus girl's. I endured it for a week. That was enough. And that, Santelle, is the secret of my failures."

"One can be too critical, of course. But a million or so, one might think, would sweeten a very sour cup."

"I have tried to close my eyes and my ears a dozen times. I never quite succeed."

"Surely," said Santelle, "there are a few charming girls . . ."

"With great fortunes? Of course. But I have a past. Now and then a wave of it overtakes me and forces me to move on. However, I am still able to amuse myself. Now, my dear Santelle, what is all this about?"

"It is about a nonpareil."

"You have a system for the wheel," suggested the fortune hunter, yawning.

"I have not. It is a lady, my friend."

"With money, of course."

"With uncounted millions."

"I suppose so."

"This is an indubitable fact."

"The whole world knows about her, then."

"Therein lies the charm. She is unknown except to a very few."

"But how large is the fortune, really?"

"At least eight millions . . . perhaps fifteen."

"This sounds like a great affair, Santelle. However, she is being courted already. . . ."

"Of course. Wherever there is honey, the bees will find it out. But they have only begun to come. They find everything so simple, however, that they are filled with doubts."

"Tell me, Santelle, what do you hope out of this?"

"One third, my dear Glanvil."

"You are modest."

"I tell you, I am leading you to a gold mine."

"Which is already staked out and claimed by others."

"Not at all. They cannot disturb her. She is a romantic little soul . . . and not one of them can stir her. But when she meets Glanvil and his old-world manner, when she encounters those brown eyes and that famous smile . . ."

"Don't talk like an ass."

"However, I tell you that you have only to appear in order to conquer. This girl knows nothing."

"Tell me the secret."

"Easily. Her father was a prospector for the bigger part of his life. His wife died young. That left Louise to play the housekeeper and take care of old Joseph Carney when he returned from his trips. He brought very little cash back with him. Sometimes she was pretty close to starvation. But she was so used to it that she didn't complain. She had books. She was a great deal alone. For a companion she finally found a blind girl, a queer thing named Kate Preston. And Kate has been the only friend of Louise Carney for several years.

"Old Joe Carney struck gold, at last. But he didn't splurge. He rebuilt the old cabin and gave Louise a cook and a maid. That was to begin with . . . and he didn't go much past it. He tore gold out of the ground as fast as his men could blast the rock away. He dumped that money into lumber lands. He built twenty miles of railroad into his lumber lands. For six years he lived in a hurricane of falling money. Then he died. Louise is twenty-one. She lives still in the cabin on the side of the mountain. Her lawyer writes to her from Denver and gives her statements, mentions large sums . . . she doesn't know what he's talking about, and I don't think that she cares. She has her house, her cook, her maid, and her garden. She has a horse to ride on and a dog to go alongside her. That's life enough for her.

"In a single word, she dreams, my dear Glanvil. And she is waiting for a man to come to her out of a dream and show her what can be done with life in the way of making it beautiful. There have been a few clumsy fellows to bother her. But they are nothing. It is you, Glanvil, who must descend like a god in a cloud of fire."

"That," said Glanvil, "is enough. Tell me only one thing. Is she at least ordinarily good-looking?"

"Glanvil, she is an exquisite beauty, made of gold and rose and blue and ivory. Do you understand?"

"I understand. A pretty face, and big feet. A charming smile and calloused hands."

Santelle waved both hands in a gesture filled with emotion. "When you see her, you will be ravished, believe me. I tell you, she is as harmonious as music."

"This begins to appear more and more promising."

"There is only the single drawback."

"What is that?"

"The blind girl."

"You are jesting."

"You will understand when you meet the household. That is the danger point. If you can defend yourself from her wit, you are safe. The blind girl is the outward fortification. Beautiful Louise is the defenseless city itself."

CHAPTER FOUR

When Glanvil first saw her, she was in the garden, that bright little patch of color that rested on the shoulder of the mountain and seemed about to slide off into the awful ravine beneath. She was training some sort of limber-armed flowering vines over an arched trellis work, weaving the vines in and out among the slats and tying them with short bits of twine.

He called to her: "Is Mister Carney at home?"

At this, she raised her head. It was brown hair, and yet there was enough light struck through it by the sun to justify what Santelle had said about gold; certainly, however, he was wrong about the rose. It was a pale, calm face, and even while she turned toward him, her eyes were lowered toward the ground.

"Mister Carney is not here," she said.

He liked her voice. He liked it very much. But it destroyed, instantly, the impression of childish impotence and innocence that Santelle had given him concerning the heiress, for there was as much self-control, as much easy surety, as there could have been in the voice of a man.

"I understood that this was Mister Carney's house."

"Mister Carney is dead, sir."

She began to work while she faced him, work without giving an apparent glance to the employment of her hands. How swiftly they drew the fragile branches through the trellis, and yet with how delicate a tenderness, also.

"I am sorry to hear of that, but perhaps it is better for me. I have admired the situation of this house so much, that I should like to buy it and all the ground around it, if possible. Do you think that it could be arranged?"

"I hardly know," she said. "Almost anything is possible, I suppose. But if you care for the place, come into the garden, please. Everyone says that the view is much finer from this point."

He dismounted and tethered his horse at the hitching rack. The ghost of Santelle seemed to be moving behind him in his shadow, laughing and clapping him on the back with a viewless hand. He himself had to bite his lip to keep from smiling. It was all so very easy.

So he crossed the garden and stood beside her. She was not such a heart stopper as Santelle had led him to expect. She was as pale as marble, not a sickly color, however, but a translucent pallor. When she looked down, the deep fringe of lashes seemed to lay a shadow beneath her eyes. When she looked up, the eyes themselves were a sort of dull black, unlike any eyes in all the world so far as he had seen.

"Here," she said as he came beside her, "you can

see a great deal of the valley itself. One can feel the wind from the mountains cutting straight across. And no matter how hard the wind blows, one can hear the river."

There was a dizzy fall of the eye, in fact, to the white waters of the river. Now the morning mist lay thick between and tinted the river with pale blue. And the dark forests hung like irregular rolling clouds of smoke along the steep sides of the mountain. A bridge, small as a child's toy, at that distance, crossed the water just before it spread across the valley in a lake. The beauties of Nature meant very little to Glanvil. But now he was stirred.

"It is more than I expected . . . a great deal more," he said truthfully. "May I give you my name? I am Winsor Glanvil. You are Miss Carney, I presume?"

"I am . . . Katherine Preston," she said. He set his teeth hard. Of course he had been the most consummate fool not to have guessed before that this was the blind girl. And yet that adroit work with her hands, the surety with which she looked straight into his face as he talked were enough to have deceived him even if he had guessed beforehand.

"Do you know if Miss Carney would sell?"

"I don't know. I hardly think so. But one never can tell. Miss Carney may move before the winter comes."

“That is a strange thing,” said Glanvil, “that a person could wish to leave such a place.”

“Are you not very young, Mister Glanvil, to wish to live in such a quiet spot among the mountains?”

And she fixed those dark eyes upon him with so much thoughtfulness in her expression that he had the uncanny feeling that she must be reading his face. He found himself forming a smile with as much care as though she could see it.

“I suppose I am,” he said, and he watched the incredible delicacy with which she passed a limber branch of the vine through her fingers, touched all of the hundred papery blossoms along its length, but not disturbing a single petal. “I suppose I am, but I want to feel what it means to be snowed in for a whole winter.”

“Miss Carney is coming,” said the blind girl.

“How can you tell?”

“By the step of her horse.”

“Is it different from other horses?”

“One can tell, somehow. But my ears have to be eyes, also, you know.”

“Do they help you to read faces?”

“Not faces . . . no. But I think they help me to find what is in the hearts of people, you see.”

He found that he had grown actually restless and ill at ease in front of this girl, as though that eye of her mind, fixed so mysteriously upon him, saw nothing of his physical being but looked clearly into the wickedness of his soul.

"At least," she said, "Miss Carney will be interested in your wish for a . . . winter home."

He looked intently at her to see if she were smiling, but her face was as grave as her great dark eyes, and these were so filled with light and with meaning that it seemed to him, for the hundredth time, that this pretended blindness was nothing but a sham.

A moment later, Louise Carney was with them. She was what Santelle had described, hardly larger than a child, and full of a child's happy carelessness, a flower-like indolence. Kate Preston introduced them. As for the work of the excellent Glanvil, he saw that it was finished almost before it was begun, for the rich man's daughter watched him with a child's openness, a child's utter fascination. She did not have sufficient art to look down to the ground, but let him see clearly in her eyes all that passed in her mind, much as a little girl stares at the image of the perfect prince that rises before her from the page of the story book.

Indeed, the work was ended before it had well begun. Another touch was all he needed to make her his. Glanvil smothered a yawn at the very thought, for, through long hours of weariness, how dearly he would have to pay for the fortune he took. However, it is impossible to get something for nothing.

"Mister Glanvil wants to spend a winter snowed

in, and he would like to buy your house, Louise," said Kate Preston.

"Oh," she said. "It was my father's house, Mister Glanvil."

"You would not sell it, then?"

"When he has left me so much money . . . how could I? It would be a shameful thing."

"I am a thousand times sorry," said Glanvil. "I merely saw the house and thought I might get it."

She nodded, watching him in that same eager, incredulous fashion, as though every feature of his face were a miracle.

"Good bye," said Glanvil.

"Wait!" called the girl. He could see her full of fear at the thought of losing him.

"The very best view is from the second story . . . isn't it, Kate?"

"I don't think so," said Kate, still with those grave, over-wise eyes fixed upon the new man.

"I'd be very happy to see it," said Glanvil.

They went into the house together, then he dropped back to the side of Kate Preston, who had followed.

"May I help you?" he asked her.

She looked up to him with the faintest of smiles upon her lips. "I don't know," she murmured. "Perhaps you had better stay with me for a little while."

What had she been able to discover—what had she been able to guess? That faint, sad smile filled him with apprehension. For, although she could have seen nothing, perhaps that ear that knew the tread of a horse and heard the voice of the river in spite of the wind had been able to read the tone of his voice and the tone of the voice of Louise.

He was so filled with that idea that he was gloomily silent as he joined Louise on the floor above. He saw that she was troubled by that silence of his; with only half of his mind he followed the chatter of her talk. He heard her, but from the corner of his eye he was watching Kate. The blind girl had gone to the window on the farther side of the room, and there she stood with her head raised and such a light in her eyes as though, in very fact, she saw the mountains before her.

He remembered the warning of Santelle, but now it had a doubly trenchant point. He had never seen another woman like her, nor another man. And he knew, above all, that nothing in his soul of souls was escaping her.

"Does she see nothing?" he could not help whispering to the girl.

She shook her head. "Kate was born blind," she declared. "Why do you ask?"

"Because she seems to be looking."

"I know what you mean. Nothing bothers me so much as that. To have her reading my mind."

A chill ran over the body of the fortune hunter. "Does she do that?" he asked.

"Oh, of course. Everyone knows that she can."

It was not true. Of course it could not be true. And yet a perspiration broke out on him.

What was Louise saying about the valley?

"The best time to see it is the break of day . . . but next to that in the late afternoon . . . you must come to have tea with us. Then you can see it with the mist gone and the shadows . . . you really must come."

"I shall be very happy to."

"This afternoon, if you wish."

She waited with her lips parted, her eyes wide, like a child begging for a favor.

Glanvil bit his lip. "Of course," he said. "That would be perfect."

And he heard Kate Preston, at her window, sigh and turn away with all the light gone from her face.

Chapter Five

When he got back to town, Santelle was already waiting at his room in the hotel, busily writing at a table. He called over his shoulder: "Well, Glanvil, you found her?"

"Yes."

"It was easier than you dreamed, eh?"

"What makes you think that?"

"I heard you whistling down the street."

"It's a pleasant day, Santelle."

"Nonsense. Weather never made that difference to you!" He added, as he finished his writing: "I hope you're a grateful fellow, Glanvil."

"I haven't the slightest idea how things could turn out," lied Glanvil.

"Well, in case they do turn out well, I have a little paper here for you." He passed it to Glanvil, who read:

> I, Winsor Terence Glanvil, agree that in case of a marriage between me and Louise Carney, one third of all the money and the value of property which I receive through that marriage shall be paid over to Paul Santelle.
>
> (Signed)

Glanvil laughed lightly and tossed the paper back. "I am not an absolute ass, my friend," he said.

"This was all agreed," Santelle reminded him. "This was all planned before I took you here to the gold mine."

"By way of conversation," said Glanvil, "one is apt to say all manner of foolish things. But as for a legal contract . . . why, Santelle, I am apt to have the entire estate, one of these days, and, if I get nine millions, you expect to have three of them? That obviously is absurd."

"Not for my work."

"You have been a mere sign post on the road to a fortune."

"I came to you in the nick of time. I tell you, this girl would have been married within a month. She's ready to be plucked. There are twenty youngsters who are as keen as fire after her. If it had not been for the sign post, Glanvil, you would have found the claim already preëmpted."

"Trust to my generosity," said Glanvil. "But as for the signing of documents . . . on my honor, I detest such a thought."

Santelle showed no passion. He kept the paper in his hand, smoothing the wrinkles from it with the most scrupulous care. "I am to be defrauded," he said carelessly. "I am to be left on the rail with nothing. Is that the plan?"

"Not at all. You know that I am generous, Santelle."

"I hear you announce that fact at present. I have never heard of it before. You are acting a very foolish part, Glanvil."

"Am I? What is your power, Santelle?"

"A great one. I simply let something concerning the past of this Winsor Glanvil escape from me. . . ."

Glanvil shook his head. "I have no fear of that. The more salt you sprinkle on the fire, the brighter the flames will burn. Opposition is the food of love, my dear fellow."

"It isn't the girl," said Santelle. "No, no. I would never dream of going to a girl to damn her lover. That is the best way to make her marry him at once. The nearest I ever came to marrying a fortune myself was by hiring some rascals to go around to her and tell her the truth about myself. That truth was really so black that she would not believe it. She would have married me instantly if the parents had not had wind of what was about to happen. They were off in an instant . . . they packed up their baggage and packed up the girl as well. In a single day they were started across the ocean. I lost at least four millions."

"Of dollars?"

"Of *francs* . . . which is fortune enough. I am of moderate tastes. I am not like you, Glanvil."

"But this news you could spread about concerning me . . . where would you go with it?"

Santelle took him to the window. "He was there a moment ago on the porch of the general merchandise store. Yes, there he is now. Not the old chap and not the boy. The big man with the hat pushed onto the back of his head."

Glanvil looked down on a Hercules, a man with the bulk of an ox and the fine finish of a greyhound; he looked big enough to lift a horse and fleet enough to outrun a dog.

"Who is that?" he asked.

"That is Jack Rutledge. Look him over with care, Glanvil. Two years ago a grizzly hugged him . . . and he killed the grizzly. Some men say he did it with his bare hands, and they are almost believed. That is the confidence that people in these mountains have in Jack Rutledge. Of course he had a knife. But a man who can kill a grizzly with a little hunting knife . . . do you know much about the big bears, Glanvil?"

"Not a thing in the world."

"I have seen a grizzly knock a three-hundred-pound black bear twenty feet, head over heels, and landed him against a tree so hard that it knocked the wind out of the black chap. Well, this is only by the way to make you appreciate what Rutledge did. Look at him again."

And Winsor Glanvil, looking again, saw the story of the bear fight at once made a possibility. The long, strong jaw of Jack Rutledge and the sharp, restless eyes placed under the shadow of a sternly arched nose were the type of the hero, the superman. Not a calm and glorious hero, such as he had seen in the family pictures of his father, Hector Glanvil, but a savage, relentless, battle-loving fellow with the ferocity of a leopard and the crushing power of a lion. Such was the appearance of Jack Rutledge.

"But what has he to do with this affair?" asked Glanvil.

"One or two things that will interest you. In the first place he is a lover of Louise Carney."

"In that capacity I don't fear him a whit. That scalped, ugly mountain, yonder, would have as good a chance of winning her."

"Perhaps. But there's another thing. He's the leader of the men in this part of the range. He's a sort of demigod here."

"And the bearing of that is . . . ?"

"Give me time, my friend. I wish to show you just how important Jack Rutledge is to you . . . and to me . . . at this stage of our little game. Jack Rutledge, you might say, is the god of justice in these mountains. He's an exceptional fellow."

"At least forty pounds above the average," said Glanvil, sneering.

"You have to hear me out. He's a college man, this Rutledge. But when he got through with college, he decided that he cared more for these mountains than he did for the law. He gave up his career . . . and a devilishly promising one it was . . . and came to these mountains to live. Here he has settled down. He has a little ranch tucked away in a hollow . . . a few hundred acres of grazing land and a quarter section of farm. He makes a living off of that land . . . no more than a living, however. So you see it isn't with money that he buys his power."

Winsor Glanvil yawned and slipped lower in his chair into a comfortable position.

"It will be over soon," said Santelle, his sharp eyes glittering at Glanvil with a suppressed anger. "I want to show you what strength this fellow Rutledge has. Two years ago, two of the oldest politicians in the county ran for sheriff. Rutledge didn't approve of either of them. They were both hand in glove with the crooks. They caught the little fellows and let the big fellows go free. Yellow curs, you see, but they were well known and well liked. However, Rutledge stepped in and put his foot down. He selected a young chap who was known simply as an ignorant hunter. He made that fellow run for sheriff and elected him by the sheer weight of his personal influence. I tell you that to show you his strength in the land."

"And what sort of a sheriff did the hunter make?"

"A hawk, a regular hunting hawk, Glanvil. He's run crime into the ground. He's caught the rustlers in traps . . . he's trailed down the longriders . . . and he's made this county a big black spot on the map of every crook in the country . . . because Rutledge knows a man when he sees one. In fact, he can do what he pleases here, and no one asks a question. If they want to raise the salary of the schoolteacher, they go to Rutledge and ask him what he thinks about it.

"I heard an odd story a little while ago. The blacksmith had trouble with his wife, chiefly because the blacksmith was too fond of moonshine. Finally the wife left and went to Denver to live with her sister's family. The blacksmith pretended that he didn't give a damn, you understand . . . until Rutledge heard about it and went to him. Nobody knows exactly what Rutledge said. But, the next day, the blacksmith started for Denver, and he came home with his wife. Rutledge had given him the price of three tickets and a new suit of clothes. They're the happiest couple in the town, now, people tell me. All because of Rutledge. You see what the fellow can do? He can reach the highest and the lowest in the country.

"The rich man, Will Clawson, was about to foreclose on the poorest devil of a rancher in the whole county . . . named Joe Carpaccio. Rutledge went upcountry and asked Clawson to hold off. Clawson told him to go to the devil. So Rutledge went away and came back with twenty men behind him. That made Clawson change his mind. He gave Carpaccio time to pay interest and principal. Rutledge and the rest helped poor Joe out of the hole. Now Carpaccio is a prosperous man, comparatively. And even Clawson is glad that he didn't foreclose."

"It looks to me that your friend Rutledge has his hand in everyone's business."

"Not *my* friend," said Santelle, with a grimace. "Because his eye is a bit too sharp for me, Glanvil. He looks through me and sees that I'm a crook, just as he would look through you and see that you're a crook."

Glanvil sat up abruptly. "Do you class me with yourself?" he asked, sneering.

"Lower," said Santelle, with the slowness of cold conviction. "Much lower. I've come out of the gutter and risen to be a . . . gentleman crook. You are the son of Hector Glanvil, and here you sit planning dirty work with me."

Glanvil smiled and sank back in the chair again, watching the other from beneath his lowered, long lashes.

"Very well," he said with a brutal terseness, although his voice was as soft as ever. "We'll let that go and get down to the point of this business. You want a third of the profits from this marriage. I say that a flat cash reward is enough."

"How much cash, my friend?"

"Say . . . five thousand?"

Santelle laughed without mirth.

"Or ten thousand at the most."

"It won't do, Glanvil."

"Then you get nothing. And now what's the gun you can put to my head?"

"The gun is Rutledge. I go to him after the

engagement is announced and tell him what I know about you."

"Suppose, my friend, that I slip away with the girl and marry her before you have time to turn around?"

"That would be extremely rash. In that case, I give you my word that Rutledge would think nothing of following you and shooting you like a dog."

"He would never take the chance," said Glanvil, growing a little pale.

"Glanvil, have I been talking in vain?"

Glanvil rose from his chair and went again to the window, and so he looked carefully down on the lounging form of big Jack Rutledge.

"Now that I have a chance to think everything over," he said at last, turning around on Santelle again, "I suppose that your services in the matter are really worth about a third of the profits."

"Ah," purred Santelle. "I knew that you would be reasonable in the end." He held forward the paper. "This is ready to be signed," he said.

Chapter Six

Glanvil had no intention of hurrying affairs. But it was impossible to go slowly. If he made a motion, Louise Carney made a whole step. She had a habit of fixing her eyes upon his face as though she were reading a book, and every change in his expression was more than words to her. By the third day he knew that he had only to speak in order to have her accept him as her fiancé. But he put that moment off because of a belated sense of the appropriate. For now and then it came over him that, although her years were the years of a woman, her mind was the mind of a child, a child delightfully done in gold and blue, in rose and ivory.

They had tea together on that first day. On the second, they rode far away through the hills and along the side of Croton Mountain. On the third day there was a walk. On the fourth day they were engaged for a picnic in the woods, and he purposely remained away and sent up a message that unexpected business detained him. But, on the fifth day, he was with her again. And big Jack Rutledge was leaving as he arrived. Louise introduced them. She laid one hand on the arm of Jack Rutledge and smiled up into his face—that arm like the trunk of a tree, that stern face, strong and immobile as the statue of an Egyptian king.

"This is my dearest and my oldest friend . . . this is Jack Rutledge," she said. "When we had hard days . . . that seems so long ago . . . we could never have gotten on if it hadn't been for Jack."

Glanvil resented that remark, for he already had a possessive sense about her. When she was his wife, however, he would very soon teach her certain differences to be observed in speech and in manners. Certainly she would never be allowed to express any sense of obligation to a rough, common fellow like this. Certainly she would never be allowed to refer to the days of her poverty.

This he registered quietly in his mind while he shook hands with Rutledge and felt fingers as hard as oak close over his own soft palm. And, moreover, the eyes of Rutledge, rather small and very bright like the eyes of a great bird of prey, stared through him. He remembered what Santelle had said, that this man would see straight into the truth of such rascals as the pair of them. And, for the moment, he almost believed Santelle.

It frightened him.

"Dear Jack . . . poor old Jack," said the girl as she led him into the garden.

He did not have to ask her why she was pitying the big man. It was simply because "poor Jack" had again proposed on this unlucky day and had been refused. He determined on the spot that he would risk no more delay. As long as those keen, determined eyes were apt to probe into his past, it was better to have the business over and done with at once. He decided that on this day he would ask Louise to marry him. And what place would be better chosen for that ceremony than the garden? It was a delightful day, the air new-washed by a rain, cool, fresh, and the sky the pure and transparent blue that lives only in the heavens above mountaintops. There was only a single blur—a mass of wind-driven cloud flying from the top of Mount Croton like a tremendous battle flag.

Kate Preston stood up as they came near. She gathered up some flowers that lay beside her and turned away toward the house.

“Do you have to go in, Kate?” asked Louise Carney in half-hearted protest.

“I have to go in,” said the blind girl. “Good afternoon, Mister Glanvil.”

“How could you possibly tell that it was I?” he broke out, amazed for the tenth time by her prescience.

“By your step,” she said. “And by the voice of Louise.”

And she went off down the garden path as freely and surely as though her dark eyes were wells of the truest sight. Only at the garden steps she made a little pause, and went slowly up them, like an old woman feeling for the stairs. They watched her pass into the house and out of sight.

"Oh," said Louise, "when I think how wonderfully beautiful she would be if she had a meaning in her eyes . . . dear Kate."

Glanvil frowned. He had never connected the blind girl with any thought of beauty. But, after all, she was beautiful, except that she was a little too pale.

"She doesn't like me, I'm afraid," he said, speaking aloud his ever-present thought.

By the guilty little start of Louise he knew that his guess had been close enough to the truth.

"Of course she does," said the girl. "Why shouldn't she?"

"I don't know," Glanvil said honestly enough. "I really don't know. But from the first day, she didn't like me."

"You must be wrong."

He turned and faced her squarely. "Am I really wrong?" he asked.

At this, she flushed. "You see," she said gently, "Kate is full of intuitions. And she lacks one sense that the rest of us have. So that if she is a little strange in her judgments now and then, we have to be gentle with her, don't we?"

"By all means," answered Glanvil.

He would provide for the blind girl, he decided, after the marriage. But Louise should never see her again. It was too dangerous—much too dangerous. He feared Jack Rutledge because of the keenness in his sharp eyes; he feared the blind girl because of some mysterious power that he could not comprehend. She had shrunk from him, spiritually, on the very first day of their meeting.

He said aloud: "What can have prejudiced her against me?"

"Almost nothing, at first. And then, just today . . . there was an ugly . . ." She stopped, and bit her lip.

"An ugly what?" asked Glanvil, with a thrill of apprehension.

"Nothing," she said.

"Will you tell me?"

"You are angry."

"It is all very odd," he said, making his voice cold.

And she melted at once. It was most miraculous that his power over her should be so complete. Other women had been subdued by that same voice, that same smile, and the beauty of Glanvil's face, but not one with such dizzy speed as Louise Carney.

"I should not say a thing about it," she pleaded. "I said that I wouldn't."

"Hasn't one a right," he demanded, "to know when there are scandals buzzed about him?"

"But I didn't believe it!" she exclaimed.

"There have been scandals brought to you about me, then?" he said.

"Ah," said Louise, "you mustn't ask."

“Some coward has tried to poison your mind against me.”

“No. You mustn’t call Jack Rutledge a coward . . . you mustn’t call him that.”

“Rutledge!” exclaimed Glanvil in much the same tone that he would have used to say: “Fate!”

“It was only a rumor that came to him.”

“But he brought you the rumor?”

“You see, Jack is very fond of me. Very. He has been more than a brother to me. And so, when he heard this ugly thing, for my sake . . . he . . . he came up and told me. And . . . oh, I should never have let you know.”

The cold thrills of fear were working like snakes up and down the back of Glanvil.

“What did he tell you?”

“I can’t tell.”

“You must. What did he say?”

“I gave him my word . . . I can’t . . . I can’t.”

Inwardly he groaned. But he must have the thing out, certainly, and bestow on her new-gained information the light of his own clever explanations. Otherwise the things she had heard were apt to grow into rooted beliefs. He must kill them while the plants were tender and young in her credence. He replaced the hat on his head.

“I have to leave you,” he said gloomily. “I’ll come back, I trust, later.” So he turned on his heel and made off toward the gate.

There was no sound behind him. Would she let him go, and without a single word of question? If so, he was lost, but he had to keep on. All was surrendered if he faltered, or turned back to her. No, the heavens be praised! There was a scurry of feet behind him; there was a rustling of clothes like the flutter of a bird's wings. Now she was beside him, holding his arm.

"What are you going to do? Winsor, Winsor, what are you going to do?"

He fairly trembled with the relish of what he was about to say.

"I am going to this Jack Rutledge," he said. "I am going to ask him to repeat what he has heard about me. And if he will not . . . I'll tear it from his dastardly throat."

It was magnificently delivered. The hot joy of that heroic speech made even Winsor Glanvil, for the moment, a hero indeed. He would almost have welcomed the conflict—his soft hand against the Herculean might of the man of the mountains.

Louise Carney was in a dreadful panic. "You must not go!" she gasped out at him. "You don't know . . . Jack Rutledge. . . ."

"I've heard of him, and his bear killing. But do you think that an honest man fears any rascal in the world?"

"Winsor. . . ."

"Let me go. I must find him."

He broke away and actually gained the gate. But

his hurry was half-hearted enough to permit her to overtake him there. She drew him around; she made him face her. If she had had only the half of her strength, it would have been enough to compel him.

"For heaven's sake, Winsor. I'm fainting. I'll die with terror if you leave me to . . ."

"Will you tell me, then?"

"Only if you swear you will not face Jack with what he has said."

"I cannot promise that. It is not honorable for a man to allow another to . . ."

"Oh, not for the sake of your honor . . . but for my sake. . . ."

He felt, then, that she could not have spoken words more perfect for his part if he had himself composed them for her. Slowly he allowed himself to melt.

"For your sake, Louise," he said with the deepest meaning, "I admit that I cannot refuse. But you are asking for my honor."

"I swore to him that I would never repeat what he told me. Because he admitted that he was not sure. . . ."

"He came to you with such talk before he himself was sure of the truth of it?"

"It was only because he was in a terrible fear about me, Winsor. . . ."

"Fear? What is threatening you?"

"He thought . . . I can't put it into words. . . ."

"But you must."

"I am too ashamed."

"Louise, for the sake of my honor . . . my self-respect, which you have dragged in the dirt. . . ."

"No, no!"

"It is true. No other person in the world could have done so much with me."

He saw her start at that and look hastily up to him, and he saw a wild light of joy flicker across her eyes.

"You must tell me, Louise. What did he fear for you?"

"I am ashamed, Winsor."

"Ah, Louise, think how you have already shamed me?"

"It was . . . how can I say it?"

"But you will."

"You will not laugh?"

"Laugh?"

She whispered: "He thought . . . that there was a danger . . . he was very foolish about it, of course . . . that if . . . that you . . . I mean that in case I were to . . . to . . . to marry someone . . . if I were to marry you . . ."

She stopped, crushed with shame. And then, feeling the chill of the silence, as he intended that she should feel it, she threw up her head and cried to him: "He had heard that you were a . . . a fortune hunter, Winsor. And he begged me not to . . . how can I say it?"

"A fortune hunter," repeated Glanvil as one dazed with horror and bewilderment. "A fortune hunter." And he struck the back of his hand across his eyes.

"You won't think that I let him suspect . . . ," she began, "that you really cared for me? I told him that we hardly knew one another . . . that you cared no more for me than for . . ." Her voice was trembling so that it fell away and he could hardly hear her.

"That is not true," said Glanvil, stepping readily into a breach so wide. "Heaven knows that after such a thing as this I can never speak. But if it had not been for this, I could have told you, dear. . . ."

What a child, what a child she was. At that single word, her head went back, and the warm flush of her joy ran over throat and face, and her lips parted, and she tilted in toward him and clung to him.

"Winsor, Winsor," she was saying. "There is no Jack Rutledge. I have never heard him speak of you. If he brought ten thousand men to swear against you, I wouldn't believe anything . . . except what I want to hear. . . ."

"I love you, Louise. No matter what cowards dare to say about me, nothing can change that. I tell you that, and I wish to heaven that you were the poorest girl that ever stood in a cottage door. But because you are rich, and because they have dared to say that I . . ."

"But I love you, Winsor. Their talking cannot change that. I have always loved you from the first day. It was just as though you had taken me in the palm of your hand."

Chapter Seven

When he reached the hotel, and that was the late dark of the twilight, with night itself close by, he went straight to Santelle. He found that worthy nervously pacing up and down his room. So wrought up was Santelle that he did not even wait to hear the news his companion might be bringing. He simply broke out with his own swelling emotion.

"Rutledge has been here. Everything is too late, and the devil take both of us and our plans!"

"Rutledge?" asked Glanvil, feeling his dreams of millions shrink to nothing on the spot. "Rutledge was here? What did he say?"

"Everything. And he said it in one minute, at the most. The incarnate devil knows all that he needs to know about the pair of us!"

"He can't," groaned Glanvil, still clinging to his dream. "He's only had four days. . . ."

"He used the telegraph. He sent out for news . . . and he got it. He had the sheriff on the job, too. I don't know what corners they got in touch with. They only have a couple of chapters about each of us, but those chapters are enough. They know about your engagement with the Purchas girl, and how it was broken."

"Damnation!"

"He told me that we have until tomorrow morning to start out of town. That's the end of my story."

"We have until tomorrow," echoed Glanvil.

"To get out of town . . . and if we're still here by noon . . . he'll answer for it that we have tar and feather as much as will stick to our skins." And Santelle made a grimace. "I had it once before in Louisiana, just outside of New Orleans. I'll never forget it. Ever happen to you, my friend?"

The face of Glanvil turned crimson with rage and with scorn and with shame.

"You may as well ask me, or any Glanvil, if I have passed through death," he said.

"Proud?" said Santelle, with his peculiar, twisted grin. "My dear Glanvil, a fox should never try the rôle of a lion. Never. Now we are to pack our grips."

"As soon as you please," said Glanvil. "Good bye now . . . I'm too busy to wait for your start."

"Busy? Just what is up your sleeve?"

"Nothing of importance, except that Louise Carney shall be married to me before midnight, if all goes as we have planned."

Santelle cast up both hands as one giving thanks to heaven. "You are miraculous, Glanvil!"

"Not at all. We simply reached an agreement, egged on by the fool, Rutledge."

"Egged on by him?"

"Exactly, for he tried to interfere and the result was a stormy scene. I became heroic and threatened to go tear Mister Rutledge into bits. This excited her. She begged me to let him live a while. At last I consented and a little later agreed to marry her this very night . . . the early marriage being her way of showing that she doesn't believe in the truth of the rumors that Rutledge brought to her about me."

"Is it possible?"

"It is finished. I have to find the minister. That is all."

"I already know the place. . . ."

"You have one located?"

"Exactly."

"Santelle, you have your uses. It must not be in this town, however."

"Certainly not. This is too close to the lion's den. But ten miles away, in a corner of the mountains, there is a crossroads village and a parson who'll make you man and wife. Until the gentle Mister Rutledge . . ."

"I shall take care of him."

"If you are fast enough to get out of the country. . . ."

"Man, man, I can guard myself. I am not helpless. I simply detest violence. That is all."

"Exactly," said Santelle, with the usual smile with which he greeted sham or fraud in his companion. "You will knock him down . . . and then break him in two."

"Strength of hand is only a small part," said Glanvil. "There are more deadly ways of striking."

"A knife, of course, when a man is looking the other way. A knife, of course, when a man is looking, let us say, flung from the flat of the hand. . . ."

"Can you do that? I have seen a Mexican, but I didn't know that you had such accomplishments."

"Or a gun," said Santelle. "Ah? But Rutledge is a famous gunfighter, Glanvil. You wouldn't risk as much as that?"

"The reason that I am not a famous gunfighter, Santelle, is that I have not lived where gunfighting is an accepted social accomplishment, but, when the time comes, I shall not be found wanting."

Santelle shook his head. "We are very understanding friends," he said, "but I wish that you would understand that I am a little more intelligent than you seem to believe. I tell you, Rutledge is an inescapable demon in a fight. You must not risk an encounter. If not for the sake of your hide, for the sake, then, of the money I expect to make out of this affair."

"I tell you, Santelle, to meet Rutledge would give me only the very greatest pleasure."

"Man, man . . . when do you practice with weapons, if you are so expert with them?"

"I don't need it. Let me tell you, Santelle, one is born with the power to kill or without that power. It is my birthright, and I have not used it. But if Rutledge pushes me too hard, he and I shall clash."

Santelle stared as though the soul of his companion were dressed with a new body before his eyes. "I believe that you mean it," he said. "On my honor, I believe that you mean it. But the clash has to be avoided. We will need fast horses for the ride."

"She has two beauties in her stable. We leave in three hours . . . as soon as she has gone up to her room. And . . . *whisht* . . . listen to that wind. This will be a true storm in a little time."

The wind had risen suddenly and, putting out a strong hand, cuffed the windows until they *jingled* like castanets.

"Weather is nothing," said Santelle. "A wet bride is as good as a dry one, if she has eight millions in her pocket. I'll tell you the road to follow. Then I'll ride on ahead and have the minister ready for the job. Take the eastern road straight on past the Carney house. It winds along for two miles. Then there's a fork and a dim trail goes straight on. Keep to the main path to your right. You come to a crossroad in another mile. Take the left-hand turn. That will carry you straight north and into this wind, if it keeps on blowing. You'll pass the light of a house on the right and two more on the left. Then, seven miles from the crossroad, you will see the lights of the town in a hollow beneath you. Keep straight on through the village. Beyond the town there is a little church and opposite the church is an old house. That is where the minister lives. Can you remember this?"

"Every word."

"Now, what next?"

"A little sleep, Santelle."

"The devil! Can you sleep at a time like this?"

"Why not? I may need strength."

"If Rutledge gets wind of what's up . . ."

"It will be better for him to keep out of the business."

Saying this, Glanvil went to his suitcase and took out a silver-mounted revolver, which he handled a moment, and then dropped into his clothes.

"I have not carried a gun," he mused, "since I was in Naples. Now I'm going to sleep for two hours. Do your part, Santelle, and I'll do mine. Good night." He lay down on the bed and turned his back on his companion.

"Your plans afterward?" asked Santelle.

"After the marriage, we keep on riding for the nearest railroad station. At that place, we take the first train East. And from the East, we are going on the first boat to France."

"I shall join you," returned Santelle, grinning, "in Paris. In the meantime, sweet dreams, my dear Glanvil."

"I shall dream a nightmare of a blind girl," said Glanvil. "It is she I fear . . . not Rutledge."

CHAPTER EIGHT

At the appointed time, Winsor Glanvil reached the stable behind the Carney house. It was the only visible sign of wealth on that little estate. All else remained as it had been in the days of their poverty, but the stable had been built after the great gold strike.

Louise, beforehand, had told him which horses to take, a tall gray gelding for himself, and a lithe-bodied chestnut mare for her. He lighted a lantern, and then hooded it with a sack. By that meager light he found and saddled them. He led them outdoors and held them under the shadow of a great spruce. Then he waited.

Moments pass slowly under the open sky with a storm wind beating through the mountains. It seemed a long hour before there was a faint sound of a closing door. But, a little later, the girl came hurrying toward him. The clouds, at that moment, had been brushed by the gale from the southern half of the sky, and the stars looked through. They glistened over the slicker that she wore. She carried another slicker over her arm, and stood hesitant before him.

"Louise," he said.

She came hurrying to him. She said: "After you left, it seemed like a great joke . . . or a dream.

There was nothing real about it . . . that you were to be here. But it is really you, dear Winsor. And no slicker . . . not even a raincoat? Foolish boy. But I knew you wouldn't think of that."

"How could you have such things in my mind, Louise, when . . . ?"

"Hush," she said, and, as he leaned above her, she held up against him small, soft hands. He pressed through them, and found her lips, warm and trembling. Then she broke away.

"We must ride. We must ride," she urged. "Every minute we stay here I am panic-stricken. I can't hide anything from Kate. She's guessed . . . I don't know what."

"I knew she would," he said gloomily.

"Here is Dad's slicker. Will it fit you?"

It was an enormous garment that he was lost in, but he huddled it over his shoulders. Then he lifted her into her saddle and sprang onto the back of the gray. She swerved the active chestnut close to his side.

"If there is a heaven, my father is there," she said. "And if he is there, he is watching over us tonight . . . and no harm can come to you or me, dear."

"We are late," said Glanvil, and he let the gray go forward at a trot.

She was after him, and then winging ahead on the mare. They rounded the side of the hill and the first blast of the coming rain rattled against them. After that, there was not time or breath for talk. He took the lead, with Louise Carney shouting to him: "Give Billy his head. He knows every cattle trail in the hills!"

He obeyed that order, and Billy went after his work like the honest horse that he was, sometimes pausing a little with lowered head as though he smelled and searched out some dangerous and broken part of the way, sometimes flaunting ahead at an easy gallop over rough and smooth as though the broadest daylight shone on the paths they traveled.

Only when they reached the first forking of the way, the gray strove to take the smaller trail and Glanvil had to turn him back on the broad way. Then they went on again, and to the crossroads, and over the seven-mile stretch toward their hidden village and the minister in it. Here they were galloping most of the way. The road was broad, and sometimes black and even, sometimes paved with tarnished sheets of silver where the rain had collected in standing pools that grew momently.

But with every instant of their ride the downpour seemed to increase. It was dashed against them in staggering bucketfuls by the gale. Or the wind fell away, and the ground trembled under the steady downbeat of the water. Sometimes it swept across them in drifts; sometimes in the throat of some narrow ravine, it whirled around them in the fierce eddy of the air.

Several times he paused to speak to the girl. Her courage never grew cold. "Are you wet?" he asked her.

"Dry and warm as toast!" she cried back to him.

He put his hand under her raincoat; the bucketing rain had found every opening, at wrist, at throat, and she was thoroughly drenched. But she laughed at that.

"You are soaked to the skin," he told her severely. "We'll have to stop."

"I wouldn't stop," she vowed, "if all this rain were sleet. But it's a warm rain, Winsor. It's a kind, friendly rain. Would you want to be married on a dull, stupid, quiet night?"

Now, as the road broadened, she rode beside him, and he marveled at her spirit. When they turned from the force of the storm, as the trail led under a mountainside, she was singing, and, when they issued into the full blast of the wind and rain again, she had no eye for what lay before her, but only for him. He could not turn his head to her without an answering wave of her hand.

Then, as the way twisted onto a sheltered shoulder of a mountain, they saw beneath them a deep hollow, dark as a pool of water, and in the center of the darkness, like reflections in the sea, a few burning lights. It was the village that was the goal of their travel this night.

They paused there a moment and he swung the panting gray to the side of the chestnut. He leaned down from his loftier place to the girl. It was not difficult, then, to put into his voice that certain deep quiver of emotion that often meant so much, but that with him meant nothing at all.

"Dear heart, dear child," said Glanvil. "How I shall keep you and care for you all my life."

He meant it, then, in a warm burst of feeling. And when he rode on with her again, he was wondering at himself. This thing that he had said had come almost from his heart—almost from the honest heart that exists even in a rogue.

Another night like this, he thought to himself, *and I shall be almost in love with her. But before another night comes, I shall have broad daylight to find out that she is simply an empty-headed little fool.*

They dropped down into the dark of the hollow; they passed through the muddy little street of the village. Beyond, they found the church with the little steeple shining faintly in the rain. In the opposite house a single light burned from the front window.

"Go in first and see if everything is all right," she begged of Glanvil. "Go in first, Winsor. Then . . . I'll come when you find . . ."

He hurried to the front door, down a path with little umbrella-topped trees on either side of it. Even the rain could not beat down all the fragrance of the wind-torn garden through which he was passing. So he came to the door under the overwhelming sweetness of a honeysuckle vine.

And as he reached for the knob, he heard a sharp cry from the street behind him.

"Who are you? Keep away from the head of my horse . . . help!"

He whirled, fumbling with cold-stiffened fingers beneath the slicker for his revolver. He turned, and lunged into the arms of two tall men, two strong men, whose grip withered away his own strength.

Now the door was cast open. In the broad shaft of light that streamed through it, other men were standing, and they ran out.

"Keep away!" called the voice of Jack Rutledge. "Let's get him inside."

The arms of Glanvil were jerked behind him and his wrists pinioned with a turn of rope, swiftly made. Then he was lifted and borne bodily into the house and set down, streaming rain water on the best rug of the minister's house. A big round-burner lamp with the shade taken off cast a dazzling brightness upon him, and around him were the forms of a dozen stalwart men whose faces were turned grimly toward him with unwinking, cruelly searching eyes. He saw, too, the startled face of the Reverend Peter Gilmore, with Mrs. Gilmore shrinking in the corner.

It was she who Rutledge first addressed.

"Missus Gilmore," he said, "there's a lady outside who you'd better see. She'll need you."

"Yes, yes, Mister Rutledge," she murmured, and hurried out of the room, giving to Winsor Glanvil, as she went by, a single startled glance, as the good housewife might have glanced at a huge spider that had crawled under her door and come to rest by the fire.

Chapter Nine

After that, nothing existed in the world, so far as that roomful of men was concerned, except Glanvil and his fate.

Rutledge stood in the center of the room and gave directions.

"Take the coat off of him," he commanded.

It was done.

"Now put him in that chair by the fire."

That order was obeyed, also.

"Jerry, you have a flask with you. Give him a swig of it, will you?"

"I keep it for snakebites, not for snakes," said Jerry slowly.

There was no chuckle in response to this sally.

"Let him have a drink," insisted Rutledge. "He'll need it, perhaps, before we're through."

Glanvil shrugged his shoulders. "I don't drink," he said.

"You're a virtuous man," said Rutledge, "a virtuous man, we can see, but some of your virtues aren't appreciated by simple people like me and my friends. Glanvil, we want to start with your confession. You stole this girl away to marry her here?"

Glanvil did not answer. There was an ugly little murmur from the others.

Rutledge silenced it with a quick gesture. "He doesn't quite understand," he said. "But we'll clear up his mind before long. You won't talk any?" he added.

"If I see a judge or any officer of the law qualified to ask questions," said Glanvil, "I'm very ready to talk and answer any proper questions."

"The law," said Rutledge, "is a thing we all respect. There's not a man here who would willingly break the law unless he had to. This is a case where we have to take the law into our own hands, however. There are a few fine points that the law doesn't adequately deal with . . . for instance, a philanderer and professional heart-breaker, like you, Glanvil."

"Give me free hands . . . give me back my gun . . . and then say that again, Rutledge."

A flush of savage emotion covered the face of Rutledge. "Do you mean it?" he asked huskily.

"I mean it."

"Then . . ."

"Wait a moment, Jack," broke in the oldest of the others. "He ain't worthy of a chance. Would you give a snake a chance to bite? It's a bluff. That's all."

"What's your name, my friend?" asked Glanvil.

"Dan Burton, young man. Why d'you want to know?"

"It's a little thing that I care to remember after tonight."

"Where'll you be after tonight? Have you made up your mind to that?"

"In purgatory, perhaps," said Glanvil. "Otherwise, I can use what I remember."

"He's cool," said Dan Burton. "But after all, his father was Hector Glanvil. Heaven only knows how a rat like this ever come to be his son."

"First of all, will you confess, Glanvil?" This from Rutledge again.

And Glanvil shrugged his shoulders and lifted his eyes again to the face of the big man. The weight of the other's glance fell upon him with a burden that made him look back to the floor. And he was afraid—not of Rutledge, but of something behind that man—a clean life and an honest heart.

But as for what was to come to him, he hardly cared. They could do nothing too great for his sins, he knew. So, like a cornered rat, he waited, and not a muscle of his face stirred.

"We don't need your confession, after all," said Rutledge. "We have your friend, Santelle. And we have a certain little paper that we took from him. One third of the profits if you marry Louise Carney, and . . ." Fury and disgust choked him. "Well," he said more quietly, "I thank heaven humbly that we were able to stop the thing."

Even then curiosity was as strong in Glanvil as any other emotion. He said calmly: "Who put you on my trail?"

"You can answer questions, not ask them," replied Rutledge, shaking his head.

"It was the blind girl," said Glanvil. "It was she. I could have guessed it clearly enough beforehand. She set you to follow Santelle."

"You should have been a detective, not a cur that deceives women," said Rutledge.

"Is Glanvil too poor a name for her to marry?" asked the prisoner.

"You can't face it out." declared Rutledge. "You can't do it, my friend. I have enough information to prove your character in the Supreme Court. You've lived on what you could get from women. You've wormed your way into their confidence and sold them worthless stock to mines that didn't exist. You've borrowed thousands from them . . . and then disappeared. You've helped them invest their estates, and then slipped half of the proceeds into your own pocket. You've done other little tricks like this, Glanvil, and we know about it. Not everything. I've only scratched the surface of your record, but I've found enough to turn the stomach of any honest man. Only . . . the law can't prove these things against you. By heavens, the very women you've deceived refuse to testify against you. So we, Glanvil, have gathered together to pass a judgment and to execute it."

He turned on the others: "Boys, what's good enough for Glanvil?"

There was a silence of thoughtfulness, after this.

"I have an old rope hangin' onto the horn of my saddle," said one brown-faced worthy. "I dunno that a little mite more stretching would do it any harm."

"Death," said Rutledge. "There's one vote for that. How do the rest of you stand? Here's a man who's sneaked inside the houses of honest men and found their women and made fools of them. If that's not worth death, what is? He's come into our own town. He's gone to the prettiest and the sweetest girl in the whole mountains. He's brought her here to marry her. Heaven knows what would become of her after that. Who else votes for death?"

"Nobody," broke in a voice from the corner of the room.

They turned toward a blond-haired youth who went on: "Nobody else votes for death. You're sort of heated up about this here, or you wouldn't listen to the talk about death for him, Rutledge. What for do we want men hung? For shootin' another gent in the back, or for liftin' a hoss, or for some trick like that? But what this here gent has done is like stealin'. Worse, you might say, but still it's like stealin'."

"Partner," said Jack Rutledge with a gloomy earnestness, "I dunno how that you can figger it, but I tell you that there is no crime so bad as marrying a woman through deceit."

"The whole point," broke in Blondy hastily, "is

right in that. He started in tryin' to marry her, but he didn't."

"He tried his best," said Lefty Garragan, he of the brown face. "That's the same as doin' it. He had her right here at the minister's house."

Young Blondy stuck by his guns, perhaps less for the sake of saving the life of Winsor Glanvil than for the sake of the argument itself.

"Is it the same," he asked, "when a gent plans to murder another one . . . and then doesn't do it? Suppose that I walk up behind a man with a gun in my hand, but then I don't pull the trigger. Is that the same as killing him? He brung Louise Carney here, but he didn't get a chance to marry her. I figger that the best thing we can do is to put our mark on him so's he'll remember us and we'll remember him. Y'understand?"

His speech had the weight that dispassionate speech nearly always has with excited men; they feel the greater justice that is with him who has no mist of red before his eyes. Rutledge himself strode across the room and back again. His big body was working with his emotion.

"Well," said Lefty Garragan, "there ain't any doubt that he's got nerve."

He strode up to Glanvil and, dropping his tanned hands on his hips, stared down at the captive, and Glanvil looked calmly back to him.

"Hanging wouldn't be the thing. It's over too soon," said Garragan. "And Blondy is right. We got to do something that'll eat into him. What'll that be?"

"Take a blacksnake to him," said Blondy. "The dog'll remember that. After about the second lick, he'll be howlin' loud and long."

That idea was taken up with enthusiasm. Lefty Garragan contributed a quirt with a heavily loaded handle and oiled thong that promised to cut like a knife. Out to the minister's barn they carried Winsor Glanvil.

Two lanterns were lighted and hung from pegs. They threw a changing light over the scene, as drafts of wind made the flames jump in the chimneys. From the back of Glanvil they tore his coat, his shirt, his undershirt. About his wrist they fastened two rope ends.

All this time he had been fighting down an agony of shame. Now at last it forced itself into words.

"My friends," he said.

They grew quiet to listen.

"My friends," said Glanvil, "I warn you now that you're doing a reckless thing. You have guns . . . and bullets in them. Pull a trigger and put an end to this thing. But if you tie me up and beat me like a dog . . . you'll suffer for it, one by one, I give you my word, and I'll never leave your trails until you've suffered for it."

"Jud Perkins and Sam Levitt!" called Rutledge. "Tie him to those uprights. The cur dares to threaten us!"

Instantly he was made fast.

He hung his head, waiting, listening. It was worse than death, a thousand times. Death was an instant, only, but he, so long as he lived, would never be able to forget this thing. Here he was stripped like a dog before other men, to be flogged. He set his teeth and shuddered.

"He's shakin' already," said Sam Levitt in his loud voice. "He's showin' yaller now. You was right, Garragan. Who takes the whip?"

"That's dirty work," broke in Jud Perkins. "But we'll take it turn and turn about . . . two licks apiece until we figger that he's got enough. When'll that be, Rutledge?"

"When the cur begins to howl and beg. It won't last long. Your turn first, Garragan."

The whip whirred behind Winsor Glanvil. He saw the thick shadow of a raised arm strike past his head and down the wall of the barn, then the lash fell.

He hardly felt it. He did not even wince from the stroke, for what happened to his body was nothing, while his heart was swelling so big with shame. They were beating him with a whip—the son of Hector Glanvil—with a whip!

He closed his eyes. The whip was falling again, and again.

"He ain't got no feeling. Levitt, you've been a muleskinner. You take the whip and see if you can make him know what's happening."

This time, it was as though a red-hot iron had been raked across his flesh.

"Blood!" someone shouted.

Again the whip fell and a shooting torment struck through his whole body. He forgot the shame then; he remembered only, with set teeth, that he must not give them the satisfaction of hearing so much as a whisper pass his lips. And he locked his teeth on that determination like a bulldog. What would Hector Glanvil have done if such an ordeal as this had been brought to him? He would have stood calm, straight, unflinching, and endure whatever they dealt upon his tortured body.

So did Winsor Glanvil stand, stiff and straight, and let the blows fall.

Lefty Garragan came and stood before him and studied his face.

"He ain't got any feeling, or else he's got more nerve than anybody I ever seen in my life," declared Lefty. "Harder, Blondy!"

A mist swam across the eyes of Winsor Glanvil. Then a sudden wave of darkness poured through his brain and he felt himself slump down to the length of his pinioned arms. That was all he remembered.

Chapter Ten

He recovered his senses with a cold dash of water over his face. And he looked up to Jack Rutledge. "Steady," said Rutledge. "Taste this."

Down his throat went a big swallow of burning whiskey. He sat up, coughing, half strangling. And, now that he was awake, he felt a thousand criss-cross trails of burning agony along his back. He writhed with the pain.

"It's not so pleasant, after all," said Rutledge. "You feel it a bit more than we thought."

"I'll kill you for it, Rutledge," said Glanvil. "I'll get you and the rest of them, one by one."

"Will you?" asked Rutledge, smiling. "There's only one thing that I pray for, Glanvil, and that's the time when I can set my hands on you. Well, lad, the flogging is not enough. Something more has to be done to you. I've sent the rest of them away. The thing that remains is too ugly for even hard-handed chaps like them to see."

"Very well," said Glanvil. "My hands are tied."

"They're tied now, but, when your hide is healed again and your hands are free, you'll be back at Louise Carney again."

"I shall," said Glanvil. "In her eyes, I'll be a martyr, of course."

Rutledge closed his eyes and groaned. "What a complacent rat you are," he said.

"I merely know my own powers," said Glanvil, "just as you know the strength of your grip."

"It's your handsome face," said Rutledge. "I've talked to her. She raged at me. Then she begged me to let her come to you."

"You are very kind to tell me all of this."

"There is an end to the story that you don't see yet."

He looked down for a moment, as though to recollect, and played with a long roweled spur that he held in his hand.

"It's the face that she can't forget. I tried to show our testimony against you to her. She kept coming back to the same thing . . . a man with an eye and a face like yours couldn't be dishonest. Well, Glanvil, my work in this little affair is not only to punish you for what you've done, but to prevent you from trying the same thing again. I'm going to spoil that face."

A cold horror struck through the prisoner at that.

"What do you mean, Rutledge?"

"I mean that I'm going to spoil that beauty that turns women into fools when they see you. I'm going to spoil it, and spoil it now. If I am wrong, heaven punish me for it. But I'm right. I know I'm right. As long as you live with that handsome face to carry around with you, you'll be poison in the lives of honest women, as you've been poison in the life of poor Louise."

"Bah!" cried Glanvil. "Do you think that I'm a blind man, Rutledge? You talk of acting for the sake of justice. It's merely because you hate me yourself. It's jealousy. That's the end of it. Don't rant to me about your high motives. But here I am helpless. If you have something to do, do it . . . but when I'm healed again, and strong again, I'll find you, Rutledge, and heaven help you then. And I'll find her."

"You dog!" gasped out Rutledge, and, seizing him by the hair of the head, he jammed him back against the floor. Then up and down the face of Glanvil he ran the rowel of the spur. Made to cut through the toughest horsehide, it puckered and tore the tender flesh of Glanvil as though it were paper.

It brought from him what the whip had not been able to bring—a cry of rage, of pain, and of horror. The iron hand of Rutledge released its grip, and Glanvil came staggering to his feet, but he was blind with the crimson flow down his face. He heard the sliding door of the barn crash shut and he knew that Rutledge was gone.

When he had wiped his eyes and looked around him, he had sight of a thing that meant more than gold to him. By the dull light of the single lantern that remained, he saw hanging in the corner of the barn, a rifle and a cartridge belt with a hunting knife appended in its holster to the ammunition girdle.

He put on the belt with trembling hands and clutched the gun. It was old in make but in good condition, and he told himself with a savage eagerness that there were bullets enough in the gun to satisfy his thirst for revenge.

When he reached the barn door, he found that he was so weak with the agony through which he had passed that he could hardly move the door back on its sliding hinges. He managed that small business at the last, and staggered out into the night.

The storm had fallen away. The wind came only in occasional puffs, and carried with it drops of rain that stung his wounded face like drops of liquid fire.

There were still lights in the house. There were still voices in it. He went slowly toward the first window—slowly, for he could feel his strength coming back upon him by degrees—a strength beyond any with which he had ever been clothed before, a might that was fed by his fury. The rifle that had hung trembling in his fingers was now like a wooden toy held in a grip stronger than adamant.

So he brushed away the crimson stains again and looked through the window.

They sat about the table in the dining-living room of the minister's house, all six men, and he wrote down their faces in his mind and in his soul—these six men he must kill. Rutledge first, of course, and then Burton, and after Burton, Garragan, Blondy, Jud Perkins, and Levitt. Six men to kill, and how many others who strove to come between him and his prey, while he performed the work of wiping out that horrid stain on the name of Glanvil? But death dealing, to him, was nothing, now.

He looked again. They were drinking coffee that Mrs. Gilmore poured for them, and they sat about smoking their cigarettes and talking—talking earnestly and with frowns, like men who had seen things that night that were not for laughter.

How little of laughter they should learn hereafter. He ground his teeth and drank in the breath of his rage. Did they dare to sit here in security? Yes, for they dreamed that because they had beaten him and tortured him and marked him with the brand of their beastly revenge he, a Glanvil, would skulk in a corner and not dare to strike back against them—he, a Glanvil, would run away to hide and tremble.

Only in the corner sat the Reverend Peter Gilmore with his head bowed and a stricken look upon his face, as though the violent doings of this night lay heavily upon his conscience. Him alone would Glanvil forgive.

But there was huge Jack Rutledge, like a giant among pygmies, like a king among his slaves, so greatly did the force of his spirit and the gleam of his eye seem to dominate the others. The rifle that Glanvil had raised in the darkness was brought to a level with his shoulder, but, when his bead was drawn on that head, he dropped the gun again.

It was not the way of a Glanvil to slay secretly from the night.

He went around to the front of the house. There were half a dozen horses tethered behind the hedge. He selected what seemed to him the best of the lot and, leading him in front of the gate, threw the reins. There the trained cow horse stood patiently. He set the gate ajar and braced it with a rock. There might be need of an open way when he returned—if he was to return.

Then he advanced up the path and crossed the porch with soundless steps. Not that he took care of his footfall, but instinct, working deeply in him, made his movements less noisy than the stalking of a velvet-footed cat. He crossed the porch. He opened the front door and stepped into the hall.

"The draft has worked the front door open," he heard a voice say from the inner room. "I'll fix it."

So Glanvil stepped to that door and tossed it wide. Sam Levitt was before him, reaching for the handle of that door, but, at the sight of the dreadful face of Glanvil, he sprang back with a cry, as though he had seen a ghost.

But his was not the form in the eye of Glanvil, nor any of the others who were rising now with startled gasps from around the table, their cigarettes falling from their unnerved hands. Upon that giant at the farther end, who had leaped up first of all, was his attention centered.

The barrel of his rifle lay across the hook of Glanvil's left arm. Here, then, was a fair start and a fair fight to please any man west of the Rockies. For yonder was the matchless Rutledge, that hero of so many battles, and only a twitch of his hand would bring out the Colt, pouting fire and death the instant its muzzle left the holster.

The heaving of his breast should have forced out a shout, but hate and savage joy half closed the throat of Glanvil and only an indescribable snarl resulted.

"Rutledge," he said.

That word and that voice broke the charm. He saw the hand of Rutledge flash back to the gun and out again with a shining length of steel. Then he jerked the butt of the rifle to his shoulder. He heard the gun explode in the hand of the other. He heard the sing of a bullet. That was Rutledge—he fired for the head alone, men said. But this time he had missed, and Glanvil would not miss. His finger curled affectionately around the trigger—a report like a hammer stroke, and Rutledge, tossing out his arms, fell backward, crashing down among the chairs like a falling tree.

Glanvil leaped backward through the doorway. He caught the edge of the door itself as he sprang and slammed it shut. Three bullets split the stout wood a fifth of a second later, but, before hands fumbling with murderous haste could tear the door open again, he was out of the house and speeding down the path.

Once more, as he dashed through the gate, they fired. Then he was in the saddle and away.

What chance had they after that? The wet, thick blanket of the storm closed around him. He heard vague voices, like sounds in a dream; he heard the rush of horses, with hoof beats muffled in mud; he even heard guns—but he had broken straight through between two houses and was riding furiously for the great mountains before him. And in his heart there was a veritable song of joy. All his wounds were forgotten; all the sting of his shame was gone. He had faced great Jack Rutledge. He had beaten him in a fair fight. And before him there was the road of long revenge still opening.

Behind him lay one man dead, except for miracle. Before him lay a man's work. And the joy of it choked him. He felt that he had not lived before. This was the beginning.

Chapter Eleven

He pressed straight ahead. He went up a slippery hill slope and halfway up found a trail, dim and broken, but intelligible enough to the sure feet of his mount. Along that small trail they worked their way. An hour, two hours—they had climbed high, they had dropped into a long, sloping decline, they were up again, climbing among the winds in the heart of high heaven. And then bad luck struck him.

It was a great white thing, looming suddenly through a blown drift of rain—only a huge slab of naked rock, but to the horse it seemed a dreadful monster, perhaps. The gelding pitched back and to the side, and wrenched the rider from his grip on the wet saddle. So Winsor Glanvil rose staggering from the mud and the clinging gravel and saw for a fleeting instant the horse dash back down the trail.

And he laughed through the storm. He still had his rifle slung across his back. He still had cartridge belt and knife at his waist. And, after all, when one starts out to deal death, it is best not to be branded first of all as a horse thief—at least it is far best to those who live among the Rockies.

He faced the storm again. And still the drops that stung his body, naked to the hips, were like whips urging him forward. Somewhere there was sure to be a house—a trail does not end in nothing.

But that, so it seemed, was exactly what this one did. Across a rocky, sandy stretch he was sure that he was following its windings, but presently he found himself on an untracked mountainside. After that, he plodded on, half exhausted, the cold, the labor beginning to tell, and the torment of wounds on face and back beginning to eat into the very strength of his soul.

But he must find help, surely. He must find help soon. For if the dreadful gash that had been torn in the flesh of his face were not bandaged and sewed together at once—he shuddered when he thought of the puckering scar that would result.

Rutledge had struck deeply, indeed. And yet, perhaps, that stroke that destroyed one Glanvil would bring into the world another, nearer to the spirit of great Hector Glanvil himself, and all the old long line of honest men, and men of might.

He must find help—but how fast his strength was waning. He stumbled on a downslope, and his legs buckled out at the knees. He came down so heavily that his hands were cut on the sharp edges of a rock. He stood up again, and it required to bring him to his feet a heavy effort that sent the blood spinning dizzily through his aching head.

Before him, dimly visible through the dark and the double dark of the storm, there was a narrow, high opening—a sort of slit in a jumbled mass of rocks that had fallen there, piled on this shoulder of the mountain by some avalanche a thousand winters old. It was at least a shelter that would keep him from the tearing hands of the wind and let the buzzing of weakness die out of his ears. He stepped through that opening. It was narrower than he had thought, and he had to turn sidewise to enter. He believed it would never do as a place to use as shelter, but here he found that the hole widened suddenly. He stepped farther in and fumbled around him. Everywhere his hand passed through empty air. By the sheerest luck he had happened upon the opening to a sort of natural cave.

He went a few strides farther, and paused, feeling about him with his feet for a comfortable place to lie down, until the dizzy weakness should leave him. His foot struck deep, soft sand, sure sign that at some time water had flowed through this subterranean channel. Here he could rest.

He had leaned down to feel for the ground with his hand when two things came upon his senses at once—first a heavy, warm, disagreeable odor, and then two points of green phosphorescence sliding slowly toward him along the floor of the cave.

He sprang back, but his shoulders struck the narrow entrance and cast him staggering forward again. He had barely time to unsling the rifle from his shoulder when a snarl grated on his ears and the green eyes lifted toward him. He could not reach the trigger or pause to level the gun. Gripping it by the barrel, he clubbed the butt downward with all his strength and chance sent the heavy blow home. He felt the butt strike against bone, and then the weight of the beast struck him and cast him on his back.

The impetus of that leap sent the animal rolling past him. He struggled to his knees, turning the rifle to get at the trigger, and then the creature charged again. The rifle was knocked from his hands. His left shoulder was slashed as by a knife. Then the charging animal shot past him. He drew the knife to meet the next attack. And when it came, he struck desperately. He felt the blade go home. There was a wolfish howl and the assailant leaped away. Again it came, and again he struck and the blade found flesh, and this time the teeth were in his thigh like metal jaws, grinding deep. He stabbed again, and again, then fainted from the sheer pressure of agony.

Something was licking at his wounded shoulder and at his bleeding face when he came to his senses, and a heavy weight lay across his body. He struck out with his hand; there was a whine of pain and fear as the hand landed in something softly furred that rolled away under his blow. He cast the weight from his body and rose to his feet, staggering, weak.

He found the box of matches in his pocket and lighted one and at his feet he saw the body of a she-wolf. And, cowering at the wall a little distance away, was a wolf cub, a bundle of yellowish fur.

A scattering of dead leaves, which had blown through the mouth of the cave, lay in niches here and there. A handful of these he ignited and fed the flame with fresh fuel; by that light he tended his own wounds. As for that gash across his face, there was nothing he could do; neither could he help the fiery cuts across his back, and the slash across his shoulder was beyond his help. He could and did, however, make a small bandage for the gash in his thigh, using a part of his clothing. And by the time that work was ended and the knot tied, he had fainted again.

And the last thought that leaped like flame across his mind was that the she-wolf, if life came back to her, would feed fat on his body, and the cub would learn the taste of flesh at that same banquet. That was the end, then, of the Glanvils.

His senses came drowsily back to him after a time. A gray light was beginning to seep through the narrow entrance to the cave. By that light he saw the mother wolf come reeling to her feet. He saw her drag herself a feeble step toward him, saw the glistening of her eyes, saw the gape of her jaws, slavering with hate. Then she dropped in her tracks, and the little cub came whining beside her.

But he could not have raised a hand against her attack. A feverish heat had spread over his body; every nerve was twisted and pinched with torment, and sick delirium crept across his brain.

It was either delirious sleep or complete faint, after that. When he wakened to reality once more, the full light of a sunny day streamed through the cave and illumined all except the farther dark end of the tunnel. Out of that gloom he heard the faint trickling of water, and with the thirst that raged in him then, the sound of the flowing water was like a voice from heaven. He dragged himself to it. He could not stand, but on hands and knees he worked his way until he found a little shining rivulet that crossed the floor of the cave and passed out again, through a crevice in the wall. He drank to repletion. There on the edge of the waters he collapsed again.

By fits and starts, as lightning showed from time to time, tearing raggedly the blackness of a stormy sky, consciousness returned to him. Whether it was one day or two, he could not tell. But it was warm weather. Of that he was sure, for another night like that of the storm would have killed him with certainty through sheer exposure and exhaustion.

But at last he was awake with a clear brain. A clear brain, but a weak one. Thoughts and sights came across his intelligence slowly trailing, like the images that enter the dim brain of a new-born infant. But by degrees he felt his way back to the truth.

There was the wolf helpless and crushed in the corner to which she had dragged herself, dying little by little, but still watching him out of a dulled eye, still turning her feeble head with desperate effort, now and again, to lick the cub that cuddled beside her. This was the end for her, the end for the little brute beside her. What had become of the rest of the litter? Perhaps, as they played around the mouth of the cave, a stooping eagle had borne one away in its steel talons. Perhaps while the mother was hunting at a little distance, some red-eyed ferret had slid like a serpent through the brush and sunk its fangs through the skull of another.

But the one life remained from all the litter. The he-wolf himself? He had forgotten the home of his family, or else the true rifle of some hunter had snuffed out his life, also.

In the meantime, there were two prime necessities, if Glanvil hoped to fight for his life. He must have food, and he must have fire.

He went about the work slowly, moving his hands and his legs with separate efforts, like a child that has not yet learned to walk.

It seemed to him, afterward, that what saved his life from the wounds that he had received was the very famine to which he had been forced to submit. Those long hours of total movelessness had given the flesh time to begin to knit, subdued the fever. Now the current of his life ran small and slow, but life it was.

Fuel was not hard to get. Near the mouth of the cave there was a great litter of dead twigs and branches, part of the ruin of a fallen tree. Yet it took him half a day to crawl out from the cave and bring back to it a small quantity of wood. After that he lay in the mouth of the cave with his rifle stretched out before him.

He had gone long, long without food, by this time. Perhaps the stabbing pains of hunger helped him back to his senses, but that same hunger would help to finish him quickly enough. Another day, perhaps, and he would be too weak to crawl even so far as to the mouth of the cave.

A red squirrel came boldly out and ventured to within a foot of the muzzle of the gun. But although his mouth ran water and his stomach clave to his back in the passion for food, he did not shoot, for the sound of the rifle might frighten away bigger and more precious game, capable of wandering in that direction and within the reach of his weapon.

But the hours ran on. The heat of the afternoon struck through the opening among the rocks and his head swam with the oven-like warmth. Still nothing came within the reach of his eye until the red hour of the sunset. And then, like a gift from heaven, a tall deer stepped lightly, confidently out of the brush and stood with high head, looking around him.

Chapter Twelve

More ran through the mind of the starved man while he lay there watching than when he had stood before great Jack Rutledge ready to fight. For when he stood before Rutledge, he had hardly cared whether he lived or whether he died. All would have been one. It was only to strike a single blow for his honor and for his shame. Here existence or a most wretched death lay on the chance of a single bullet.

And he remembered, now, with a dreadful qualm of fear that he had not looked to the gun and its loading before he prepared for the hunting. What if it misfired, and this gift of life raced lightly away from him?

Or what if his aim missed? To be sure, the long barrel of the gun rested upon the stones, and the muzzle was trained fully upon the big stag, but indeed it well might be that he should miss, for his hands were quivering with eagerness and with weakness, and his whole body shuddered with excitement. He set his teeth to assure himself the more, but the effort made him tremble still more violently. If he missed—yes, if his bullet were not instantly fatal—he was lost. He dared not try for the body. For after a wound in the body the stag was almost sure to run, and, even if he went only a few long strides, it would be too far for Glanvil to follow.

The head was the target, and toward the head, furtively, with a prayer on his lips, he turned the sights of the gun. He saw the big, quivering ears, he saw the large brown eyes, full of tenderness and trust in the world that was about to strike at his life. He saw the wet, shining muzzle. Just between those eyes he drew his bead—and as his finger curled around the trigger, the stag bounded off sidewise and stood a quivering instant, alive with terror. It could have seen nothing. Only that extra sense that warns the dumb beasts of approaching destruction had telegraphed a warning to its brain, and now it paused a single instant to search the mountainside to find the terror, if it could, before it whirled and raced away through the brush.

Glanvil turned the muzzle of the gun enough to catch a hasty bead again, and that small movement was enough to startle the deer. It wheeled with a snort; mid-leap, the bullet from the rifle struck it through the head, and it dropped from the air and lay like a senseless stone upon the ground.

"Life," whispered the man. "Life."

He lay for a moment, gathering his strength, which was far spent indeed, and moistened his white, dry lips. Then, leaving the rifle behind him, he issued forth, on hands and knees, and crawled to the deer. The keen hunting knife pierced through strong hide and flesh. He carved an ample portion from the haunch. And with that prize he dragged himself back to the cave. Now, as the hope of food grew stronger in him, the torment in which he lived from his wounds disappeared. There was room in his soul for that one raging appetite only, and he could hardly wait to kindle the fire. It was burning, at last. He hacked the meat into chunks and spitted them on a pointed twig. That twig he held straight into the flames.

And the wolf cub came at the smell of the meat and crawled near on its belly with savage, restless eyes. It had not eaten for very long, and its growing body was making a torment of the need of food. The exquisite agony that gripped the stomach of the man made him stir with compassion. He tossed the cub a fragment of raw food, and watched it sneak furtively upon the morsel—then bolt it whole and stand up with glistening eyes of hunger.

And Glanvil lolled back his head and laughed with a savage joy, a savage sympathy. What time before in all of his life had he given away aught of value to him? But now, like a reckless spendthrift, he tossed away what was more valuable than gold itself. He turned the stick above the fire. The meat *hissed* and spat forth its juices, and a rich fragrance, more richly delightful than all that had met the nostrils of Glanvil in his life entered his lungs, his soul. Life, life.

And the starved wolf cub crept nearer.

It lay on its belly and watched with burning eyes and slavering mouth while the man withdrew the spit and began to devour the gobbets of cooked meat—half-cooked flesh, indeed, but what Paris chef had ever prepared a dish more to the taste of Winsor Glanvil?

Still gnawing a mouthful, he sliced off another bit of the raw flesh and held it forth in his hand. The knife was raised in the other. If a tooth of the cub touched his fingers, he would bury that knife blade in its back—and then laugh as it writhed forth the last of its life on the sands of the cave.

It worked closer to that meat—it stretched forth its neck with the fur bristling. Then it picked the meat cleanly from his palm and bolted the mouthful whole. And Glanvil grinned again, mirthlessly, drinking deep the joy of the beast that was his joy, also. Ah, how close they were to one another now, with only a single thought shining like a star before them out of that threatening night of famine.

He finished his own cooked flesh; he reached for the unfinished chunk of raw meat and then paused. To those who gorged themselves after long famine there came a bitter time of repentance, and here were no doctors to aid him in his time of need.

He set his teeth and fought back the raging appetite. But here was one that could eat and eat to repletion and no danger to nature. He held forth flesh again, and again the cub came close. It caught the meat again and swallowed it. It crowded near, watching not the hand that gave, but the face behind the hand, as though reading the soul of the man, and Glanvil, with a dreadful and ravening joy, fed it again and again, and made it tear the morsels from the clutch of his hand, into which the strength was returning.

He left the cave when the meat was gone. He came back with more, and fed the cub until the little beast, with puffed sides, rolled itself into a ball and slept, slept there beside him, only grunting faintly in its slumber when his hand fell upon and stroked fur softer than down.

Yonder was hunger, too. The red tongue of the old wolf lolled from her mouth and a faint glimmer of life had returned to her dying eyes as she watched the cub eat—and live. He crossed to her, dizzily, with weaving legs, but strong enough now to walk. He crouched before her, and tossed a bit of meat. She let it lie unregarded before her—but only a moment. All of her instincts were crying out in her that the taint of man on this much-needed food was the certain promise of death, but just beneath her nose was the sweet breath of flesh, raw flesh, rich with life-giving blood.

She snatched it covertly, and swallowed. She devoured another bit. He laid a fragment a few inches from her nose. Then curiously, half tortured and half delighted by the agony of her efforts, he watched her writhe forward and gain the food, and swallow again. And now her eyes, like the eyes of the cub, were raised to watch the face of the man who, against all the precepts of her wild training, was giving her life instead of taking it from her.

Through the dusk he staggered to the body of the deer again, and brought back a load of meat that he laid before the starved creature, and he sat back and watched her eat with heaving sides, watched until sudden sleep struck in a wave over him.

It was broad morning when he wakened again. Every movement was still most exquisite perfection of pain, but his brain was clear, and his body was filled with new strength. He breakfasted again on roasted flesh, but this time it was a huge and careless meal. And again he fed the cub and the mother wolf.

After that, he came close to her, the knife ready in case she tried to snap. But although strength was returning to her, also, she was still too weak to lift her body, still too certain of her weakness to try her teeth against the creature that had conquered her once before when she was dressed in all of her strength. She let him examine her, only warning him back, now and again, with a deep-throated snarl.

And the cub went with him, and sniffed curiously at the crimson stains on her long fur, mixed with sand and gravel. And the grit had worked deep into the knife slashes. There was a hollow-topped rock that might hold about a gallon of water. In a bark cup he brought water from the rivulet and filled the receptacle. Around the stone he built a strong fire, and, when the water was warm, he bathed his own wounds. It was like the touch of a god, that ablution, easing the draw of the cold, stiff flesh against the lips of his wounds. He washed and renewed the bandage on his thigh. All his other wounds were nothing compared with that deep incision. Then he turned to the she-wolf.

What was his agony compared with hers? What were his shallow wounds contrasted with the deep gashes that had drained away her strength and left her more helpless than her cub—she a veritable queen of her race. For she was well-nigh a hundred pounds of sinew and bone and iron-hard muscle. Had it not been for the first chance blow that half stunned her, he could not have survived ten seconds of battle with her. She would have knocked him on his back and slashed his throat across.

All this he knew as he stared at her, and she at him. For, if he brought her back to strength and life, might he not be restoring the snake that would bite him?

But the ache of his own wounds urged him on,

just as the sharp tooth of his own famine had forced him to feed the two brutes. With the warmed water, he washed the blood from her pelt. A dozen times she turned her head, with yawning teeth and a devil in her eyes. But the teeth never closed. And at last she lay motionless, her head fallen on the sands, her eyes closed, and shudders of deep, deep content shaking her body while he tended those wounds.

He spread the mouths of the wounds wide. He washed out the gravel and the sand that choked them. He brought armfuls of dead leaves and bedded her softly in them. And at the last he sat down at her side.

He surveyed his work carefully with unspeakable pride. For, having lain at the door of death himself, being only a scant stride away from it even now, indeed, yet he had been able to preserve himself and to save two other lives.

They were more than brute beasts to Glanvil. Indeed, as he turned his eye back through his life, he knew that they were dearer and nearer to him than any humans he had ever known. For all his life he had been taking, taking, with a cunning, greedy hand, and now for the first time he had given, given freely of what was most priceless to himself, given without the hope of a reward, and he found that a strange new joy had risen and made his heart warm within him. He had fed them both; he had cared for the wounds of the she-wolf—even she who had put her teeth in him. Now he sat beside her, with his hand on her thick mane, and the wolf cub? It lay snuggled against his leg and licked the hand that he held before it.

Chapter Thirteen

There began for Winsor Glanvil the existence not of a man but of a beast. Though food had brought him some strength, he was still filled with a deadly weakness, as though his blood had been turned to the palest, clearest water. Only by the most dreadful effort was he able to work off enough of the hide of the stag to furnish him with a buckskin jacket, and take sinew enough to supply him with thread—dried before the fire in front of the cave and made supple by rubbing in the fat of the deer's body. But still that hide had to cure in the sun, stretched out among four pegs that he had driven into the ground, and, after that, it would have to be worked supple, and then sewed together before he could use it as a covering for his upper body.

In the meantime, he was half naked, and naked, above all, where his wounds most needed covering. From the flagellation, the muscles of his back were stiff, sore, weak, and from the slashing teeth of the she-wolf, his shoulder was badly gashed. And these wounds were open to the air. In the heat of the day, he lay out in the sun, drinking up the heat that it showered down on him. But when the evening came, the mountain winds at once blew, cold and sharp, and found a way through the entrance to the cave, and brought up from the ground a deadly dampness that penetrated his body to the heart, and his spirit to the innermost soul. He could not sleep. If he warmed his shoulder at the blaze, his back began to ache. If he warmed his back, from the deeply gashed shoulder, shooting pains thrust themselves through and through him. So he drowsed before a wretched fire through the night, wondering what made him cling to existence so like a blind animal, when, by a stroke, he could end all of this misery and be free.

Aye, a dozen times he took up his rifle and looked calmly down into the black deeps of the barrel where death lay. But something held him back—not love of life—but an instinct lying even deeper than the thirst for life itself.

As for the fire, it was never a very successful thing. Sometimes sharp drafts blew through the entrance to the cave and thrust the flames aside, and usually, after it had been burning for a little while, a dense cloud of smoke gathered in the cave and made him lie down close to the ground in order to breathe. A horrible life, surely.

And ever he had with him the ceaseless anxiety as to the manner in which his wounds were healing. His back, he felt, was recovering slowly but surely, after the first severe inflammation subsided, but the wound in his left shoulder, as it began to heal, pulled horribly at his flesh, and the deep cuts in his thigh were beginning to fester. He warmed water, forced open the mouth of the wound, enduring the most horrible agony, and washed the interior of that hurt as well as he was able. But, a day later, a throbbing ache in it told him that he had not searched the cut deeply enough. For fear of death, he was forced to go to work again. He whittled two clean, thick-ended sticks. With these he forced the mouth of the wound to yawn wide open and he cleansed the inside of the hurt. Twice he fainted through the sheer weight of that pain. But he completed the operation, and, the following day, he knew that he had effectually removed the danger of poisoning—at least for the time being.

But he had before him, now, another vital danger, for the food supply was done for him. The meat of the stag had turned so rank that he could no longer touch it. He had dried himself a small portion in the sun. If he had had the strength and the sense, he knew that he should have tried to cure the entire body in the same fashion, making it into jerky. He had not done so, and here was famine before him, again.

There was still a quantity of the flesh left, unspeakable to him, but apparently more acceptable than ever to the wolves. By this time, the wounds of the wolf had responded most marvelously to his first care. She was able to turn and lick them, as they began to close and heal. Her returning strength enabled her to rise and walk from place to place, although slowly and stiffly, and, as her strength returned, there seemed to return with it a greater distrust of him. She never went near him of her own volition. But now and then, as she dragged herself past him at the mouth of the cave to lie in the sun, which was curing her wounds as it was curing the wounds of the man, she submitted to the touch of his hand—submitted, always, with a sinking of her whole body, and a lightning turn of the head, and baring of the fangs.

As for the cub, that was another matter. He was turning dark and darker every day, and promised to be that prized rarity of the trapper, a black wolf. Every day, too, he grew visibly bigger, visibly brighter, visibly more interested and more daringly familiar with this new member of the family.

For if the mother wolf were a wise creature, full of lore for the young wolf to learn, the man was a thing of utter mystery, to be wondered over, to be reverenced. The man had no gaping rows of teeth; his mouth was not a weapon; he was a poor, weak, slow-moving thing. When the scent of game came fresh and heavy on the evening wind, through the mouth of the cave, he showed no emotion at all, and even when the dreadful odor of the grizzly was wafted into the cave as the king of the forest and the mountain-desert strode by, the stranger did not cower in terror.

But he carried with him a thing that made a noise like small thunder and that killed with a flash, leaving behind only a pungent, stinging breath to tell of the work it had accomplished. And he carried, too, a long and shining tooth more trenchant, far, than even the fangs of mother wolf, which could hamstring a steer at a single stroke. With that tooth, he could slash through tough wood, and whenever mother wolf smelled it, she shrank, and her hair bristled. And whenever she saw it bared, she cowered and snarled, and her eyes turned green. So that the cub learned to dread the knife by watching his mother. He knew that it meant trouble of some kind.

The man himself was a thing to be dreaded, no doubt. For mother wolf acted as though he were the living lightning bolt itself. But the cub could not understand this. Indeed, there was nothing about the man that he could understand. Only he knew that when the hand of Glanvil touched his head and ran down his neck and along his back, a thrill of joy passed through all of his body, and, when the voice of Glanvil sounded soft and deep in his throat, something like a sweet, hushed echo of the sound passed through the little wolf's body and into his heart. And, just as that tender-touching hand could arm itself with the metal stick that slew afar, or with the long bright tooth of steel, so the voice itself could change and ring with a command that made the cub's tail drop between his legs and brought him swiftly to the feet of the man, full of awe, full of fear.

He was a tyrant, too, this creature that lifted its forelegs and walked upon its hind legs only. Behold how, at times, it spoke with a light voice and moved a dancing hand that invited one to play, to frolic about, to lay hold with teeth. But if those teeth closed a trifle too hard, instantly the voice turned sharp with a ring like the ring of metal against metal, and the hand struck. And if, in response, he snapped at the hand that struck, the hand forthwith armed itself with a stout stick, and he, the son of the wild wolf, was caught by the scruff of the neck, and beaten until he licked the dreadful hand and promised obedience and gentleness thereafter.

After such tyranny, there were rewards, too. There were strokings of the hand, there was the gentle voice that touched his heart again. There were bits of meat given from the fingertips. Sometimes mother wolf, at the beginning, had snarled horribly, deep in her throat, when she saw the man handle her cub so roughly. Sometimes she had drawn near, dragging herself on her belly, her weakened limbs trembling as she strove to gather them for a spring that would launch her at his throat. But, after a time, she seemed to take it as a matter of course, and she would lie by, grinning wide, as though she said to herself: *This is well . . . this is a lesson in the lore of man. How mysterious are his ways, and how wise. The cub learns apace. This is well.*

In the meantime, mother wolf grew stronger and stronger still. No nurse, however skillful, supplies what Nature has given to its wild things —the ability to cure their own hurts swiftly. The wounds closed as by magic. With good food and plenty of it, her rough coat grew smoother, her belly grew fat, her eye brightened, and some of the stiffness was leaving her step.

But the food gave out; the mother minded not these famines. One large meal in a week's time was enough for her, but for the cub, that was quite another matter, for it needed sustenance on account of its growing bulk as well as on account of the daily expenditure of its strength playing and gamboling every day in front of the cave.

So, at night, they lay down near the warmth of the fire, the she-wolf, the man, and the cub nearest the flame, with its nose tucked into the deerskin jacket that now covered his nakedness.

But the food was gone, and Winsor Glanvil could not renew the supply. All day he lay near the mouth of the cave, or else he ventured out as far as he dared to drag his wounded leg, ventured out with infinite agonies. But he found nothing, only the trail of the mountain grouse in the grass told of food on foot near him. He wondered at the absence of all other living things near him. How could he know that the message had gone abroad, and that from the smoke of his fire near the mouth of the cave the message had gone abroad through the woods, lingering for the nose of every wild creature to read it plainly: *Man has come! Beware! Beware!*

Two days he lay thus in the open, and a third day brought nothing.

Then, in the dusk, mother wolf rose and shook her stiff flanks and stalked forth. She was gone until midnight, and then she returned and dropped wearily on the floor of the cave. Before the cub she had laid the body of a jack rabbit. What stealthy hunting had given her such a prize, the man could not guess. Certainly speed had never won it for her. But the kill was new, and the body was limp and warm. He took away from the ravenous cub enough to make a meal for himself and roasted the flesh at his fire. Then he sat up and thought over his problems.

He had been here many days, now, and it would be many days more before he was healed enough to leave the place definitely. There seemed no progress for the better in his wounded thigh, although his back was fast recovering. It might be weary long weeks before he could walk easily, to say nothing of running. Even if he could find game to shoot, his ammunition might give out. He must find some other means of gaining a livelihood—some other means, too, to help the weak mother support her cub.

For if he had helped her, she, in turn, had helped him. In time of need he had given her food that saved her life. In time of need when he was famished, she had brought flesh to him, also. A deep and quiet wonder passed through the soul of the man. Indeed, what a fool he had been to question that there is justice in the world when among the very dumb beasts of the universe there is such a scrupulous desire to return good for good and even good for evil. For he had invaded her home, he had struck her down in misery and brought her near to death. Now she carried home food for her cub, and for the man who had injured her. Glanvil felt a little awed as he considered it.

But it came to Glanvil, at the last, that there are other weapons than knife and gun. There is rod and line—there is the trap. He made little wooden snares along the trails of the grouse in the grass and caught the great fat birds easily enough. He cut with his knife stout hooks out of the bone of the deer's skeleton. Trailers from strong vines were his lines. A little down the mountainside a stream rushed by with murmur and shout, and on the bank of it he lay to fish. The little fish he cast over his shoulder. And mother wolf, lying there with pricked ears, watching, delighted with this master work, caught them out of the air and swallowed them. Or else the growing cub snatched them and tore them to bits. The larger fish he brought back and roasted to a delicious tenderness in the coals and the ashes of his fire.

These were uninvaded preserves. Man had not been this way to hunt for pleasure very often, and Glanvil only had to reach forth and take what he would.

And, in those happy evenings, when he sat near the fire, with the well-fed wolf beside him, and the well-fed cub prowling and gamboling nearby, he looked upon himself as though from afar and wondered. He, from the plains, had looked up many a time to these mountains and thought them now bare and stiffly cold and uninviting. Yet had he been thrown down in a city among men, could he have found his living with his bare hands?

Chapter Fourteen

Tedious weeks must pass for even the cleanest bullet wound to heal, when it has cut deeply through human flesh, but the wound in the thigh of Glanvil was a poisoned one to begin with, and he had no healing drugs to lay upon it in the second place. Neither could he lie still to allow it to heal. Flat upon his back he should have lain for days and days. But in the cave and out of it, he was forced to stir constantly, fighting for the food that kept him alive.

So the whip cuts on his back healed first and grew sound. And the corrugated scar from the spur cut healed on his face next. Thirdly the slash of the wolf's fangs closed and grew sound in his left shoulder. But as for the wound in his thigh, surely it progressed, and yet from day to day, as he examined it, it seemed to him that it made no progress. Still he could not walk except with an individual effort for every step.

A journey of half a mile would have been to him an endless trip. He dared not look forward to it without a shudder. Sometimes he thought of trying to make a signal to other men by building a great fire on the mountaintop, and repeating it every night until help came to him, as it surely would. But he told himself that, if help came, the men would carry him back to civilization only to try him for the slaying of big Jack Rutledge.

No, with all the miseries that he was forced to endure, it was better to remain where he was.

The weeks turned into months; the summer ended; the sharp nights told of autumn. How long he had been there, he could not tell. But he knew that mother wolf was long ago healed. She slid back and forth to the cave and out again with a silken smoothness. She was fat, strong as a lioness, for her own hunting was only for her pleasure and to give her variety, perhaps. As for the necessities of life, she had food enough from the fishing and the trapping of her human companion.

So did the black cub. What with all the food he could gorge—a rare, rare thing in the history of any young wolf—and nothing to do except find exercise and pleasure where he would, the cub had grown amazingly. He had a black coat, now, a thick, deep undercoat of fur for the winter that was coming, and the longer hairs were tipped with white. So, prospering in food and a happy home, with a great frame given him by a giant mother and perhaps a still more gigantic father, he promised to be a monster indeed of his race. And the man watched him with pride.

He left the cave in the company of his mother, now. Sometimes they were gone for two or three days at a time, and, when they came back, often their sides were leaner and always their eyes were wilder. But, as a rule, there was a fleck of dark blood on the coat of the black wolf, and the man knew that he had killed for himself.

Then, on a night, the wind blew up cold and sharp, and, when the morning came, he found that all of the mountains were white with snow. It was a gloomy spectacle for Glanvil. That day he tried his strength down the mountainside, but, when he had covered a few furlongs, he was forced to turn back, and it took him until dark to regain shelter, regain it on his hands and knees, dragging a numbed, useless leg behind him.

It required a week to undo the disastrous effects of that sally from the cave, and, when the week was over—a week of wretched starvation and suffering—he found that the mountains were knee-deep in snow. He was snowbound for God alone could tell how long a time to come.

There followed for Glanvil a season of the blackest despair. A season of near starvation, too. But the very pangs of hunger at last forced him out to make an effort for his life, and he was rewarded at once. On his very first expedition, not a hundred paces from the entrance to the cave—upwind, according to the prevailing gales, he saw a thin column of steam arising from between two naked old trees, and the air, when he drew near, was rank with the smell of bear.

Mother wolf, following at his heels, snarled and

fled with her tail between her legs, but the King Silver, as he had come to call the cub, remained nearby, curious although frightened. To Glanvil, it was danger indeed, but it was possibly a supply of food, and therefore he ventured the chance. A stone or two thrown at the right place and the shouting that he raised, suddenly brought forth a fine young grizzly, newly entered upon his winter's sleep, and with fat rolling sides from the last of his labors among the nuts and the roots and the insects of the late fall.

He stood blinking in the morning sun, bewildered, but growling, still half stupefied with sleep. And he was an easy mark for Glanvil. Down in the snow the man sank, steadied the gun, and fired. The first shot brought the grizzly lumbering toward him with a roar that sent King Silver squealing for shelter. The second shot brought him down in his tracks.

An hour later the man was dining on roasted bear's meat. Then, the rest of that day and all of the next, he was laboring at the enormous skin, worth more than gold to him for the rigors of the winter that lay ahead. By dint of prying the body over with long poles, he managed to turn the skin loose, at the last, and peg it down in the floor of the cave to cure by the heat of the fire. Thereafter, for a week or more—the count of days meant nothing to Glanvil now—he worked over the frozen body, carving out the meat in long strips and bringing it to the fire that he kept before the mouth of the cave during that stretch of fine weather, to dry and cure it with heat and with smoke.

It was hard provision, when the labor was ended. This was no crisp-smoked venison, but a food as hard as wood, with a fearfully rank taste. However, there was a quantity of it. More than he could use, surely, through the course of the winter, eked out with what fish he could catch in the streams, and what mountain grouse he could find.

But the labor itself was a chief delight. It gave him so much to do that from dawn until the dark he was busy, and at night he slept soundly, exhausted. In the meantime there was enough of the big body and the bones left to supply the two wolves amply during a pinched season for them. They did not hunt that week, so gorged were they with food. And that experience fixed in the minds of mother wolf and the cub that the man was an invincible god, surely, for only a god, of course, could face and destroy with a blow the king of the mountains.

When the store of bear's meat was dried, he began to regulate his life carefully. His strength was not yet his by a great deal. The wounded thigh was healing fast, now, to be sure, but he had to guard against every sudden move, for fear lest the torn flesh should be set gaping again as had happened so often before.

He apportioned his hours. Some time he spent in making an opening through the smaller rocks that covered the top of the cave—a labor of infinite exertion and the greatest care, for he must not make too large an aperture, and yet he wanted one great enough to permit the smoke from his fire to rise through it and so to escape.

A part of each day for a long time went to the creation of this vitally necessary chimney. For the big fires that he would need in the bitterest heart of the winter would stifle him, otherwise, with the smoke.

The chimney was one labor, and the making of a bearskin all-over garment was another. To fashion and sew that ponderous suit, and to make from fragments of the skin stout bear-hide moccasins, and thick leggings that wrapped him to the hips was a thing that tasked all of his ingenuity. And when the work was done, the weight of the hide was almost unbearably great. And the smell of it was far from a perfume. However, it was warm, unbelievably warm. Equipped in it, like an armored knight among barbarians, he could defy the cold no matter how sharp the wind blew.

But even these two tasks were not all. He had to forage for wood. And that was a great labor indeed. He had no axe. All he could do was to hunt for branches small enough to drag back to the cave and store away in its depths, and break down dead shrubs. But he was never able, in this manner, to accumulate enough wood to give him any feeling of considerable safety. He could not use that wood for anything other than cooking, he found at last. As for mere warmth of his body, for that he had to trust to the bearskin and, at night, the body of King Silver stretched upon one side of him, and the mother wolf curled on the other.

Neither were these preparations all that he had before him. Every day he went out to tend his little traps and deadfalls, and take in the decreasing amount of small game that they furnished to him. Until, at the last, rabbits were almost all that he could expect to find, and these came sparingly indeed to his traps. He could fish, however, to the last.

And it was the fish that eventually saved his life. For, as the heart of the winter came, he found that the entire stock of his bear's meat was spoiled by the damp. The wolves had it to feast upon, and even they took it reluctantly. But, no matter how great the cold grew, and it became of an Arctic intensity, he could break through the ice where the streams were frosted over with a thick armor, and drop his baited hooks of bone into the depths where still some life remained. And he made himself a long lance-like pole of light, dried wood, with a prong of bone. Then, like an Eskimo, he speared his fish through the openings that he broke in the upper ice above the streams.

In the meantime, the heavy winter set in. And it was unbelievably severe. Even in the lowest and most sheltered valleys, that season, the cattle died by the thousands, but up there among the battlements of the mountains, where the wind was king, bellowing and thundering day and night, to leave the mouth of the cave was to enter upon a dreadful battle.

Weeks and endless weeks followed. He dared not leave the cave except when the need of fuel and of food drove him out. And he would have gone mad from sluggish idleness and the lack of food for his thoughts had it not been for the King Silver.

Never an animal had such a schooling as the education that Glanvil lavished upon the cub, not even the most prized circus performers had such attention poured upon them. For the trick animal of the circus is, after all, only the meal ticket of its trainer, but the silver wolf was food for the very soul of Glanvil. When he spoke, there was no answer except from the active eyes and the pricking ears of the big brute. For it had grown big by this time. It sallied out with its mother, from time to time, and sometimes it went out to hunt by itself. But the vast majority of its time was spent in the chilly shelter of that cave with the man.

It came to understand him by gestures. It became a serviceable slave, with this difference, that its services were a happy game to the silver wolf. If he beckoned toward the back of the cave, big Silver learned to go into the shadows and come back dragging a branch. Mother wolf could never be taught. But the big cub learned lightning fast with an open and a supple brain. He learned to go abroad, too, and drag home at the command of the master branches that would have exhausted Glanvil's strength to manage. And the King Silver, like a hunting dog, would stalk and strike down a rabbit, and then bring it back to Glanvil. Once he came home trailing, with infinite effort, the quarter of a sheep. How far from the deep valleys beneath had it carried that prize? And what ranch was there to be preyed upon?

It brought a new thought to Glanvil. He had felt that no human habitation could be within many, many miles of his refuge on the mountainside, but now there was proof that he had been wrong.

He was in no haste to take advantage of the information, however. His leg was healed, now, but it was still stiff and withered. Every night he exposed it to the fire and rubbed it with grease to make the hardened flesh supple. Every day he exercised it carefully, and, little by little, he could put more confidence in it. Not until he was an active man again, however, dared he to venture among other men. For what his reception might be, he could not tell.

CHAPTER FIFTEEN

All was one in those wild mountains that winter. December, January, February, and March stormed and raged and howled, and the snow was deep and the wind was filled with teeth of ice. In April, the weather began to change and break. And in April, Winsor Glanvil made his first descent upon the houses of men.

He was new-made, by this time. And when a bright morning came and the air was softer and the sun was brighter and nearer, he cast off the great cumbersome bearskin. There had been a day when the weight of that garment was a ponderous load to him. But now it was nothing. Those who live the life of the wilderness gain the strength of the wild things. His muscles were no bigger than they had been in the summer, perhaps, but they were supple as the body of a snake, and they were tough as a young hickory bush. There was not even a hint of a limp in his gait. The wound in his leg was long since healed, and the flesh had grown straight and the suppleness had returned to his muscles.

So he stood up strong and tall and cast away the bear robe. In its place he put on the deer-skin trousers and jacket that were his latest manufacture. He had killed that deer himself, in hand-to-hand conflict, when he found the poor creature struggling in a deep drift of snow into which it had slid on the bosom of a little avalanche. And because of the battle, he prized that skin as a symbol of his new manhood. Now, in these lighter, tighter garments, he stood at the mouth of his cave and looked forth on the day. There was sound everywhere. Among the loftier mountain heads, winter was still strong and thick with a helmet of ice, but here the strong April sun was beginning to work its way. There was a whispering of running water beneath the snow crusts. There was a furtive whistle from a bird from time to time. Insects *hummed* and darted like lightning across the air. And even in the woods there was a difference—not an actual stir of life, but the near approach of awakening, like the face of a sleeper just before the dawn. Spring was already there. Another few weeks and it would quite fling aside the white garments of the dreary winter.

Glanvil, from the height, read all of these signs, and felt a stir of happiness in his heart. He combed with his fingers the long black beard that had grown about his face in the last months, and like a king he looked slowly around him.

Far off, from the hollow, he heard the wail of a wolf—the King Silver squatted on his haunches and lifted his big head to the sky.

"Be quiet," said the man.

And the huge yearling wolf stood up again and watched his face,

"We are going on a journey," said Glanvil. "Are you ready?"

King Silver canted his head upon one side and looked on with wistful eyes, as he always did when a new word came that was not in his extensive vocabulary.

"We are going down," said the man, "to see what we can see. We have been here long enough, freezing and starving."

The young wolf, tormented by this flow of speech that he did not understand, looked anxiously around him. Yonder was a fallen dead branch. He leaped to it and came back carrying it in his mouth to the opening of the cave. But the master shook his head.

"Your mother will miss us," he said. "I know as well as you that she is coming back from her hunting, the old vagabond. Well, call her. Call her, Silver!"

The King dropped on his haunches readily, tilted his nose up, closed his eyes, and opened a mouth glittering with snowy fangs. Out from his quivering throat came the smooth, deep bay of a male wolf; the echo flew across the ravine and came faintly clanging back again; immediately after a short howl blew down the wind.

"She is running," said Glanvil. "She will be here at once."

He had barely time to go into the cave and come out again, bearing his rifle, when the timber wolf broke from the edge of the woods and slunk up beside him. He eyed her quietly.

"The old fool has missed her kill," said Glanvil. "Go bring her meat, Silver . . . meat!"

The King shot into the cave; he reappeared at once dragging the partially consumed quarter of a deer. This he dropped at the feet of the master, and Glanvil kicked it toward the she-wolf.

"Your belly is too thin for happiness," he said. "Eat!"

Her fangs were instantly in the meat. She ripped it off in long chunks and bolted them whole. It was amazing to see her melt her way down to the bone swifter than flame, but Glanvil stopped the process. If she were to accompany them, it would not do to have her belly too full. He laid hold on the end of the bone, a maneuver that she greeted with a snarl of rage, but he, chuckling, took her by the upper jaw and loosed her grip. She shrank away, skulking on her belly, raging inwardly, her eyes squinted as though in expectation of a blow. Truly he had gained a wonderful power over her in that winter, but she was still far from the perfect understanding of his orders that the King had. The wild devil in her was pushed back behind a veil, and she paid him only that obedience that was forced from her by the dread of his superior strength of cunning.

"Take it back," said Glanvil, and the young wolf caught up the half-eaten fragment and darted with it into the cave. He came back licking his lips, and the man grinned down at him.

"You have stolen one bite, you scoundrel," said Glanvil. "Well, you will work for that before the day is over. Now, heel!"

He walked off down the mountainside, and they fell in behind him, the King at his heels, and the gray mother in the distance, unseen. He could never teach her to stay close. And, although she was never far away and always within the reach of his voice, she preferred to skulk from shrub to shrub and covert to covert, rather as though she were hunting them than as if she followed them at the man's command.

Halfway down the mountainside a red squirrel peeked above a stone, ducked down again, and then with the foolhardy recklessness of his race decided to take a chance and try to cross the clearing in front of these enemies and gain the nearest tree trunk.

At the first flash of the scurrying body—"Take it!" cried Glanvil.

The King dissolved into a black streak. Fast ran the squirrel, with tail streaming behind it, but faster rushed that impending doom. The red squirrel had reached the trunk of the tree before the King caught it. Then there was one snap of the resistless teeth and a headless little body dropped back on the ground. The King carried that body proudly to his master, and Glanvil laid it by under some brush and against the snow. He smiled as he went on, for the gray mother was sure to find that body and yearn for it, but she was equally sure to know the scent of his hand upon it and go on, leaving it untouched. Many a cruel lesson it had cost to teach her so much as this.

They crossed the first valley. They climbed the narrow ridge beyond and dropped into the farther hollow and here a whine from the King gave him warning. He turned and found the young wolf looking back up the slope over which they had come, quivering with terror. Then he saw the coming danger.

Perhaps their own footfalls had started the trouble by unbalancing a little stone that was the key to the situation and which, as it rolled, had loosened a tiny bit of snow, and this, sliding slowly forward, had disturbed the balance of a larger rock, and that rock, lumbering leisurely forward, had dislodged a still greater mass of snow. At any rate, just behind them a young snowslide was in full career, and now its rumbling voice grew about them. It was still high, high up the steep side of the mountain, but with every instant it was gathering speed, and with every instant its heavy front, plowing deeper in the piled and frozen masses of the snow, was gathering bulk, gathering breadth. It caught a little group of saplings, shore them off, tossed them upon its back, and went rushing on.

There was no time to stand and gaze longer; the King still waited for the word, but he was quivering with dread. His wisdom in this case would be great, but the wisdom of the mother would be greater still. Where was she? As for Glanvil, if he strove to flee, he was as apt as not to run straight into the path of the thundering menace. Ah, here was the she-wolf, leaping toward them out of a clump of trees.

She sped straight past them with a whine of warning, and then ran ahead. It seemed the sheerest madness to Glanvil. It seemed that she was running in the very path where the avalanche would sweep in another moment. But he had learned long before this to trust to her instinct rather than to his own reason in such emergencies as this. So he followed her at full speed, and that was a speed that would have amazed a sprinting athlete.

They darted straight down the mountainside, and then up to the top of a little hill. Not a hill—hardly more than a little hummock of ground. Surely the old wolf did not think that this was a sufficient protection to keep the mass of snow from washing across them. Yes, here she paused and squatted on her haunches, her red tongue lolling out, her whole body quivering as she looked up on the approaching destruction. And the man, against his will, paused there, also.

The snowslide was under full way now. The

thunder of its coming, heavily repeated from the echoing opposite wall of the valley, was a continuous roar. The King shrank against the side of the man and looked up to his all-knowing face. And he, feeling that his last hour had come, patted the noble head and set his teeth.

The slide had a great front, now, like the forehead of some enormous tidal wave, churned to the whitest foam. Nothing could stop it, it seemed. The veteran trees of the forest, feet thick in the trunk and stanchly rooted, were plucked up by the heel and sucked into the writhing masses, or else they were cut short at the ground and tossed aloft. And from the squirming back of the slide, now and again, the stripped trunks of trees were flung into the air as though the hands of giants hurled them, javelin-wise.

Straight on for the crouched trio that destruction raced, like a monstrous whale, huge headed, and tapering to the tail that, at the last, was a high boiling flag of snow dust fluttering in the air. The noise of the trees breaking was like the crackle of enormous machine-guns, or the volleying of whole armaments of great twelve-inch rifles. Like a wall arose the white head of the mischief as it swept nearer—faster, now, than a racing blood horse—yes, faster than a thrown stone. No living thing could vie with that speed. And closer, closer, it cast its white brows above the tops of the dark evergreens nearby.

There followed a shock that made the ground rock beneath the feet of the man. Then, with a wild roaring greater than a hundred hurricanes, the front of the snowslide staggered, reeled, and then pitched away to the side, casting a far-flying shower of snow dust across them.

Down and down it lurched, still gathering new speed. The whole front of that monster was by and the long, twisting, writhing, thundering body followed along a ravine that, heaped across with the crusted snow, Glanvil had not dreamed of as he ran across it. But the she-wolf had known and used it to save their lives.

Now the white ruin reached the pit of the valley. Now it flung itself far up along the opposite slope and there at last came to a stop, making a heap like a newly risen white mountain, stuck about on the face with the protruding hulks of tree trunks, like little matches that children stick into the cheeks of the snowman.

The path down which the snowslide had come was now a raw welt across the surface of the mountain. The trees were stripped away along its entire length, and in the end, digging deeper and deeper, it had stripped away all the earth down to the bedrock itself and left this wet and shining in the morning sun.

The she-wolf rose and shook herself as though issuing from cold water. But the cub edged closer to Glanvil and licked his hand with a faint whine.

This miracle, in his eyes, must be owing to the consummate wisdom of the man. There could be no explanation—how wise and great a master, how like a god he was.

And Glanvil, looking down at the beautiful head of the brute, and the eyes now abashed and tender with submission and love, felt a little sharp-pricking pang of shame. He would have explained if he could. But all he could do was to vow silently to himself that this night the gray mother should feast till her insatiable maw was crammed.

Then they went on. Once more the she-wolf hung back behind them, skirting through the trees. It would need a wary foot, indeed, to surprise this hunting party from the rear.

"Go on!" called the master to the King.

Up the farther slope, which Glanvil himself had never topped, the silver wolf shot, but at the top he paused suddenly and flattened himself on the ground. Glanvil hurried after, and from the crest he found himself looking down on a little mountain village.

CHAPTER SIXTEEN

He brushed from his eyes the long mass of hair that, from time to time, he had roughly trimmed by hacking it away with his sharp hunting knife. It was marvelously altered from the shining black of the summer before when he won the heart of Louise Carney, for now it was a deep gray. So much the long agony of that fall and that winter had worked upon him.

Surely not even his oldest friend in the world could have known him now. But, for that matter, what friend had he worth noting? None at all. There was the wolf cub at his heels, and no human had ever meant so much to him as did the King. He thought of that with a touch of wonder, running his hand through the rich fur of the young wolf. And, in the meantime, his eye feasted on the village. It was very small, very poverty-stricken in appearance, but from the chimneys the smoke curled up and a faint chiming of voices came hollowly up to him—the piercing voices of children playing in the snow. It seemed very wonderful indeed that this small town had managed to exist through all the rigors of the winter. But there it stood. No doubt the greatest period of the snows had buried the houses to their eaves. Now they had been shoveled away, and the village appeared. A little more, and the snow would be melting under the warm suns of May.

All the pangs of his long torment came back to him now. The forgotten pangs of back and shoulder and deeply gashed thigh worked through his quivering flesh again, and here, so very near, there had been abundant help if he could have reached it. Surely if he had built a signal fire at night he would have had abundant rescuers about him by the next morning. But he was fiercely glad that he had fought out his own battle in his own way, single-handed. Now the world that, he felt, had so savagely wronged him could not make a counterclaim against him. He felt between himself and all the universe, not a single binding obligation—except, perhaps, to the mother wolf. Yet there arose in him a strange hunger to see human faces again. And, since he knew that they could never recognize in him the destroyer of Jack Rutledge, he started straight down to the town.

The silver cub began to draw back. Not that he had ever had actual experience of man other than his master, but because, in his hunting through the woods with the gray mother, there had been one overpowering scent that never failed to make her shrink against the ground with bristling hair and with green hate in her eyes. That was the scent of man and of steel that lay, often, thickly about on the surface of the snow. And, straight down into the deadly peril of that scent, which reeked up in the smoke from the houses, the master was going.

The King began to whine, but a sharp word from the master reminded him that his own poor wits were not needed, and he slunk along at the heels of Glanvil. There was another and a bolder interference now, however. Gray mother shot out suddenly from the woods in front of them and faced them with teeth snarled bare, and with green-lighted eyes of rage. She advanced on them with little stiff-legged bounds, as though ready to rush at their throats.

She, too, apparently wished to warn the master back. Until she was at the very edge of the village she persisted, but then the sudden voice of a child, playing nearby, made her bound into the shadow with a silent baring of her teeth. She was gone without a sound.

A big, square-muzzled hound, half Great Dane and half bloodhound, from the look of it, came hastily through the brush, apparently drawn by something its nose had caught high in the air—for it came with head up until it saw the man and the young wolf skulking behind him. At that, bristling and savage, it would have rushed the King, but Glanvil interfered with a sharp word.

The human voice made the big brute pause and shrink with ears suddenly lowered, but then the very scent of the man seemed to change. No doubt, to those cunning nostrils of the dog, Glanvil was rank with the scent that of all is most loathsome to the canine race—the scent of the wild dogs, the tameless wolves. He came snarling to the very feet of the man, until the waved rifle of Glanvil made him shrink away again.

The King Silver, in the meantime, stood perfectly erect, head high, tail aloft, and the upper lip grinned back a little to show a glint of the ready fangs. He was a very statue for beauty, a very statue for pride and for flawless courage. He was not anxious to begin the battle with that burly monster that far outweighed his own undeveloped strength, but he would not give back an inch, and, if the master spoke but a single word of encouragement, the fight would begin. All of this the master saw, and appreciated it with all of his heart.

But he warned the dog back again, he spoke to the King, and went slowly forward. He suspected what would happen, and he was not wrong. Balked of the immediate prey that was before him by the presence of the man—that irresistible authority—the great fighting dog followed up another trail of interest and rushed off through the brush. There was only a moment of that noisy trailing, then sudden snarls of two varieties—the guttural, savage growl of the dog that says: "Let me get you by the throat, you brute! Let me close with you! Let me put my teeth into you in one good grip and hold and hold with my jaws locked, no matter what happens . . . or until men come!

Stand still, you rascal, you renegade, you traitor! Stand still and fight! *G-r-r!* How I hate you!"

The snarl of the wolf, pitched higher, blood-curdling in its effect: "Man-tamed rat! Sneaking fool! Now I have you single-handed at last! Now your brothers and sisters are not standing by to help you! Now I have you weeded out from your cousins and your uncles and your aunts, I'll teach you a thing or two about fighting that you never dreamed of, you bloodless cur . . . you eater of table scraps . . . you herd hunter . . . you, you, dog! *Ah-r-r-rah!* How I despise you. Now catch me if you can while I knife you to ribbons!"

The fight began. It was a crashing whirl in the underbrush. And Glanvil did not stir. He had a suppressed confidence in the result of that fight. And he only hoped that the hound would be destroyed utterly.

The snarling of the wolf was intermingled, now, with the short howls of agony and rage from the hound. Only a moment more—then the brindled brute burst out into the clearing, open-mouthed, yelping at every stride, and kiting along with all his might.

On his flank slid a smooth gray shadow, her head jerking sidewise as the long fangs ripped and slashed. She had written a pretty story on that burly beast already, and she was still busy writing. His shoulders were gashed, his neck was torn, he was streaked and flowing with crimson. To the edge of the brush she followed in silent savagery. Then the hound rushed on, howling, to find safety, and gray mother plunged to one side into the shadowy brush and was gone silently, as she had gone before.

"Good girl," said the man. "You are the jewel of my eye, old wisdom. That was a red lesson for him."

Then he went on into the street of the little town, with King Silver licking his lips in memory of the delectable picture that he had just seen, and following close, close behind the heels of his master. For, upon either side, new wonders and new terrors darted out toward him, or shouted at him.

In the first place there was a cluster of children who had raised a ringing peal of terror and of wonder when they saw the great hound rush from the wood so thoroughly thrashed. For he was the fighting champion of that town, was the hound. He had beaten every dog that dared to challenge his supremacy. Even among the people there was an air of awe when they looked upon the brindled monster, and his owner was fond of telling how, on a day, that hound, single-handed, had conquered a timber wolf—a real gray lobo. He had never added that it was only a cub wolf that had been beaten. But, after seeing the great dog so thoroughly beaten, there presently stepped out from the woods a wild man with a long rifle in his hand and a dog that looked like a wolf following at his heels. The conclusion was too obvious—this black wolfish creature, which was not even panting with exertion, must have done the fighting.

They yelled with their wonder. And their yells brought their parents first to windows and then to door and then running out onto the street. They saw the strangest picture that had met their eyes in many a year—a man, dressed in a ragged, home-made deerskin suit, with the hair turned out, and rude moccasins on his feet, his gray hair chopped away from his forehead and falling long and wild about his shoulders. At his feet slunk the King Silver looking, indeed, like a monstrous silver fox.

They were too astonished to come to the stranger with questions—all of them, that is to say, except the owner of the burly hound. He was a big man, who loved his savage dog because their natures were akin, and, when he saw his dog cowering at his feet, covered with crimson, he thought of one thing only, caught up a revolver, and plunged into the street. There he saw the wild man, and halted only an instant in his wonder. For, if the man was wild, his gray head seemed to say that he was old, also, and therefore weak. So he came running to Glanvil.

"Stranger," he shouted, "have you been settin' your wolf-dogs on my hound? By the heavens, you'll pay for that!"

Glanvil reached into the little deerskin wallet at his belt, and in which he kept the money that, by good fortune, he had not lost in his flight after the shooting of Rutledge. He drew out a nickel and tossed it at the big man.

"Your dog is worth about that price, I suppose," he said. And he passed on.

As for the other, he had come close enough to notice, under the thatch of the gray hair, the bright brown eyes, young and keen, and the young black beard. And something about the fierce steadiness of those eyes, like the fixed stare of a mountain lion, made him turn and step back while Glanvil went on.

As for Glanvil, it was one of the sweetest moments of his life. He was strong of hand, he well knew, from those labors in the long winter of the mountains, but for the strength of his spirit he could not vouch. Now he had ample testimony, for with a mere touch of his eyes he had chained up the strength of a fighting man. He went on, and at his heels the King Silver walked with a higher head and a more watchful eye. All of this was merely a proof, to him, of what he had already suspected—that his master, although shaped like other men, was different—just as the gray lobo is shaped like the prowling, sneaking coyote—but how different are their fighting hearts.

Under the barber's pole he turned in; he saw the fat barber, and that worthy was gaping at him with great round eyes. Glanvil sat down in the chair.

"I am not a wild man," he said, smiling at the pale face of the barber. "I want a shave and a haircut, and all the talk, sir, that you can spare while you work."

Chapter Seventeen

The fear of the barber was short-lived, for he felt at once that a man who valued his talk was an extraordinarily sensible person. As for the wild clothes, they did not at all match with the polite talk. He sensed an adventure and poured forth, in the beginning, a babble of questioning. The answer of Winsor Glanvil was perfectly smooth and perfectly simple.

"I decided to try my hand at trapping," he said, "and so I did. But my clothes were burned by accident, I was snowed in so that I couldn't move far from my camp, and altogether I have had a rocky time of it. The worst of it was when a deer that I thought I had killed with my rifle started up and gashed me across the face with his horn."

And, with this, he ran his finger along the hard furrow that the scar had left across his face. As for the gray hair, he could forgive the fate that had bestowed upon him that change, but he was filled with a soul-consuming curiosity to see the effect of the scar on his face. The ladies might find gray hair quite a romantic attraction. But as for the scar—he shuddered when he thought of it. Sometimes, on a cold morning, he could feel it drawing all the flesh on that side of his face and tugging at the corner of his mouth. And still, he had seen even large scars that were not unattractive. And perhaps the smooth beauty that had been his before might be exchanged, now, for a wildly romantic air that would be more instantly fatal to the hearts of the weaker sex. In the meantime, as he sat in the chair, he vowed to himself that he would not look into the glass until his hair was trimmed and his beard was shaved.

The talk of the barber flowed on in an uninterrupted stream. When he heard that this man had not seen a newspaper for six months, his heart swelled with joy. Out of his brain poured a vast tide of information.

"But," said Glanvil, "I don't care about politics as much as I do about what has happened in these same mountains around us. I wonder if some of those storms . . ."

"It's been a wild winter," said the barber, "but . . . good heavens, that has the look of a wolf, that dog of yours."

"I think there may be a touch of wolf blood in it," said Glanvil carelessly. "But you rarely see black wolves."

"I've heard tell of a silver wolf no further back than last fall. Jem Turner trapped a big one right backcountry, yonder, a dog-gone' whopper of a wolf. He swears that it weighed a hundred and twenty pounds."

"A hundred and twenty pounds?" asked Glanvil. "That's a good deal more than I thought they ever went. You see," he added, "I'm entirely an amateur at trapping."

The barber grinned. "I reckon maybe you are. What made you do it?"

"I was weak and sick," said Glanvil. "Bad lungs . . . and the doctors recommended the mountains. I took the mountains in my own way. How big do the timber wolves go?"

"The biggest that I ever clapped eyes on myself went just ninety-five pounds, but then they come bigger'n that, I know. Jud Harper, he caught one and weighed it right on Welling's scales. That ran up to a hundred and seven pounds, but it was a pretty fat wolf. A hundred and twenty pounds don't seem hardly nacheral for a wolf to weigh, but I got to say that Jem Turner is an honest man . . . why, he nailed that wolf only about ten miles from here. I seen the skin. Looked like a black bear rug."

It was not hard to put two and two together, after all. This was the father, beyond a shadow of a doubt, of the silver cub that now followed Glanvil, and with such a Herculean father and such a giant of a mother, with such special care and feeding as it had had, it should be a monster of its kind. Already, hardly more than fourteen months old, it looked simply too big to be a wolf. It lay in the farthest and the darkest corner of the room and watched the process of the shaving of the master until the gleam of the razor at the throat of Glanvil was too much for it. It slipped out and stood, bristling nearby, its head turning a fraction back and forth as it marked every turn of the hand of the fat man. How marvelous that the master should submit to this near neighborhood of death without a struggle.

"Well," said the barber, "if you want to know what's been happening through the mountains, I dunno that there's much excitement. When was it that you went up into the hills?"

"Along in August."

"August? Lemme look back. Was that after the big forest fire up the range that cleaned out the Slocums?"

"Yes, it was after that."

"I guess that you was around after Glanvil shot Rutledge?"

Glanvil closed his eyes. "I don't think that I've heard anything about that. What Rutledge do you mean?"

"*The* Rutledge. Jack Rutledge!"

"Not the man . . . ?"

"That's him . . . it was big Jack Rutledge himself. And you ain't heard no talk about the shooting and what come up to it?"

"Not a word."

"Well, well, seems like everybody must've knowed about that. This here Glanvil . . ."

"I never heard of him."

"A lucky thing for a lot of folks if they'd never

seen or heard tell of him. He was one of these smooth-talkin' Eastern gents, mighty good-lookin', they say he was. I never seen so much as his picture, though. But folks says that he was fine enough lookin' to've . . . hey, mister, will you send that dog away? He makes me sort of a mite nervous, I'll tell a man, snoopin' around and sniffin' at my leg as though he was pickin' out a spot where he'd take his dinner from. He's got a good deal of bitin' power, I s'pose?"

A word from the master sent the big wolf to a corner of the room, and there he sank down again, but with his head stretched forth upon his paws and his legs well drawn under him, ready to launch himself at the throat of the stranger in case the master should seem in need.

"All I warn you of," said Glanvil, controlling a smile, "is that if your razor draws so much as one dot of blood while you're shaving me, the dog yonder will have your throat torn ragged in a fraction of a second."

The barber groaned, but then he went on with both his work and his chatter.

"This here Glanvil was a real heart-breaker. Seems that that was the way he got along. Nothin' immoral, I suppose. But just get the women interested in him, and then pick their pockets. That sort of a cur. He come up this way and the first thing right off that he spotted was Louise Carney, of course. You've heard about her?"

"Her father made something in mines?"

"How many millions I'd hate to guess, I tell you. This Glanvil, he comes along and makes a pretty big play for her, and dog-gone me if he don't get her. After all, she's a pretty simple girl and don't know much about these fortune hunters. She sees how good-lookin' he is."

"This," said Glanvil, "doesn't sound particularly interesting. By the way you started, I thought that there might be a murder or some such story in it."

"Hold yourself together, stranger," said the barber with a sort of gloomy intensity of delight. "Just you hold yourself together and listen right hard and you'll hear all that you want to hear about trouble. Well, this Glanvil finally got things fixed, and the girl had said that she would marry him, but, right about at the same time, old Jack Rutledge begun to smell trouble. Jack was in love with Louise Carney, of course. Everybody on the range knowed that he had been . . . and back in the days before her dad made so much money, too. He begun to pry back into the history of this here Glanvil, and he found out plenty . . . enough to've turned your stomach to've heard them."

"What happened, then?"

"He give warnin' to a pal of this Glanvil that he knowed about the two of them and that they'd better start along if they didn't want a lynchin' party after 'em. But Glanvil decided to make his play, anyway. He got ready to make his start that same night with the girl.

"Now, there is a blind girl named Kate Preston that lives up yonder with Louise Carney . . . a sort of a queer thing, they say that she is. Sort of able to look at the insides of things . . . and people. Nothing like her nowheres else in the mountains, I guess. This here Kate Preston, she sort of read the mind of Glanvil and the girl. She up and left the house and she walked right down the road to town, in the dark, and all by herself. Mind you that . . . right down a trail, and her not able to see. But she felt her way along and, though she got some pretty bad falls, she got to the town and asked somebody to lead her to Jack Rutledge. They took her there, and she told Jack that she thought everything was about to start. Jack, he has everybody watched. They see Glanvil's pal leave town early, and ride away and they foller him over the hills to the minister's house there. Then they see what's comin' and send for Rutledge. They go on and grab Santelle . . . that was his name . . . and make him tell what he knows . . . used a blacksnake to make him talk." The barber laughed. "After that, along comes this here smart gent Glanvil and falls right into the trap . . . they grab him and figger on givin' him a beatin' that will last him for a while. They lace him down good, and then they go back into the house, leavin' him in the barn.

“Now, son, here’s where the queer part of that yarn begins. This here soft-lookin’ Glanvil, while they’re layin’ the quirt onto him, doesn’t make so much as a peep of sound. He takes it all till he faints. Then while the boys are in the house drinkin’ coffee and thankin’ heaven that they saved Louise Carney from such a skunk, but wonderin’ at the nerve of him, the door is throwed open, and they see this here Glanvil standin’ in front of them, naked to the waist, and with a mighty bad-lookin’ cut on his face. Looked like he’d fallen against a nail and ripped his face right wide open. He yells out to Rutledge and gives Jack a mighty free chance to pull his gun. And then he beats him and puts a bullet into him and turns and runs away.”

“Very odd,” said Glanvil through his teeth.

“That ain’t more’n the start, friend. The boys thought that Rutledge was dead, and they open up with their gats on Glanvil. They chase him right on out of the town and they must’ve sunk one of their bullets in him, for by and by, the next morning, the hoss he’d swiped come back to them in the town. Glanvil must’ve rode until he dropped dead offen the back of the hoss. About a week later, a cowpuncher come across a body that was in pretty bad shape and partly eat up by wolves or coyotes, or something. It was a gent about the size of Glanvil that had black hair like him . . . and in fact it must’ve been Glanvil’s body.”

"Well," said Glanvil, "it seems as though he paid for that little party pretty well."

"Mighty queer, that part of it. Everybody put him down for a yaller skunk, but in the end he turned around and fought like a devil."

"And Rutledge . . . he was dead, I suppose?" said Glanvil.

"Dead? Him? Of course not!"

Black mist spun before the eyes of Glanvil. Had the long agony of that winter been for nothing, then? Had he accomplished nothing by that facing down of Rutledge?

"Of course not," said the barber. "The bullet hit him fair and square, but it glanced around off his ribs. He was up and walkin' in three weeks."

"It doesn't seem possible," murmured Glanvil.

"Jack Rutledge ain't like other men. Besides, he had something to do, and that was to cheer up Louise Carney."

Hot fury stormed through Glanvil. "I suppose that he managed to accomplish that?" he said faintly.

"Sure. I suppose that he put before her all of the facts that he knowed about Glanvil. Anyways, she grieved a lot at first, and, when the body was brung in, she put a fine big stone over his grave in the churchyard and put his name on it. And she said on it that he'd died fightin' like a man, which nobody could very well deny. But afterward, she forgave Rutledge and seen that he was acting by his best lights, I suppose. And now, what would you think has happened?"

"Where there's a woman concerned, one never can tell," said Glanvil.

"That's a true thing. Well, she up and got herself engaged to get married to Rutledge, and the thing is comin' off next week."

Chapter Eighteen

The voice of the barber went on, but the man in his chair, although he nodded from time to time, heard nothing but the sound of it like a distant stream of wind through the trees in the mountains, for his mind was too filled with his own thoughts.

All the thing that had comforted him during the long agony of the winter was undone at a stroke. At least, he had been able to tell himself, he had paid a price, but he had brought down one enemy and a great one, to his death. Now it seemed that his blow had been struck in vain. And there wakened in the heart of Glanvil a deep and implacable rage that was never to die away, again, until many a grim thing had been done by his hand.

Then, at last, he heard the barber say: "And there you are, sir. Ain't able to recognize yourself, I guess. Tell me if you like the job." And he thrust a big hand mirror before Glanvil's face.

What the latter saw was a nightmare, not himself. The black beard was gone; the gray hair was neatly trimmed. The aspect of an old man was gone and his youth was restored to him—but what youth it was. Ten years had been added to his age, but the apparent passing of time was the least of what he saw. All the right side of his face, as he looked at it in profile, was as it had ever been—handsome and even beautiful beyond the right of men—save that the smooth grace was ended, and in its place there was a closer chiseling, a lean look of strength. But the left side? It was a ghastly grimace. A great white scar ran down over the flesh, twisting in beside the eye and then zig-zagging down near the corner of the mouth and so to the chin. The nostril was drawn a little, the corner of the mouth was pulled into a faint smile that seemed the very incarnation of sardonic rage and hatred, even the eye was drawn and narrowed, so that he seemed, from that side, to be peering out with a look of settled and penetrating malice.

In all the world, he had never seen a face more terribly repellent. The barber himself was biting his lip and standing back with a faint frown of pain, as though he himself felt the stroke that had left this scar.

"That deer," he said, "you had ought to've burned alive, partner."

But Glanvil, rising hastily, paid the man double and hurried from the room as he would have hurried from a torture chamber. In the street there were a number of hangers-on and idlers, pausing here and there in little settled groups, and all gathered, beyond doubt, for the sake of seeing the wild man and his wild dog at closer range.

But every face changed color as he went by, and every eye widened in staring upon him. No, they could not even look steadily upon him, these mountain yokels, but turned their heads hastily away as though ashamed of the horror that they felt. And the marked man went by them with a raging devil in his soul.

He could revolve only one thing in his mind. What could be done to Jack Rutledge to make him pay for this desecration? The barber had named it—death by fire—slow fire—that was the thing. Or, better still, some mark upon the soul of the man that would never wear away.

Here was the end, then, in a single stroke, of all the power that had been poured into his hands by Nature. God had so framed him that merely to look upon his face had been a delight, and now that delight was turned into horror and fear. Aye, and he would teach the world that he was truly to be feared.

First, however, he must be dressed as a man, not as a wild beast. He went into the general merchandise store. There he bought the best-fitting clothes that he could find. In a back room he donned them. After that, he bought a horse and saddle, mounted, and started directly on his way.

A pack of the village dogs, which had gathered at a respectful distance behind his heels, as soon as he spurred his horse to a gallop, broke into a clamor and swept around the King Silver. So he drew rein and, turning, looked back.

"Take them, boy!" he called.

And King Silver obediently, joyously "took" them.

First there was a whirling black shadow, like a spinning pool of night, in the midst of the pack of the dogs, and out of the central circle they leaped away with loud howls of pain. A dozen dogs, and many a proved fighter among them, they stood off and snarled and howled, but they had tasted of the steel of the King Silver, and they were wary, now. One, bolder than the rest from a random strain of bulldog blood in it, leaped in at the young wolf. Glanvil saw his warrior meet the rush with a heavy-turned shoulder, saw the dog sprawl on its back—then one flash of the gleaming white sabers that the King wore, and the throat of the dog was ripped across. He rolled in his death agony, kicking among the pack of his comrades, and they gave back again.

But King Silver had the taste of blood, now, and he flew at the circle in a fury. It did not last half a minute. But, when the circle of the village dogs dissolved, three of them were stretched lifeless on the snow, and the rest were kiting back for the houses as fast as their trained legs and backs would carry them, with the King in hot pursuit. Another and another went down in a cloud of snow dust, and then lay still under the assaults of the tyrant—until the sharp whistle of the master called him off and drew him back.

But at all of this, Glanvil looked on with the utmost satisfaction. He, among men, must live as the King Silver would live among dogs—a slayer, a heartless destroyer. But, if he were to live safely, he must do his destroying without bringing upon his head the penalties of the law. That was obvious. No outright murders, but destruction carefully planned and carefully executed, so that the blame should seem to fall always upon the other man.

He conned that scheme quietly over and over while he rode on. He sent the King ahead, and the big wolf scoured away with a swift gallop over hill and dale, through bush and grove, coming back again, repeatedly, and standing on some little eminence in the trail to watch the oncoming of his master. He was the master hand, this King Silver. He was the matchless destroyer. From him Glanvil would learn.

So he came, at the last, to the little town in the hollow. How well he remembered how he and Louise Carney had looked down upon that place through the black of the storm. He rode on down the hill. He passed the minister's house opposite the church. Yonder was the minister himself, working in his little garden, but he did not so much as wave his hand at the rider who passed, with the big black dog running ahead.

Besides, how could he have guessed that the gray-headed rider was that man who had figured most prominently in what was the minister's strangest day in all of his life?

Glanvil paused, then dropped from the saddle

and strolled idly into the churchyard. It was a quiet place. The naked shadows of the stripped trees lay in a mottling pattern across the graves. Here were new stones and old. Here were weather-worn head markings inscribed with rough mottoes. Some of them he read.

> Here lies Bill Granger.
> He beat Sam Waldron and Marty Kline
> and died game when the Indians came
> down.

> Here lies John Winter.
> He did his share. He was a square man
> and his word was better than a balance
> scales.

Then there were more formal and more neatly inscribed stones that told of later and of more prosperous years that had come for Sacketville. Glanvil wandered slowly among them. For somewhere, unless the barber had lied, was the tombstone that marked the psuedo-remains of himself.

He went on, therefore, pondering over each legend, until he came before a great, smooth, granite shaft, and on the shaft was written:

> Here lies the body of Winsor Terence
> Glanvil.

He died as a man should die, fighting bravely.
May God forgive his sins.

He read it over and over again. *He died as a man should die, fighting bravely. May God forgive his sins.*

Had she found this inscription in her own gentle mind and prepared it for the writing on the stone? And he thought again, how she had ridden with him through the storm, bravely and gaily, and laughing at the fury of the wind and the beating of the rain. And a sudden breath of her sweetness swept up to him like the breath of a spring wind over fields rich with new flowers. There was a new touch of sad gravity in Glanvil as he turned from the tomb of the unknown man who bore his name.

He was dead, so utterly dead that the woman who had loved him had built this monument to his name and now was preparing to marry another. At that, a red stroke of rage almost blinded him, and he found his way out to the horse, mounted, and went swiftly on.

Chapter Nineteen

Darkness found him on the road, and he turned in at the first house. When he rapped at the kitchen door, it was opened by a busy housewife covered in a blue gingham apron. From the kitchen lamp a broad, soft shaft of light fell upon his face. At that, she screamed and fled, slamming the door in his face.

Glanvil waited, grinding his teeth. For all of this, Jack Rutledge should pay. Presently he heard excited voices, and then a heavy footfall of a big man. The door was opened, and there the householder stood before him, with his big fist gripping the revolver that hung in the holster over his hip.

"What're you?" he growled out at Glanvil.

The wanderer stepped into the light and watched the face of the big man as the latter shrank and changed color. It was always the same—woman or man—they could not endure that startling ugliness of feature that seemed to let the hidden vices of the very soul shine through most patently.

At least the matchless voice of Glanvil remained to him, velvet smooth and quietly musical. "I'm caught by the night," he said. "I want to get a meal here, if I may."

"Ha?" cried the other, still rallying himself

from the start that the vision had given him. “You want food?”

“I’ll pay,” said Glanvil. “I’ll be glad to pay.”

The rancher shook his head. Perhaps he was one who would never have sent a man hungry from his door—but this was very different. The echo of his wife’s scream was still at his ear, and before his eyes was a type of ugliness such as he had never seen before.

“We got nothing to spare,” he said, and closed the door heavily.

Now the new-born devil in Glanvil urged him to dash that door open and spring into the room, gun in hand; he felt the delicious taste of the evil impulse raging against his very teeth, but he choked it back. Instead, after a moment, as he heard the voices of man and wife begin again in the house, he knocked once more at the door.

“Who’s that?” called the man of the house.

“The same man, sir. Still here waiting for his supper.”

“Is that you? Be off with you. We got nothing for you here, stranger.”

“My friend,” said Glanvil, “suppose that I touch a match to this shack and send it up in smoke?”

“Ah,” cried the other, “is that your tune?” He jerked the door open and stood there with his revolver in his hand, ready. “Now,” he said, “you little rat, lemme hear you say that ag’in?”

“Put up your gun,” said Glanvil. “Put up your

gun, my friend. I'm in a peaceful frame of mind tonight. I don't want your blood on my head. Put up your gun, I say."

He had begun gently enough, but, before he ended, there was the raging devil issuing from his throat and making his whole body shake. The effect upon the big rancher was strange enough. First he drew back half a step. Then he appeared to falter. Twice he gripped the butt of the gun tighter, as though he were about to use it. But then he appeared to change his mind.

He stood from the door, muttering: "After all, if a gent is hungry, we got to feed him, I suppose. We got to feed him, wife. Come in, stranger."

So Glanvil stepped lightly through the door. "My dog comes with me, as a rule," he said.

The King slipped behind him and stood at his side as he closed the door.

"Dog?" cried the rancher, turning paler than ever. "It looks like a wolf . . . only bigger. What sort of a man are you, stranger?"

"A hungry one," said Glanvil, and sat down at the kitchen table. "And very sorry to force myself upon you. Steady, boy!"

The wolf lay across his feet, his bright eyes fixed on the face of the rancher.

As for the frightened woman, she had fled at once to the front of the house and left her husband to tend upon the wants of the newcomer. And this he did with trembling hands, always avoiding the eye of Glanvil. As for the latter, he took a keen pleasure in staring at the big fellow. In a way, he was glad that the latter had shown so much of the white feather, for otherwise there would have been a tragedy. For there was a new spirit in him, which startled and amazed him. It was as though a soul within a soul took charge of him and hurried him on toward deeds of violence. For a brief instant, as he stood at that door, he had felt that there would be nothing sweeter in the world than to snatch out his gun and drive a bullet through the hulking body before him. And still he tingled with the thought. There had been no possibility of failure, no thought of it. In his heart, in his hand there was an absolute certainty. He could not miss if he chose to fire.

So he told himself that this new-born demon must be guarded against with the greatest of care. Otherwise, he would find himself knee-deep in blood before he had taken many more steps on the trail of Rutledge, and then the law would step between him and his intended victim. This he told himself while he ate.

"Now," he said to the rancher, "what do I owe you?"

"Nothing," said the other gloomily. "Nothing at all."

Glanvil threw down $1.

"We are quits," he said. "I have frightened your wife . . . and you have looked at my scar. But the next time we meet, my friend, keep your eyes on the ground or there'll be a cause for you to regret it."

With that parting insult, he turned deliberately on his heel and left the house. He had hardly closed the door, when he could hear the voice of the woman as she ran into her husband, a voice gasping with relief and gratitude.

"Thank God that he didn't murder you, Charlie! He ain't a man . . . he's a ghost!"

"He's a devil," muttered her husband. "He's on his way to a murder, or else he's coming fresh from one."

Glanvil mounted and rode off. He whistled, and the mother wolf slipped instantly out of the dark and ran down the trail before him. Her black-coated son lurked in the shadows behind. So, escorted in this fashion before and behind and secure against surprise or attack, the master kept on his way.

It was the close of the first day of his new life, for nothing connected him with the old ways and the old days. He was a new-made man. He had left behind him that gift of beauty; he had in its place the gift of a strength that, he felt, was limitless, and he only yearned for a chance to use it. He had quelled two strong men, two brave men, by the mere touch of his eye. But what would happen when he met the hero, Rutledge?

For that encounter he waited hungrily.

He slept by the roadside; with the dawn he was up again and on the trail once more, with Croton Mountain hanging, huge and blue, in the sky before him. Still it was early when he turned the shoulder of the great peak and rode down into the village.

"I want to find Rutledge," he said to the first man he met. "Can you show me his house?"

It was an old fellow of whom he asked the question, and the ancient man was turned into a staring child as he watched the strange ugliness of the face of the stranger.

"Might you be a friend of Rutledge?" he asked gently.

"Do you know his house, or do you not?" asked Glanvil sharply. "That's the question that I ask you. Can you answer me?"

From this flare of senseless fury, the other recoiled.

"It's yonder," he said, "through the town and down the road that heads into the main street. You'll see his house in the first valley over that range of hills. There ain't no other house in the valley where he lives. He's all by himself."

So Glanvil spurred hard down the road. He went through the town with a rush of hoof beats. He swept up the road beyond and over the ridge. In the little hollow beneath him, he saw the lands and the house of his arch-enemy.

Straight up to the front door of the house he

rode, and, leaning, he beat against the door with the butt of his gun.

"Hello!" he called. "Rutledge!"

There was an answering hail, low and cheerful. Then Jack Rutledge himself came, calling out as he did so: "Is that you, Henry? Is that you?"

Glanvil dropped from the back of the horse. His revolver was loose in the holster.

"By gad," he heard the voice of Rutledge call before the latter reached the door. "A silver wolf!"

Then Rutledge stood before him, his hand gripping the butt of his gun.

"Is that your dog?' he asked, without glancing at Glanvil.

"That's mine."

Rutledge turned to him, and started with that little shudder that all men gave when they stared into the face of Glanvil.

"Have you got business with me, stranger?" asked Rutledge.

"I have business," said Glanvil.

"Well?" asked the big fellow curiously.

"The main business will follow later. This is simply an introductory talk, I hope, Mister Rutledge."

"I'll be glad to know your name."

"It's a name that you ought to guess, sir."

"Guess?"

"Exactly. You and I have talked together, before."

"I can't remember."

"You should, Rutledge."

"In fact, I remember your voice, I almost think. But never your face." He stopped short, an apologetic expression in his face.

"As for that," said Glanvil, "I have no feelings that are easily hurt. I'm not a whit insulted. But you should remember me for a good many reasons, among others the fact that you are my heir, sir."

"You are joking now," said Rutledge, beginning to frown. "What is the point, sir?"

"You will see it directly. I might say that you are my heir, because you have inherited the woman who was to marry me."

"You?" gasped out Rutledge, staring out through the doorway toward him.

King Silver slipped before the feet of his master and lay crouched, ready to turn himself into a thunderbolt aimed at the throat of the stranger.

"My dog," said Glanvil, "doesn't like your way of talking. He prefers a soft voice. Look again, Rutledge. You ought to know me. If my face has changed, you had a hand in the changing!"

Then realization appeared in the ashen face of Rutledge.

"Glanvil!" he cried. "It's Glanvil come back from the dead!"

Chapter Twenty

"It is I come back from the dead for you, Rutledge."

"I am glad of it," said Rutledge, although the perspiration gleamed on his forehead. "I am heartily glad of it. Man, I think I could swear that you are the only person in the world that I have ever wronged in a true sense of the word and in a full sense of the word. I have vowed that, if I should ever have the chance of finding you again, I should tell you that I acted to you like a savage devil. I intended to ask your forgiveness, Glanvil, and I ask it now. Only tell where in the name of all that is wonderful you have been these many months?"

"I have been collecting household pets," said Glanvil. "Here is a sample of them. Do you like the breed, sir?"

"It is like a wolf."

"It is a wolf. I have been studying the breed, you see, and learning a great many very valuable lessons from them. I have been learning how to hunt, you might say, and, now that I have got the lesson by heart, I have come down here to see you, Rutledge."

"You have come to hunt me," said Rutledge sternly. "Very well, Glanvil. The thing I did to you, God knows I was provoked to. I knew that if you were not marred, you would come back to find the girl and that a glance from you would win her again as it had won her before. Very well, Glanvil. I acted a beastly cruel part with you. And I tell you frankly that I want nothing more than to fight this out with you on even terms. If you are ready, go for your gun."

"You are a politic murderer, Rutledge," said the smaller man. "No, this is not the even terms that I want."

"What will you have? I give you the first move, Glanvil, and I can't do more than that."

"If I win, as I shall surely win, what do you think would happen? They would join together and hunt me down. They would make a virtue out of revenging you. They would call me a murderer, Rutledge, because, my friend, I am so much faster with my gun than you, that your Colt would never be discharged. They would call it murder and come for me by the score. No, Rutledge, what I wish to do today is simply to let you know that I have come back here to stay for a time until you and I are able to meet before other people. In the meantime, I have a different name. I am no longer Glanvil. My name is simply . . . John Glenn. No one will know, other than you. My face and my hair have changed too much. Even my voice, I suppose, is a bit different. I shall never be known. And you, Rutledge, will not dare to make me known, because, if you do, you will have to confess the unspeakable thing that you did to me when my hands were tied and I was helpless on the floor of that barn."

The head of Rutledge dropped, and he shuddered. "It was a ghastly thing," he muttered. "I did not know how horrible . . . until today. If I could undo it, I would give ten years of my life willingly."

"You will give more than that. You will meet me in front of eyewitnesses who will see us fight fairly and squarely according to the custom of this land. And when I have killed you, Rutledge, I shall think that a part of the debt is paid off. Only the girl will remain."

"The girl?" breathed Rutledge.

"You, I see," said the younger man, "see nothing in what she has done except what is normal, natural, and right. She has left me for you. That is all. However, as I see it, she has betrayed me. There is an account between us."

Rutledge stared at the other and then, instinctively, down to the keen, cruel eyes of the wolf. "I almost believe," he muttered, "that you would treat her as you would treat me?"

"One does not use bullets on women," said Glanvil. "One does not need to." And he smiled. It was a ghastly thing to see that smile working with the tension of the scar to distort his face on the one side, far more ghastly because the other profile was a perfect and unmarred beauty, although far, far changed from the former luster of the heart-breaker. Rutledge moistened his white lips.

"Very well," he said. "The more you speak, the more you expose to me the devil that is in you, Glanvil. Do you expect to live, sir, after this? Do you expect to live?"

"What will *you* do?" asked Glanvil.

"It is my duty," said Rutledge. "If God ever created a fiend and put him on earth dressed out in the flesh of a man, it is you, and therefore . . . defend yourself, Glanvil!" As he spoke, he snatched out his revolver and covered Glanvil, covered him with a working face, and with a hard-set jaw.

But the smaller man merely smiled again, that blasted and hideous smile.

"I haven't the slightest intention of killing you today," he said. "I have explained beforehand that it does not fall in with my needs. But another time will come. Do you hear me? Another time will come."

"Are you a coward, too?" asked Rutledge, breathing hard.

"Keep back," said Glanvil to the wolf, and the black beauty that had been crawling ominously toward Rutledge shrank behind his master. Then he lay again, crouched, ready as an arrow on the string to leap at the enemy at a moment's notice. "As for cowardice," Glanvil continued, "you are not fool enough to accuse me of that. I met you once, Rutledge, fairly and squarely, and I shot you down. I'll meet you again at my convenience, and the second time, one of us shall not rise."

"I should do it," said the big man behind his gun. "By the heavens, I should do it. It would be a deed worthy of a reward. But something keeps me back."

"Fear," said Glanvil. "Fear of what people would say if they found me dead with my gun not drawn and you standing over me. A fool's fear, Rutledge . . . for you are a fool in all things, after all. Chiefly a fool in thinking that you could keep the love of a girl who once promised to marry me." This he said in the face of the steady gun in the hand of Rutledge.

But the latter suddenly thrust the gun back in its holster. "You are cool enough," he admitted.

"But if we meet in the presence of other people," said Glanvil calmly, "day or night, on foot or on horseback, with gun or knife . . . or bare hands . . . I promise to kill you, Rutledge. Do you understand? In the meantime, you will do what I tell you to do."

"You are quite mad," said Rutledge, and yet he shrank back a little from the other, as though he feared a sort of magic influence that could compel him against his will.

"Do I seem mad? Nevertheless, you will do as I dictate."

"What power, then, have you over me?"

"Do you not see even this?" He laid his finger on the course of the hideous scar that marred his face.

"And what of that?" asked Rutledge, shuddering in spite of himself.

"Simply that it is my hold on you, through the girl."

"Ah?"

"Still you don't see? Well, Rutledge, let me explain in words of one syllable. I know how you came to be engaged to her. It wasn't love. Not at all. But simply having you constantly near her, day after day."

"That is a broad lie," said Rutledge, but his voice was shaken.

"Propinquity, Rutledge, propinquity! And nothing else. Besides, she has been saying to herself . . . 'Glanvil is dead, and what am I to do with my life?' "

"You lie again," gasped out the big man. "She has forgotten you . . . at least she has heard so much infernal mischief that you have done that she understands, now, that you were simply a fortune hunter."

"Does she? But there is something else that she can never forget . . . which was that she loved me, and that she will forever. Oh, man, I tell you I know women. I have studied them all my life, and a clear-running life like that of this girl can hold only one passion. She loved me. There is simply not depth enough in her to contain a second love. As for you, she pities you."

Truth suddenly touched the very soul of Rutledge, and he groaned aloud.

"Very well," went on the victor, "she pities you. Day after day she has seen you near her. She says to herself . . . 'This good man loves me. This good man will be unhappy all the days of his life unless I marry him.' Besides that, there is the blind girl looking into the heart of poor Louise Carney every hour of her life and saying . . . 'Rutledge is a hero. Where could you expect to find a nobler man? What right have you to torture such a great soul as his?' "

"That is all false!" cried Rutledge, but it was the agonized voice of one who cries aloud to shut out from his heart a truth that he bitterly recognizes.

"Come, come," said Glanvil. "I see through it all like window glass. So you must not try to pull the wool over my eyes. You must not, sir. We come to this point, simply . . . that you have persisted in hanging around the girl like a beaten dog until at last she has said, like an echo of blind Kate Preston . . . 'I have no right to torture this good man, this great man, who the entire world admires and looks up to.' *Bah!* That is it. And now I show you my power over you. In order to annihilate you, if I choose, I have only to go to poor Louise and say to her . . . 'I am Winsor Glanvil. This horrible white gash that puckers my face and gives me the look of an incarnate devil was given to me by the good man, the great and pure soul . . . by your lover Rutledge. And what do you think will pass through her mind?"

"She will not believe it," faltered Rutledge. "Or, if she does, she will realize that I was terribly driven and tempted . . . for her own sake."

"For her own sake? Furthermore, I shall tell her how, for her own sake, when I was helpless, and my hands had been bound behind me by other men, you and the rest lashed me like a dog until I collapsed with pain and the loss of blood and the eating shame of it. And how, after the rest had gone, you remained, and how you turned me on my back, and how you took a spur . . ."

"It was a foul thing," muttered Rutledge. "And God forgive me for it."

"If even you can see some wrong in it, what will she see, when she hears me speak and looks to find the man she loved, the man she still loves, and finds this wrecked and distorted face. What will she feel? And what will her first thought be? Simply this, Rutledge, that you are a cur, a cruel, tyrannous cur. She will send you back your ring, if she wears one of yours. She will tell you that she never wishes to see your face again."

Rutledge, white and stricken, stared helplessly at the other, for the truth of what he had said was an inescapable thing.

"And?" he suggested.

"You wish to know the way of escape? It is very simple. You pay me a small price, and I give you my word that the story shall not reach her ears."

"Money?" cried Rutledge, throwing out his arms and letting them fall heavily against his sides again in the greatness of his relief. "Money? Man, you may have what you want . . . enough to take you to Africa. . . ."

"Money?" asked Glanvil sneeringly. "*Tush,* man . . . while you are playing for millions, you are willing to buy me a railroad ticket? You are too kind. No, you will simply give me a note something after this fashion . . . 'Dear Louise . . . This will introduce to you my friend, John Glenn. You must not let his looks bother you. Poor fellow. A deer gashed him with an antler and has disfigured him for life. He is poverty-stricken. He needs work. I cannot keep him here as a cowpuncher. He does not understand the work. But he would make an excellent gardener. He understands such things. Besides, if you ever want fresh venison, you will find that he can get it for you when no one else can find it, for he is a remarkable hunter and a wonderful shot. I hope you can put him to work as a roustabout around your place. I am sending this sealed letter by his hand, and I have not ridden over to talk to you about it in person, because I don't want to prejudice you too much or put too much pressure upon you. If you think that you can endure the strain of that hideous face every day, please take him. If you cannot, let him go. He has no expectations. With love . . . Jack.' "

He ended his dictation. Then he added: "You might put in a postscript that I have an odd-looking dog with me, a savage creature, but that I have it perfectly under control, and she need fear nothing from it. Besides, it will watch the house perfectly at night. Is all of this clear to you, Rutledge?"

"I am to give you a free pass to go into the interior of my fort and plant your bombs?"

"Exactly."

"Do you think that I am mad?"

"Not at all. But I think that you will be willing to gamble for such a large stake. Am I wrong? You have everything to gain. And you can lose nothing more than you would lose at a stroke if I went to her and told her my story. In the meantime, you are to marry her within five days. It is my part to prevent that marriage within the five days if I can . . . my wits against yours. But if you are once married to her, you need fear nothing from me. I leave that instant."

"In the meantime," Rutledge said, "if you find yourself losing, how shall I know that you will not go to her and tell the story anyway, in spite of your promise?"

"You will not know how strong my sense of honor is. That will be another torture to endure. And you will also have to expect to be on your guard whenever you come into public among other men. Because, before the five days are over, and after I have accomplished certain other things, you may be mortally sure that I shall kill you, Rutledge. But as for my promise, I can tell you this . . . until this time I have often forgotten that I am a Glanvil. After this moment, I shall never forget again. I shall make the world groan by knowing me."

Back and forth in front of the door of the house strode Rutledge, deep in thought, pausing now and again, his brow black with wrinkles, his mouth working; back and forth opposite him, his head down, his eyes full of green light, slid the huge silver wolf, making pause for pause with the big man, turning when he turned, keeping always exactly even. A strange and grim picture, with the master of the wolf for the background, perfectly calm, perfectly indifferent, and beginning to smoke a cigarette as though he had not the slightest interest in the final response of Rutledge.

Then the rancher came to an abrupt halt and faced his enemy, towering hugely above him.

"I think that you have cornered me," he muttered.

"To say trapped would be more accurate."

"You are right, I have to surrender. I have to give you that letter and send you to Louise. And now it is definite, Glanvil. One of us must surely kill the other. We both cannot live in this world."

"Exactly. So keep your nerves calm. Do not worry during the next few days, Rutledge. Do not lie awake, wondering if I am at that very moment pouring forth the whole true and ugly story at the ear of the lady. Be calm, indifferent . . . take your exercise . . . sleep well . . . have no dreams . . . and practice with your gun every day. Because when I kill you, I don't want to be facing a nervous wreck, a poor caricature of the great Rutledge. Now go into the house and write out the letter I have suggested. No, I'll go with you, and dictate it over your shoulder."

Rutledge gave him a glance black with rage and hate and despair, but finally, with a shrug of the shoulders, he submitted and turned on his heel, turned with his head fallen forward between his shoulders.

Glanvil walked lightly in behind him. And the slinking wolf moved in at the heels of the master.

CHAPTER TWENTY-ONE

Here in the lower valleys the snow was gone, and the warm sun of the early May day showed the soil of the earth, newly emerged from its winter white cloaking, all black, soaked, and filled with richness to the brim, with the new grass pushing up hastily, making a tender flush of yellow-green on every hillside. Only under the trees the snow still remained in banks.

But from the garden of Louise Carney all the snow had long since been removed. The soil was newly turned and pulverized and leveled. All was ready for the growing season that was already coming upon them. But the birds were there even now, sometimes sitting on the eaves of the house or on the naked branches of the fruit trees, and sometimes darting down over the soft sod of the garden to scratch and delve for worms. But the only color, except for little beds of delicate wildflowers sowed here and there, was in the pots behind the windows of the house. The house was new-painted—white with green shutters and red roof, itself like a great flower on the shoulder of the mountain.

Over all of this, Glanvil looked with that new eye that had been created during the winter in the wilderness. He looked, and found all was well.

Not a detail missed him. For when one has been schooled to search a whole landscape for game—game on which life depends—the details must be seen. It is not the mountain and the groves upon it—it is the stir of a shadow, the glint of a leaf, the small dint on the surface of the snow that counts. And so it was with Glanvil, as he looked over the house and then down to the great red barn in the hollow.

There was a very atmosphere of cheer and happiness about all of this. In the new-growing pasture there were no horses—their hoofs would have slashed the tender sod to pieces and ruined it for the season, but in the corrals they had their heads over the fences, staring at the coming of spring with hungry eyes.

No, it truly seemed that he had not been missed. And he bit his lip. It might be, after all, that what he had said to Rutledge was not true. It might be all a fiction, with which Rutledge agreed simply because he was congenitally unsure of himself with the girl. Upon this, everything depended. The way that lay before Glanvil was difficult, only to be covered with consummate diplomacy. But the thought of the struggle only increased his love of the fight.

Here the side door of the house opened and out came Kate Preston. He started at the sight of her. Always, from the first day of their meeting, that pale, lovely face had filled him with unwilling awe. Now, returned from the wilderness and clad in the armor of his new strength, he had hoped that she would have no effect upon him. But it was not so. The old thrill of dread went through him. And beneath the broad shadow under the brim of her hat, it seemed to him that the dark eyes were looking down the hill to him, finding him, and penetrating once more to his soul of souls. He was ashamed of that weakness and scorned himself for it, but the real dread remained.

He determined to take danger by the ears, so to speak, and know the worst at once. As for Louise Carney, there was no danger that she would know his gray head and his deformed face, but the blind girl, having only strange, profound instincts to guide her, and hearing in the place of sight, might break through his disguise at a stroke. In that case, his work was probably ended before it began. So, to know the worst at once, he went straight up to the garden where Kate Preston was busy.

He leaned at the fence for a time to watch her, for, much as he had always feared and disliked her, she exercised a singular fascination over him. She was using a trowel to make shallow troughs in the soft ground inside of one of the beds. And she did it with such a bent head of interest and with such sure hands, that again, for the thousandth time, he swore to himself that she had eyes, and that blindness was merely her affectation. Yet all was nothing but the perfection of touch. Now and again, as the trowel was at work, he watched her other hand skim over the surface of the soil, fingers outspread, not seeming to touch it, yet feeling every slightest undulation of the surface. Or, again, one hand dipped like a swallow behind the trowel and by those touches he knew that she was reading the surface of the ground just as another read by sight. How strange were those hands, full of prescience, eloquent, like the face of most people.

She made the trench, and then she dropped into it the seeds, one by one. No other mortal in the world could have done the work so very deftly, dropping the seeds at regular intervals, dabbing each seed firmly down with a sure touch. No, there she missed a single seed, this dainty gardener. Was it lost under one of the tiny clods? With fingers lighter than floating down she searched for it. And he looked quickly into her face. There was a faint, sad smile of resignation.

It meant a great deal to the watcher. He had always felt that, like some rare ones among those born blind, she felt nothing of her affliction, but now he could see her gently enduring. Oh, wonderful, inhuman, feminine patience. For a long minute, bent quietly in her place, nothing stirring except the delicately floating fingers, she looked for the seed.

Surely here was someone to be feared, and feared immensely. Here was a tact and a patience that might well prove mortal to her enemies. And the cold touch of anger and of fear passed through him again, like a stabbing ghost of steel.

He leaped the fence with one light bound and was at her side. And even as his shadow fell across her, he saw her questing hand drop, saw her face raised toward him, with question, with mute, blank question. It was very pitiful, for, had she had life in those great eyes, who could have compared with her? Only one danger—she would have seen too much.

He saw the seed that had strayed at once. It had tumbled against a tiny rock and recoiled into a farther corner of the trench. He picked it up and dropped it into her palm. She smiled. It seemed to him, now, that he had never before seen in her face a smile of real happiness. And again, smiling up to him, how very living those eyes seemed.

"You are very kind," she said.

He paused before he answered. All depended on how she received the sound of his voice, and how much recognition showed in her face. So, staring fixedly at her, he said: "This is nothing."

She started a little, and the faintest of clouds passed over her forehead.

Then: "I know your voice."

He set his teeth before he could answer: "I think not."

"No? Perhaps I am wrong. At least . . . I can't place it. And yet . . . well, I suppose that my ears are playing me a trick. No, your voice is different. Will you tell me who you are?"

"My name is John Glenn."

"I never heard that name before. I am Kate Preston."

"I've heard of you, Miss Preston."

"You've come to see Miss Carney, I suppose?"

"Certainly."

She rose and led him.

"We've been re-paving this part of the path with stones, you see. You'll have to step carefully. They are very treacherous and turn under one's foot."

He marveled at her own step crossing them—light, light beyond imagining, seeming to touch and test each stone beneath her, before her full weight fell upon it. Now she stood at the side door. She set it wide for him.

"Walk in, Mister Glenn. I'll call Miss Carney."

"I have a letter for her."

"Oh, yes." She held out her hand. Still she had that marvelous instinct of location that made her turn directly toward him, that startling sense that enabled her to keep her face always toward an auditor.

"It is from Jack Rutledge," he said.

"Jack Rutledge! Oh, yes." And a light spread across her face. Then she disappeared up the stairs.

"It will be all the blind girl," he said to himself.

"All Kate Preston. If I can fool her, I'll fool the other one . . . as long as I care to fool her. But the blind girl may see through me."

In the midst of these thoughts he heard a light, quick step on the stairs and there was Louise Carney hurrying down, with the letter open in her hand. He studied her with perfect gravity and with a deep interest. She was much changed. And although of course all the features were the same, he could hardly recognize the spirit in her, it was so sobered. So much of girlhood had died, so much of womanhood had come to life in her since he saw her last. She seemed a little thinner, a little taller. And her eyes were calmer, and looked at people with an easier directness. More like the eyes of Kate Preston, he thought. Yes, one would have thought that she had gone to school to the blind girl. Or else they had had the same teacher, in differing degrees, pain being their master.

She was quite at the bottom of the stairs before she seemed to see him so clearly that the full details of his scar struck home in her. And then she blanched a little, to be sure—blanched a little and paused in her last step to reach the floor.

It was only a moment's hesitation. The Louise Carney he had known could hardly have forborne a word of horror or of fear at this sight, but this new woman came straight forward to him, smiling, and took his hand.

"If you are a friend of Jack Rutledge," she said,

"you are a friend of me and my house. Of course I shall be glad to have you. Have you known him long?"

"Not very long," he said, and then watched carefully. But there was no darkening or brightening of her eyes. His voice was so altered that to her it meant nothing—at least, linked as it was to that hideous mask of a face.

"But first I want to see that dog out there. I love dogs, John Glenn."

"I'll call him to the door."

He set the door wide and spoke his name. Instantly, in the frame of the open daylight, stood the glorious picture of the King Silver, like a king indeed, with his great ruff standing up above his neck—more lion than wolf as he stared proudly at the girl.

"Heavens!" cried the girl. "He's like a wolf, isn't he? Kate, Kate! You must come to see King Silver, Mister Glenn's dog!" She said afterward, clasping her contrite hands together: "I always forget. What a terrible thing to have said. You know that she does not see?"

"Not with her eyes," he said.

At this, Louise started, as Kate had done when she heard his voice.

"Can you see so much in her so soon? Then you have a very rare gift of reading the minds of people. It's true, of course. She doesn't need eyes. She has something better."

Kate Preston came down the stairs in haste. In spite of blindness, her step was as swift and as sure as that of her friend.

"Where is he? Where is the dog?" she asked, and held out both her hands, like an infant feeling toward the kind warmth of a fire. Never before had Glanvil seen her so helpless in attitude.

But King Silver spared only one glance for her. Then he turned into a shadowy bolt aimed at her throat, with great fangs shining as he sprang, and with such a snarl issuing from his great body that it froze even the blood of the master.

"*Ha,* down!" shouted Glanvil.

It was as though a great magic hand had struck the wolf aside. He swerved from his mark, veritably in mid-air, and landed like a huge soft bundle in a corner of the room. The scream of Louise Carney pierced the brain like a stabbing needle.

"Don't be afraid!" called Glanvil, full of wonder and of rage at the brute.

"I'm not a bit afraid," said the blind girl. "Only sad. I've never had a dog so much as growl at me before. But reassure poor Louise. I'm quite unhurt."

Chapter Twenty-Two

Reassuring Louise Carney was no easy thing. In the first flight of her terror, she wanted King Silver destroyed at once.

That brought from Glanvil the terse reply: "I'd rather shoot myself, madam!"

He was startled beyond measure when he listened to his own voice. As though those words had been spoken by another, without his volition at all. What was a wolf cub to him that he should sacrifice his interests to its life? What was the dumb beast to him? And here, in fact, he had cut the very throat of his own affairs.

For the girl answered angrily: "He ought to be shot . . . for the sake of other people who may be near you . . . oh, Kate, those terrible teeth would have torn your throat out. Mister Glenn, of course I can't employ you here with such a beast as that in your company."

He was furiously angry. For the time being the two creatures he hated most in the world were Louise Carney and the silver wolf.

"As for that," he said stiffly, "of course you must have your own way . . . and equally, of course, the dog will not be shot."

"Dog?" she said. "It is a wolf if I've ever seen one."

"Did you ever see a wolf take orders? Come here, Silver."

Silver came and dropped at his feet with long red tongue lolled out, looking like a devil, indeed, as he stared back over his shoulder toward the blind girl, but like the most beautiful devil in the world.

"I can't have him," reiterated Louise. "Dear Kate, you are not hurt? Not in the least? Not frightened to death?"

"I only heard him . . . I didn't see him, you know," said the blind girl in her quiet way. "But I'd like to see him now. May I touch him, Mister Glenn?"

"Kate!"

"I mean it, Louise. I think that Mister Glenn has his dog under perfect control."

"Do you really wish to touch him?" asked Glanvil, now deeply filled with wonder.

"I do, indeed."

"It may be dangerous. I've never seen such an ugly streak in the brute."

"I'm not in the least afraid, if you are by to watch him."

"Kate, I absolutely forbid . . ."

"You mustn't forbid me . . . because I intend to touch King Silver."

The brain of Glanvil spun about. This calm defiance of danger on the one hand and of her protectress on the other was far beyond all his conception of her, keen as that conception had been in the past. Now she went straight to the big wolf and kneeled down in front of him. He snarled like a veritable demon, but she merely dropped her hand on his throat and smiled up to the master.

"It is quivering like an organ," she said. "What a huge, strong dog he is. Louise, please don't be absurd. Mister Glenn won't let him hurt me. What breed is he, Mister Glenn?"

"I don't know. Shepherd and wolf, I suppose."

"There's not much sheep dog about him. Why, he's built as strong as a lion. And such fur! You could make money on his pelt."

"I suppose that one could."

Over him—head and throat and shoulders and quivering body—her hands worked, touching lightly. Then she stood up. And still his snarling hummed deeply in his throat.

"I know him now," she said. "If I had seen him jump, I should have been frightened. Louise, you mustn't think of letting such a glorious animal be destroyed."

"Do you want it to do a murder, Kate dear?"

"There was something wrong about me that meant something to the mind of King Silver. I don't know what it was. That's what I want to find out. What made it jump at me? In three days, Louise, I'll have the King a fast friend, if you'll let me."

"Kate, you fill me with terror. Do you mean it?"

"Every word. And I think that I can do it."

"I don't know what to say."

"He's a glorious thing, Louise."

"A glorious devil!"

"Such a glorious thing has a right to exist. There's a place for beauty in the world, Louise. Just beauty and nothing else!"

There was a little pause.

"You haven't always thought that," said Louise Carney faintly.

And Glanvil, understanding her meaning, set his teeth.

"It's true. Most ugly things should be destroyed."

"Kate," protested the girl in a whisper, and, glancing at Glanvil and then down at the floor, her face flamed. "If you will stay, Mister Glenn," she said, "I'll be very happy to have you. You'll find the man who takes care of the horses down at the barn. He'll show you your quarters."

He thanked her and left at once. His brain was quite in a muddle. He had never seen the wolf act in such fashion. And still, as the King went down the hill, he was growling softly to himself, and his hair was bristling. It was very odd. What could have excited him, the master could not dream.

In the barn, the stable man showed him his room.

"If that dog of yours gets loose," he said, "somebody in the village is apt take a potshot at him and skin him for wolf."

"Then somebody in the village," said Glanvil dryly, "is apt to be shot and skinned for a fool."

The other glanced askance at him, as much as to say: "*Ah,* is that the kind you are?"

But Glanvil paid no attention to him. For he was still digesting the first glance that Louise Carney had given him, and taking home the horror and the fear in her eyes. In his room he counted his money. He had $8 remaining. And he smiled at the sight of them, smiled sourly. That should have been eight millions by this time, had not Rutledge and his men interfered. And the balance of the sum was due to him from the world, he told himself.

After that, he left the wolf in the room and went up to the house to report, but Louise Carney was kindness itself. He must have the remainder of the day to familiarize himself with the place and its way, she said. Besides, there was the village that he must come to know, in case he needed to run any errands for the household there.

Back he went for the King. Become familiar with the village, indeed. But, while he was there, might he not encounter Jack Rutledge? That was to be hoped for, fervently, devoutly hoped for. He looked to his guns. They were well oiled, in perfect condition, and they balanced familiarly in his palm.

Then, with the King at his heels, he went down to the little town. School was out by the time he reached it. A swirl of home-bound youngsters curled around him, wild young spirits foaming with joyous liberty, and at once a chorus greeted him: "Hey, look at the gent with the funny face! Who stepped on you, stranger?"

For boys respect nothing, not even grief, not even the crippled and the blind. All that is not ordinary is to be mocked. And Glanvil was not framed by nature to endure mockery. He snatched two of the older lads and knocked their heads together. He spanked a little one, and sent them yelling up the street. But Glanvil went on more content, with the hungry devil in him a little appeased.

At the very next corner the youngsters had their revenge prepared. Two huge wolf hounds—the greyhound breed crossed on the great Dane—leaped out from a corner and shot at the King. The latter barely waited to hear from his master—"Take them, boy!"—and then he set about his work in cool earnest.

He needed no instruction in battle. Gray mother had worked in his view many and many a time, and she was a matchless artist with her snowy fangs, but the learning that was in the brain of the King was owed to time-old ancestry. The two came with a rush, heads down, great mouths gaping. And, in the distance, a dozen curious, grinning men stood by to watch the fight. They had seen what had happened to the boys at the hands of the stranger. They were perfectly willing to have his dog torn to pieces, now, in revenge.

But Silver did not stay to be torn. He leaped lightly in the air and landed in the rear of their charge. Before they could wheel about he had laid open the flank of one of the brutes. Now they came and bolted at him with savage yells. He danced like a boxer to the side and gave the unhurt animal his shoulder with such force that it went down in a sliding cloud of dust. Before it was up, Silver had darted in and out, and the throat of the dog was torn wide. That was enough. The second dog, gaping, choking, already half dead, slunk away toward friendly faces, while the voice of Glanvil called back the King and the hand of Glanvil patted his dark head.

He said to the gaping men: "This seems to be a lively town, my friends. I hope I don't tame it."

Then he walked on, leaving them too stunned by his insolence to speak back to his challenge. It was very pleasant to Glanvil. And yet, of course, these things were not enough. Well enough for him to scatter insults and blows here and there, but for every whiplash that had fallen on his back, what sort of payment should he make? They would learn, in time—they would all learn.

Chapter Twenty-Three

Even as he insulted them, he knew that there would be no opposition. Their minds were not active enough to understand this insolence and react to it. And so it proved. They grew first red, and then white. They looked at one another—and they allowed their enemy to pass. He walked in this leisurely fashion beyond them and turned in at the hotel. One might have said that, by this time, he had ridden down the enemy's front and come off without a single challenge. In the hotel he went back to the rear room where, on another day, he had taken his share in the card games. Usually a flock of little gullible birds and one large-winged hawk making prey of them.

So it was now, except that, in this case, two were working in harmony. Five chairs were occupied in that poker game and the stakes were running high, for three of the chairs were occupied by three brothers, recently come down from the lumber woods with their pockets full of money. For they, in turn, were the smaller sharpers who went out to the firing line and, enduring the hardships of work by day and cards by night, took the money from honest laborers by petty devices. Now all three of them were combined against these two prosperous travelers who, it appeared, were both looking for a ranch or lumber lands to buy. The three combined and had decided, apparently, to strip the pair of every cent they possessed.

All of this was almost instantly intelligible to Glanvil after he had come into the room. The scheme was too obvious. It was too utterly apparent. And he smiled up his sleeve when he recognized in the two tenderfeet none other than the celebrated reprobates, Dan Lightner and Marty Kern. Those cardsharpers had worked the country for many years, and always with profit except for those times when they had rested brain and body in jail. Now they were out again and making up for a deal of lost time. Their maneuvers were perfect. Not one person in ten million, unless they had been known to him, could have suspected that they were working in concert. All that was apparent was that the three were losing and that the other pair, alternately, was winning. So matters went from bad to worse. Suddenly alarm and suspicion began to take hold upon the three. Their little tricks were not working. Something was very wrong. It seemed as though fate was working against them. Fate was at this moment in the form of two exceedingly clever card manipulators. By this time—against such stupid opposition—they had probably marked the cards. Certainly their manner was one of the most perfect ease. They could not make a mistake, so it seemed.

Glanvil listened to them with the wicked pleasure that one criminal takes in observing the course of another.

"I've never had such a run of luck in my life," Dan Lightner was saying. "If this keeps up, I'm going to give up ranching and take to cards. But in a minute or two, I suppose that the luck will all change again."

"Of course it will," put in Mr. Marty Kern. "Of course it will. But you've had no better luck than I. I suppose this will wind up when I'm cleaned out." So saying, he put down a full house and raked in a very fat stake.

The three sparrow hawks stared at one another in amazement and the deepest concern. They were too far committed to this game to withdraw from it now. And yet every moment they continued to participate brought fresh ruin upon them. It was all most strange. And in his nervous excitement, one of the three brothers while he shuffled the cards, flicked one of them in the air, and it fell at the feet of Winsor Glanvil.

He could not help examining the back of the card with those hawk eyes of his. And as he laid the card back on the table, he saw what he wanted—it was a red-patterned card, and toward one corner there was a little smudge of red, hardly perceptible even after one's attention was called to it, and even then looking most like a faint imperfection in the printing.

But: "Will you let me see some of that pack?" said Glanvil.

The dealer looked up with a scowl.

"What's wrong with the pack?" he snarled out. "And what's it to you? You ain't in this game!"

"Neither are you, I think," said Glanvil with such pointed calm that the other, forgetting his anger, suddenly began to stare, first at Glanvil, and then at his two companions, and finally at the tenderfeet. The latter were doing their best to carry the thing off with a high hand. Dan Lightner was tapping on the table with a restless forefinger.

"Friend," he was saying, "I don't understand your interruption. Keep your hands off the cards."

But already the lightning inspection of Glanvil had found what he wanted. In the first three cards he looked at, he identified the markings easily enough. And he pointed them out to the gull who had been about to deal. In the meantime, Lightner and Kern had risen, violently protesting, but backing toward the door.

"Here you are," said Glanvil. "There's the ace marked, and there's the king. This is a jack. Do you understand? You're being plucked, stranger."

There was a shout of rage from the sparrow hawk and his two brothers.

"Guns, Marty!" snapped out Dan Lightner. "Get the scarface first!" And, as he spoke, he sprang backward toward the door and snatched out his gun.

It was very fast work, but just a trifle too slow to keep pace with the lightning hand of Glanvil. The gun of Dan was in the air when the Colt spoke from Glanvil's hip and the gambler, with a groan, sank to the floor and clutched at his shoulder.

The other men had dived at Kern. His gun had caught in the holster and before he could free it, he was under a twisting, shouting mass of humanity. Glanvil, in the meantime, had leaned above his particular victim, leaned apparently in order to see how seriously he had been wounded, but, in making the examination, he saw the fat wallet in the inside coat pocket and instantly the treasure was his. After that, he left the hubbub stirring and retreated from the noise with King Silver at his heels, and so up the street and up the hill to his room on the Carney place. There he counted his spoils. He had an even $4,000 in that wallet. The money he put under the mattress, except for some smaller bills. The wallet he promptly burned.

And then he sat down to laugh. For, altogether, he was very satisfied with himself. He had gone out empty-handed and he had come back with a supply that should last him until his adventure was ended, at least. And how simple it had all been. More than this, he had established himself in the eyes of the villagers as an honest man with a keen eye to detect fraud. Nothing could possibly have been any better.

News of violence moves on wings of lightning.

He had not been an hour in his room before there was a rap at his door, and he opened it on Louise Carney's stableman, Harry Buxton. He was a quiet little man, very broad and strong, with a curious way of canting his head to one side and looking up with a searching glance as he talked. But he never had much to say.

"You might be coming over to the kitchen," he said. "It's about time to eat."

So Glanvil went with him and sat down in Martha Buxton's kitchen, for he was to have his meals with the Buxton family, by the arrangement of Louise. And as he sat at the little table, the King lay across his feet and snarled a deep and gloomy warning when other feet trod too close. What Buxton himself could keep in, his wife at once let out.

"Mister Glenn, we been hearin' about you in the village. I guess that there's one pair of rascals that'll remember you for a long time. If they ain't put away where they'll be safe, I suppose the fear of 'em will be hauntin' you the rest of your life, John Glenn."

Her husband put in calmly: "Don't talk foolish, Martha. Mister Glenn, he ain't the kind that minds danger. I'll bet that he's been livin' in it for years. Ain't you, Glenn?"

"I love quiet and peace," said Glanvil, a little embarrassed. "This little affair in the village was forced on me, you might say."

"*Little* affair!" Mrs. Buxton cried, clasping her

hands. "Hear the man talk! Set on by two cut-throat gamblers . . . and he calls it a little affair. Lord love us, I hope no harm ever comes to you out of it. You're a very brave man, John Glenn."

"They'll keep clear of him," said Buxton. "He's give them their lesson, I guess, the same way as his dog gave the Kinney dogs a lesson. I would've give a good deal to've seen that fight. Silver must've cut 'em up bad. They say the biggest dog is gonna die, his throat was tore so bad."

"I hope he does, the snarlin' brute," said Mrs. Martha Buxton. "I hope you don't mind liver, Mister Glenn?"

"Why, I eat anything at all," said Glanvil.

"Well, that's a man after my own heart. That was what the man said that tried to hold up the Glaston stage. When they had him in jail . . . 'All I want is food,' said he. 'Lots of it . . . I don't care what.' "

"Who held up the Glaston stage?" asked Glanvil. "And what is the stage?"

"Why, it runs here from Glaston, you know, through the Glaston Pass, right around the side of Croton Mountain. It's been running for eight years, now, come the Fourth of July. And there ain't been one single robbery on it yet."

"A good record," said Glanvil. "I suppose that not much money is carried over the line, though?"

"Not much money!" exclaimed Mrs. Buxton. "Why, most all the pay for the lumber camps and the miners come up this way every Friday night.

What's today? Why, today's Friday. And they'll have about forty or fifty thousand dollars coming up in that stage."

"It's very heavily guarded, then?" asked Glanvil.

"It used to be. But they've had so much luck for eight years that they've got to be sort of careless. Didn't Tom Cracken tell us that they only had the guard and the driver, now, along with the man that brings up the cash? Only the three of 'em carried guns, and one of them three ain't any use with weapons. That's old Kenning, the driver, Harry."

"You're talking big and foolish, Martha," said her husband very sternly. "I'd hate the job of stopping and robbing that stage, I'd tell a man."

"You're a peace lover, Harry Buxton. I'd laugh at the idea of you robbing anything."

"You know nothin' at all," said Harry Buxton sullenly, and lapsed into silence.

But he was unregarded by his wife. She had turned her attention to the King, and babbled out questions like the chiding of running water. She wanted to know if he would really bite, and Glanvil had to assure her that he really would. Should she feed him? No, he hunted for his own food. Could he catch a rabbit? By cunning, not by speed.

And so they sat over the supper table late, until the windows were polished ebony with the black of the night, then word came from the house up the hill that Miss Carney wanted John Glenn.

Chapter Twenty-Four

It was a brisk, bright night, with all the stars glittering, no wind abroad, and the snowy upper mountains breathing cold into the valleys. All was frozen. The murmurs and the millions of stirring sounds of the day were gone, and the earth, freshly and thinly crusted over since the setting of the sun, *crunched* faintly under the foot of Glanvil.

He went gaily, confidently up the hill. There was only one shadow over his mind, and this was the fear lest Louise should have taken too high a displeasure because of his last exploits in the village that afternoon. However, he had his explanations ready, and certainly she would never discharge him without listening to what he had to say. He was not prepared, however, for what awaited him. Louise herself opened the door to him.

"I have a friend of yours here," she said.

She took him into the living room, and there, with the ruddy firelight making his stern features more rugged than ever, was Jack Rutledge. He stirred suddenly in his chair when he saw Glanvil.

Louise Carney was as pleased as a child over bringing them together. "I'm going away for a while and let you chat together. Since Mister

Glenn only arrived today, I know that you have thousands of things to talk over. And Jack is a silent man. He won't even tell me how he first met you, Mister Glenn."

"It's bad luck to remember trouble," said Glanvil, looking steadily at Rutledge.

"Trouble?" echoed the girl, a little bewildered.

"There was a cañon between us," Glanvil said as calmly as ever. "So that Jack was only a hundred and fifty yards away from me by air line . . . but half a mile by walking. And when I saw him, he had just put two bullets into a grizzly and the old rascal was charging. An unlucky time to have a rifle jam, wasn't it, Jack?"

"Oh, oh!" This from Louise Carney. "And you shot the monster, Mister Glenn?"

"It was a lucky shot and stopped the brute. That was our way of being introduced. You can't blame a man for not wanting to remember such things."

The hand of Louise fell on the shoulder of Rutledge. "Why, Jack, then he has saved your life."

Rutledge cast at his tormentor a glance full of the darkest vindictiveness. But there was nothing he could do except to authorize the lie that had been told so blandly.

"I suppose you may say that he did," muttered Rutledge.

"But, Jack, why didn't you tell me? I knew he was your friend because that was such an exceptional letter you wrote to me about him. But . . . a man who saved your life?"

She came hastily to Glanvil. She took both his hands, and her eyes went warmly, kindly, searchingly over his face, as though all of its ugliness had suddenly disappeared. She said, smiling on him in that tenderly intimate manner: "When I first saw you, Mister Glenn, I knew that I should like you, but since I know what you have done for Jack, of course you're a part of our life, at once. I . . . I didn't guess, you see, or I should never have sent you down there with . . . with Harry Buxton."

"I am very happy there," said Glanvil.

"We'll talk of that tomorrow," she said. "Of course you must come up to the house. But now I must leave you two together. Sit here, Mister Glenn. Here is an ashtray. Here are some cigars. They are a kind that Jack likes very well. Here are cigarettes . . . his vintage too, you know. Now be comfortable, and talk your hearts out. Oh, we're so glad, so glad to have you with us, John Glenn."

So she left them. And as the door closed behind her, they stared at one another, Rutledge in despair, in fury, in hate, and Glanvil smiling on the larger man.

"How glad she is to have me with her," said Glanvil, mocking. "The very man who saved the life of dear Jack."

"Bah!" gasped out Rutledge. "What a devilish

natural liar you are. What a poisonous rat, Glanvil!"

"You begin to see, dear Jack, why I wanted your introduction to the little lady. Upon the body of dear Jack, I, with my deformed face and my gray head, step into the life and the good esteem of . . . some eight or fifteen millions of dollars. *Tush,* man, you were an idiot not to have seen it before. I shall climb higher, too, and every step of the way I shall be thrusting you deeper and deeper into the mud." He rubbed his hands, and, over the tips of his joined fingers, he smiled upon Rutledge with the greatest complacency.

"I have been a fool," admitted Rutledge savagely. "All of your villainy no honest man could see in a dream, even."

"These are the cigars that dear Jack likes." He raised one and examined it. "Dear Jack smokes cheap tobacco . . . and likes it. Let me see his cigarettes. Oh, very poor, also. What a man, what a man you are, Rutledge, to have eight millions of dollars poured away to waste on you. As well give a man an ocean so that he will take a bath in it. Dear Jack, what would you do with so much money? You have no taste, no soul that responds to beauty. What would you do with it? More acres and more beef to put fattening on the acreage . . . then more acres and more beef . . . all hides and horns and tallow and beef. That is what dear Jack would do with his eight millions. No, Jack

. . . no, no, dear Jack . . . you must not have the money. In the interests of beauty . . . in the interests of art, you must not have it."

Rutledge leaned forward in his chair, and his great shapeless shadow, quivering with the restlessness of the firelight, swayed forward, trembling on the floor.

"Do you look even as high as that, Glanvil? Do you even think that you can stop the marriage?"

"I have four more days," said Glanvil. "I could kill you at any time, but I prefer to wait. I much prefer to wait. And when you have served your last purpose with me . . . when I have finished using you as the ladder by which I climb into the esteem of the lady, then, dear Jack . . . then, my dear boy, I shall kill you, and what will the answer be?"

Rutledge, perspiring, fascinated, hung forward in his chair.

"I shall tell you, then," said Glanvil, "since your fat brains cannot work it out. The lady will be shocked. Not by your death, but by the base ingratitude that made you stand up before John Glenn, that good man who preserved your life once before . . . made you stand up and assail him, gun in hand. Oh, she will be horrified by the corruption and the evil that she shall find in dear Jack before the end. She shall bless God that she was delivered from the hands of such a man. She shall bless God that she could find such virtues behind a scarred face."

"You are a devil," breathed Rutledge.

Glanvil began to laugh softly, gloatingly. "There is the trap exposed to you. Free yourself from it if you can, dear Jack. Sweat and groan and writhe and lash your dull brain into a gallop. Because it might take you to a solution of the mystery, you know."

"I shall go to her immediately and tell her the whole truth!" said Rutledge, springing up. "I shall tell her that you are Glanvil, and that it was I who scarred your face."

"When she comes to me for the confirmation, I shall tell her that it is a mad lie. And she will believe me, dear Jack. I shall tell her with sadness and with gravity. Oh, I have ways of making her believe me. I could wish for nothing better. It would entangle you at once and make her despise you. Such a feeble lie, Rutledge. Woman like bold, glaring, giant untruths . . . but, if she hears you say such a thing, she will only be moved to scorn. No, you have committed yourself inevitably. Honesty bids you tell the truth about me, but your love of her forbids. You *do* love her, dear Jack. Her blue eyes and her bright hair never leave your mind. They are lodged in your soul. Her voice sends quavers of music through your body. You are weak with joy at the mere thought of her. No, dear Jack, you will never risk telling her the truth."

"You are right," groaned Rutledge. "I cannot tell her."

"So you will wait," said Glanvil, "until I have chosen my time. Then, in the presence of many men, I shall kill you, and make the quarrel seem of your commencement, dear Jack. Oh, yes, I shall shoot in self-defense only. And, in the meantime, while I am waiting for that right time to come, you must remain calm and cool, dear Jack. You must not grow edgy. You must not let your sleep be broken. Always remember that. You must not let the inner man be broken, as it seems to be broken now. For there are shadows under your eyes. Your hands are restless. You cannot sit quiet. Your lips twitch. Your eyes are as uneasy as the eyes of a hunted rabbit. And if you should continue in this way for a little time . . . why, dear Jack, a child of five years could beat you to the draw."

The whole body of Rutledge lunged forward, but he checked himself. "I have done you one great wrong," he said, "and for that I am suffering now. But through it all, I meant nothing but honesty, and God fights on the side of honesty. He will help me, Glanvil, and put you down in the end."

"Wrong, wrong, wrong!" Glanvil laughed. "God favors brains, Rutledge. God has always favored brains in spite of what slaves and cowards say. And when He sees what I am doing now, He will rub his hands with pleasure as I rub mine now, and He will say . . . 'This is a man indeed. He makes even his misfortune a source of power.' "

"You lie!" groaned Rutledge. "She has told me herself that she cannot look on you without a shudder."

"Of course," said Glanvil, his calm unbroken. "She has been talking of very little else than John Glenn. This evening her dear Jack has been filled with her chatter about the new man. She thinks it is horror, but it is really pity, sorrow, wonder. The gates of her mind have been opened. They are standing wide ajar and ready for me to make a great thought enter them. Trust me, dear Jack."

"I am going," said Rutledge suddenly.

"She will be hurt if you leave."

"Curse you, hypocrite." And he strode from the room.

Glanvil heard him speak tersely to the girl, and then the outer door closed heavily. He himself, of course, went out at once, and in the hall the girl hurried to meet him.

"What is wrong?" she asked. "What has happened?"

"Nothing."

"Oh, but I saw Jack. He is worked up over something. Something that must have come between the two of you. You must come back with me."

CHAPTER TWENTY-FIVE

Standing there with one half of her hair in shadow like tarnished gold, and half in light that made it burn softly, she made a picture that Glanvil enjoyed quietly, soberly. Certainly she had become something more than a foolish girl since he had first known her and made love to her.

"Something went wrong," she was saying. "It was almost . . . as if you two had quarreled. Is that true?"

He shook his head. "Let me put it this way. He and I have disagreed. There has been no quarrel. That's the end of it."

"But it can't be the end," she insisted. "You who have saved his life . . ."

He made a little grimace. How sinister a sneer it appeared on his scarred face. "Men forget such things," he said. "You see, it's what might be called an obligation, and men hate obligations. If you lend a man five dollars, it's a pretty sure way of losing his friendship. And with a greater thing, so much the worse. If you lend him his life, he's nearly sure to hate you."

"It's all very strange," she said, frowning at him. "I know only one thing . . . that you are good and kind, John Glenn, and that Jack Rutledge owes his life to you."

"Do you know that much?"

"Of course. I suppose that compliments are foolish things, but, when I've seen you handle a wild dog as you handle King Silver . . . and when I hear such a story as came up from the village today . . . of how you stepped in between two rascals and their poor victims . . . well, it doesn't take a great many things like that to help one to a picture of a man. That's why I wanted you to trust me with the real story of what's made Jack so excited tonight."

"He'll tell you in his own way," said Glanvil. "And that's much the best. He'll have plenty of time to choose his own occasions, because I'll be getting on in the morning."

"You mean that you are leaving me?"

"Yes."

"You couldn't be happy here?"

He threw out both his hands, palm up. "What does that matter?"

"It matters everything. Tell me, are you sure you could not be happy here?"

"Ah," said Glanvil, "if I should say what I feel, you would not understand. There is no use talking about it."

"Do you think so? It makes me sad to hear you talk like this, John Glenn."

"After all, since I'm going so soon, why shouldn't I tell you? Well, since I was disfigured by the antler of that stag, I have gone about the world, meeting nothing but hate and scorn, you see. People shuddered when they looked at me. And when I met you today, I waited to see you shrink and turn pale at the sight of me. But you didn't. You came down all gentleness and kindness, and, that moment, I blessed you with all my soul. Is it true, Miss Carney? Did you feel no horror when you first saw me?"

Even now, as she stood before him, watching his face, she was filled with fear and with distaste, and yet she managed to falter a "no".

"Ah," said Glanvil, "what else could I ask for? To find one human being who could look at me without disgust, who could see in me something more than a scarecrow and a ghost . . . that is a happiness that you cannot understand. Happy here? Here is everything that I care most about . . . the free mountains, and the open sky . . . and kindness."

He felt that in all his life he had never rendered any speech so perfectly, and, although he might have wished to change the words somewhat, yet after all in speech the language is the smallest part and the manner of speaking is all in all. So when he spoke of the free mountains and the open sky, there was a thrill in his voice that made the girl tremble, and, when he lowered his tones to say that one word "kindness", her eyes filled with tears, as though she saw before her a brilliant picture of this poor man hounded through the world with many brutalities.

"There will be some time," she said, "when I may know you well enough to tell you a whole story . . . but I can only tell you now, that I have known one man whose face was like the face of an angel, but he was a demon at heart . . . a cold-blooded devil. He taught me that beauty is the smallest thing in the world. It is the heart that counts."

"Dear Miss Carney," he said, bowing his head, "I shall keep the thought of you always."

"You speak as if you were still determined to go at once."

"In the morning. I must."

"For fear of Jack Rutledge?"

He threw back his head. "I am not the slightest bit afraid of Rutledge," he said.

And he could see the perfect belief in her face. No matter what her faith in Jack Rutledge as the man of men, the king of the fighters might have been, it seemed impossible for her to doubt this scarred face, these brilliant and searching brown eyes.

"But," he added, "you are to marry Rutledge in a few days. That would break everything up, I suppose. Every way you look at this, it's a great deal better for me to go on."

"You and Jack Rutledge," she said, shaking her head with the profundity of her conviction, "have had a falling out over some little matter, I don't know what. Because high-spirited people are sure to have quarrels. And neither of you will give way. But when both are honest and both are brave, it only needs a little time. This trouble, I'll wager, is the smallest thing in the world."

"I can't talk about it," he said. "But Rutledge may if he wishes. God knows, there is nothing I wish more than that we should be friends."

She flushed a little at this, and her eyes shone with a spark of angry enthusiasm.

"Whatever it is, Jack is wrong, and I know he's wrong. I'll never let him rest until he's explained everything. Because I feel that I have a right to interfere here. Why, it makes me heartsick to think that such an old friendship as that between you and Jack Rutledge should be broken up . . . in twenty minutes of quiet talk. It simply must not be."

"I hope you can do it," he said simply. "I hope it with all my heart."

"You'll stay, then? You won't go, John Glenn?"

"I am the happiest man in the world," said the hypocrite.

She followed him to the door.

"When I hear how sad your life has been and when I see the sadness in your face," she said, "it makes me want to do some great thing to make it all up to you. And we *will* be friends."

"With all my heart."

"That great shadow of a dog . . . where has he gone?"

"King Silver? He smelled a rabbit somewhere. He won't go far, I think. Good night."

"I'll put it all before Jack in the morning, when I see him."

"I shouldn't do it, if I were you."

"Why not?"

"It's better to let people work out of their own troubles."

"I know," she said, "that I can untwist the whole tangle in five minutes. I have a perfect faith in myself."

"And, after all," he said, "so have I."

He left her and went out into the cold blackness of the night. There on the walk he remained for a moment with his head tilted back, drinking in the pure, cold air, and rejoicing in it. He had not dreamed how necessary to him had become the great outdoors during that bitter winter, for now, when he was in a house, he felt crushed and walled in, confined with his whole soul in a narrow compass. So the flare of the firelight died away before his eyes, and they grew accustomed to the stars. The wall of blackness that had at first confronted him gave way, melting back into far prospects of the dim, distant mountains against the sky. So it was always with nature, he felt, a cold and unpleasing and mysterious exterior, and behind that first appearance, wonderful and simple and new beauties for those who stayed to look and to listen.

He was so full of happiness, now, that he could have cried out, he could have shouted and sung. Half the battle had been fought, and it was his victory—it was wholly his victory. When he thought of Jack Rutledge and how that unfortunate would be confronted with a mysterious maze of questions about matters of which poor Jack was in the most perfect ignorance, he had to set his teeth to keep from breaking into loud and joyous laughter. And the more he thought of it, the more he admired his own cleverness. For, upon the merest nothings, he had built up a danger beneath the water that very well might wreck the noble ship of the fortunes of Jack Rutledge.

In the first place, that gentleman would be taken utterly unawares. In the second place, he had not the agility of mind to adapt himself suddenly to such new and to such unknown possibilities. Even if the girl were to sit down and tell Rutledge the plain story of exactly what she had heard and of what she surmised, he would be too dumbfounded to make a rejoinder. But there was no danger that she would do any such thing. She would break out into exclamations. She would begin, perhaps, by asking him to give her one simple favor, and, when he said that he would, she would tell him that he had to be friends with the new man. There was no doubt that the matter would run in this fashion, for she was impulsive. And he, poor fellow, would probably ask her promptly what she was talking about.

So the war would begin.

It was such a delightful structure of nothingnesses that Glanvil felt he had constructed his masterpiece of knavery. He was able to pay himself the greatest compliment that lay within the reach of his mind, for he could say to himself—I am satisfied.

In the meantime, where was the King Silver? He might be in a neighboring field cutting the throats of sheep, by this time, or he might be hunting down the village dogs and slaying them one by one with the savage slashing of his great fangs.

He hurried around the corner of the house, and there he saw the missing animal—there was King Silver like a mighty statue of blackness touched with a gray and glimmering mist, his big body poised and his head high, looking up into the face of a girl—blind Kate Preston.

Chapter Twenty-Six

Perhaps it has been sufficiently seen that Mr. Winsor Glanvil was not an impressionable soul, but he stood for a long moment staring at this picture with something very like cold chills running up and down his spine. He had thought, at first, that the black monster was about to leap again at Kate, as he had done when he first met her. But now there seemed another meaning behind the scene, a meaning that Glanvil utterly refused to give admittance into his mind, at the first. However, he presently saw her put out her hand, and, to his bewilderment, the big animal crouched under it. More and more marvelous, she slipped to one knee, and King Silver stepped closer to her, still crouched a little, but put up his head and seemed to lick her hands.

A sense of weakness spread through the master. He had too recently seen Silver rip open the throat of a great hound; he had too recently seen the monster in fighting action, and this was a new and undreamed of side to his character. It was not Silver that disturbed him the most, however. It was the blind girl.

Once before, when his plans were ripening to perfection and when all the strength of Rutledge could not have defeated him, she had been the moving power that destroyed him. It was her slender hand, after all, that had gouged the scar upon his face. He grew hot with rage at the thought, but a moment later he was cold again. She was not like other women—oh, most unlike them. As she had beaten him once before, would she find a way of beating him once again?

All in the garden, while he stood there, became more visible, and the naked plants and bushes stood out in darker silhouette, for in the east above the mountains there was a dull glow of yellow light, and now the moon was rising. Under that dull light he went to her, and at the soft sound of his steps she rose and faced him.

But King Silver? The blood of the master turned colder still when he saw that the big wolf remained facing the girl and gave him not so much as a glance. He could not help the question. It broke from his lips of its own strength.

"What have you done with the King?"

"He came to meet me," said the girl. "All at once there was a cold nose in my hand . . . and that was the King Silver. He and I have been talking. All in a moment we were friends."

He re-sketched the picture that she had drawn so carelessly—that slender girl and that black monster stealing upon her.

"Were you afraid?" he asked.

"I thought it was my last moment on earth. But

he seems to have changed his mind about me. He hasn't moved, has he?"

"He's still facing you."

"I thought that I could still feel his eyes on me. I really don't know what has happened."

"You have put a charm on him," answered Glanvil, with a poor attempt at lightness.

"Or he upon me. I don't know which way it has worked. What made him jump at me the first time, do you know?"

"No. I can't imagine. But . . . why are you out here in the cold?"

"I'm wrapped warm, you see. And I have a foolish happiness in coming out into the world when I can see almost as much of things as even the best pair of eyes will show."

"What do you see, then?"

"The stars," she answered, "and the big mountains across the valley." She waved to them, and, at the gesture, the wolf reached up his head toward her hand.

"There is a moon coming up. It is barely above Mount Croton now," said Glanvil.

"Well"—she sighed—"I left that out of the picture. I suppose there is a glint of the Croton River in the heart of the valley, then?"

"A dull streak of white. You can barely guess at it through the shadows . . . much fainter than the sound of it."

"Oh, that is very clear."

"Good night, Miss Preston."

"Good night."

He had turned away, and King Silver was gliding at his heels, when the girl spoke again, and he turned back to her. There was enough moon shine to show him the trouble in her face.

"I have something to say to you which is hard to get out," she said. "Will you forgive me if I am rude?"

"Of course."

"I want to ask you, simply, if you can really be happy here?"

"I? Of course I can be."

She shook her head, and for the hundredth time he felt life and light in the dark eyes that were fixed upon him.

"I don't think so," she said.

"But why not? Here is everything that a man could want."

"What is that?"

"Freedom, and pure air, and not too much work."

He put as much conviction into his voice as he had ever managed to do in his life, but again she merely shook her head.

"That isn't enough."

"Why? Hundreds of millions of men are contented with a great deal less than that."

"You are not like the hundreds of millions."

"Do you think not?"

"You are only like yourself."

"Are you flattering me, Miss Preston?"

She sighed again. "I'm afraid that I don't know whether it's a compliment or not."

"If we are to be very frank," he said, "tell me just what is in your mind about me."

"Will you do the same for me?"

"That is hardly a bargain."

She answered suddenly: "You are too strong and too big to live happily in such a small and enclosed existence."

"Enclosed?"

"Oh, there is air and space enough. But I think you understand what I mean much better than I do. You want an environment of people rather than things. You want to control people. Aren't you that sort of a man?"

"I've never found that in myself."

"You are no longer frank," she said. "And you are a little angry, too."

"Not the least in the world."

"I must go in," she said. "I am sorry to have hurt you."

"I should be sorry if I were such a fool as to be hurt by a little talk. I am interested, Miss Preston."

"Are you?" She paused and turned back to him with that mysterious surety with which she was always able to face the person with whom she talked.

"What else do you find in me?"

"I don't know," she said. "Usually when I meet

people, I know what I am to think of them at once. When one has no eyes to see the face, one has to use the ears, and then listen carefully to every word. Every word and every whisper means a good deal. Little things sink deep."

"I believe it," he said. "You are the deepest-looking person, man or woman, I have ever met."

"Most people are shadowy things," she said. "But now and then someone comes with voice and a personality as clear as the blaze of the sun. I can see the sun, you know, when my face is turned straight up to it . . . I mean, I can feel a strange haze, enough to know what the beauty of seeing must be like."

"That is a sad thing," he said.

"I can't talk about it," said the girl. "And yet I want to . . . with you. But we must talk of you, not of me."

"Why is that?"

"Oh, I know that you understand. Dear Louise Carney is far blinder than I am blind. And I must try to see for her and for myself, also . . . which is very hard."

"So you must try to find out what I am?"

"I should not dare to speak of these things to any other person. But there is something so keen and cold and hard about you that I know you will be as much amused by this as you are shocked."

"You are quite right."

"There was one other man I have met who gave

me as clear an impression as you do . . . but he was all evil. He was like red fire before my mind."

"And I am only chiefly evil?"

"You are very strong," she said. "And mixed in with the strength there is a clear and gentle soul. If I could not guess that, King Silver would have taught me."

"How could he teach you anything about me?"

"You have taught a wild wolf lessons without using blows. That is a rather wonderful thing to have done, I suppose. And if you have the strength to do such a thing as that, you have the strength, also, to do very great harm wherever you choose. Frankly I am afraid of you, Mister Glenn. And I am afraid of what may bring you here. And what makes me most afraid of all, is that you fear me, a little."

"I fear you?" he cried.

"Yes."

He fought with himself for a moment, then something from her passed through his spirit and seemed to subdue him. He felt, for the moment, looking into her pale, lifted face, as though he were growing smaller and crouching before her as the wolf had done.

"It is useless for us to talk any further," he said sullenly. "Good night again."

She did not return any answer; he left her standing where she was and hurried down the hill. At the corner of the house, he turned again, full of some vindictive answer to make to her. Then he saw that her head had fallen, and that both hands were pressed against her face, a very picture of despair.

If her failure struck so heavy a blow in her, it meant how much she had hoped for from that talk. And the greatness of her hope augured the greatness of her distrust of him. In that case, in any crisis, she would side with big Jack Rutledge against him, and what might seem perfectly simple on the side of Glenn to the mistress of the house might seem with equal certainty a convincing argument of his deceit to the blind girl. At least her hand was against him, and her clear, quiet brain was fighting on the other side. He felt, at once, that the victory that had been almost in his hand was removed to a distance once more. He must beat aside this danger. But how should he go about it?

Even as the idea came to him, an answer rose in his brain. Too late for this night. Tomorrow he might try his skill against her.

Chapter Twenty-Seven

He was almost at the barn again, with the lights of Mrs. Buxton shining from the second-story rooms, when the King saw a rabbit and shot away after it. He followed, glad of the chance to run off some of his anxiety. This was like the old days in the mountains.

He ran for a furlong into the woods before the King came back to him, baffled as usual, but happy from the hunting. And Glanvil was about to turn back toward the barn and his room when a gray shadow slipped out before him and lay down panting at his feet. It was the mother wolf, her reddened eyes glittering up at him, and her sides heaving from her run.

He greeted her with a word and a touch of the hand from under which she slipped up and headed back through the trees, looking back toward him over her shoulder. As plain as could be, she was giving warning that among the trees there was some danger toward which she wished to lead him, some danger with which she could not cope, just as in the old days she would come back to him to give tidings of some monstrous grizzly across whose walk she had come.

But there was not apt to be a grizzly in such nearness to the homes of men, where all the woods, to the nostrils of the wild, were rank with the smell of wood smoke and of cooked food. With quite other expectations, Glanvil followed her, and King Silver, as usual, slid along at his heels, watchful, waiting for the battle, and ready to add his teeth to the argument.

They had not gone far through the bushes when, at the edge of a little clearing, strongly barred by the shadows of the tall trees that the moon cast across it, mother wolf sank upon her belly. Her master, revolver in hand, followed her example. King Silver lay at his side, with long head thrust forward to watch.

A shudder through the body of the young wolf told Glanvil that the danger was near. Then, into the clearing, stole the furtive figure of a man. He was trailing a long rifle in his hand, running half stooped, his head thrust forward as he strained his eyes among the brush and the trees. There was no shadow of a doubt that he followed the trail of Glanvil himself.

The latter worked himself softly to hands and knees. The trailer was near, was past—and then Glanvil sprang like a cat. He saw the hunter wheel with a stifled shout and put up his arm against the flying shadow. Then Glanvil struck with all his weight and the fellow went down with a crash.

"Back!" cried Glanvil to the rushing wolves on either side of him, and at the same time he thrust his revolver under the chin of the fallen man.

"For heaven's sake, man, behind you . . . look! A wolf!" gasped out the hunter.

"A wolf," answered Glanvil sneeringly, "but not your sort of wolf, my friend."

So saying, he went through the clothes of the other and took away a heavy hunting knife and a revolver. The rifle had fallen on the clearing, at the first attack.

Glanvil rose. "Stand up!" he commanded.

The stranger obeyed. He had no eye for Glanvil, still, but only for the ravening forms of King Silver and the King's mother.

"Get away and watch," commanded Glanvil.

At that familiar word, the two disappeared, each in a different direction, to take up the watch among the shadows. It would be a soft foot indeed that stole upon Glanvil.

"Now," said Glanvil, "we are alone."

Only one thought possessed the brain of the other. "Timber wolves," he stammered. "And acting like dogs. What are you, stranger? What are you?"

"You know my name," said Glanvil. "You were on my trail."

"A poor day for me," groaned the other. "Those devils told you I was comin', I suppose?"

"I suppose they did. What sent you after me? A plain hold-up, man?"

"I was broke," said the other gloomily. "I had to have some coin."

"You could have sold a gun. You could have

pawned this knife. Your clothes look new. And . . . isn't that your money pouch at your belt?"

"No. . . ."

"Unbuckle that belt and throw it to me."

The steady mouth of the revolver seconded that word, so, reluctantly, the other did as he was told, and the heavy belt dropped at the feet of the conqueror. Glanvil undid the buckle that secured the mouth of the little pouch—he took from it a tight wad of greenbacks.

"You needed money, eh?" he said.

The other was silent.

"We'll start in at your name. What's your name, my friend?"

There was no answer.

"Here, boy!" called Glanvil.

The King Silver leaped into the clearing and, standing beside his master, showed his long white fangs in a silent snarl.

"He'll cut you up like butter," said Glanvil, "if I give him the word. Now will you talk?"

"My name is Lefty Hewitt," said the other, keeping his fascinated eyes upon the King.

"Lefty, you have a good deal of coin in your pouch, and it looks like new money to me. Is it blood money, Lefty?"

"Take me in," said Lefty sullenly. "Take me in and turn me over to the sheriff, if you want to. But I ain't gonna talk no more. I'm through, all through."

From his pocket, without a word, Glanvil took a length of stout twine, and with this he secured Lefty's hands strongly behind his back. After that, he made the man sit down while he kindled a fire. It was blazing in an instant, and into the fire he put the muzzle of Hewitt's rifle.

Lefty, in the meantime, looked on with growing concern and nervousness. "What's in your head?" he asked. "What's the main drift, partner?"

Glanvil waited until the steel of the barrel had changed color. Then he drew it forth and tried the muzzle against a twig. There was a *hissing* sound at once, and a small column of vapor, like a puff of smoke from the lips of a man, went up into the air. Then Glanvil turned to his companion.

"It's about the right temperature now," he said. "Just about the right heat for branding."

"Branding?" said Lefty, his face growing haggard.

"Unless," said Glanvil, smiling, "you've changed your mind about talking."

"It's a bluff," gasped out Lefty. "You don't dare! They'd . . . they'd lynch you in the town. They's some already that don't think none too much of you there."

"Do they like sneaks who hunt men by night?" asked Glanvil. "Come, come, you fool. I'd feed you into the fire inch by inch and let the wolves finish you when the meat was cooked, except that I want to get some information from you. But if you have any real doubt about it . . . we'll make the first mark for the sake of convincing you."

Lefty Hewitt collapsed at once. He threw up both his hands, and his little gray eyes gaped wide in terror. "I'll talk," he said. "He said that you was a devil, Glenn. But he didn't put it strong enough. . . ." He paused abruptly. "Glenn, I can't talk."

"You'll burn, then, you fool."

"Heaven help me," said the wretched man.

"As a matter of fact," went on Glanvil smoothly, "I know the whole story already. I simply want confirmation from you. You're not giving away secrets, Hewitt."

"If I talk, what do I get out of it?"

"Your life, you cur," snarled out Glanvil. "Now open up and let me have the yarn."

"I was down and out," said Lefty, staring at the ground, his long and drooping mustaches working as he spoke. "I was down and out. The boys had cleaned me out the night before. You know Benton?"

"No."

"That sneak can talk to the cards and make them understand him. It was him that busted me. We was playing blackjack."

"Very well. You went flat then, Lefty. What next?"

"I figgered where I could make a raise. I ain't got many friends around here, but there's one man that I knowed. He'd been with me when I did the most part in the catching of Lew Cook, that yegg."

"Very well. You have been an upholder of the law, then?"

"I never done a crooked turn in my life," whined Lefty, staring again at the dreadful snarl that curled, from time to time, on the lips of the wolf.

"Except now that you were really broke . . ."

"I . . . well, maybe you know already. I went to Jack Rutledge, the way most folks go when they're down and out."

Glanvil drew in a great breath. After all, the premonitions that had been floating through his mind had not prepared him for such a shock as this. How utterly broken the big man must be to sink to such methods as these for the working of his will.

"Rutledge heard me out and shook his head. He said that he couldn't do more'n stake me to a railroad ticket to go south to better parts. I was about to take ten dollars and leave when he called me back again. He says to me that he knows of a good turn I could do for him that would make him my friend for life. Well, it's worthwhile being the friend of Jack Rutledge for five minutes . . . let alone for life. I didn't wait long. I told him to blaze away.

"He told me that he had an enemy that was such a low skunk that he couldn't fight him hand to hand. But he had to get rid of that man, and he had to get rid of him pretty secret. It sort of surprised me. He was the last man in the world that I ever expected would act like that . . . and the way he looked was pretty bad. He looked like a sick man, bitin' his lips and rollin' his eyes from one side to the other to keep from lookin' me square in the face.

"But I listened. A man has got to listen when Jack Rutledge talks up, I guess. I listened and pretty soon he begun to talk money. He ain't a cheap man. He took me down to the bank and give me a thousand dollars cash, right off. What could I do? It looked like pretty bad work, but then almost anything that Jack Rutledge puts his hand to is figgered on as being good enough for any man in these here parts to foller up. I up and told Jack that I'd do what he wanted me to do. I guess that it was wrong for me to say it, but I couldn't dodge. I was broke, I was flat. And I figgered that this man Glenn must've been a pretty low sort of a snake if Jack Rutledge was out for his scalp. So I said that I'd do it."

"And you came up to the hill and waited for me there?"

"I did that."

"When I went by, you decided that you'd wait until I was deeper in the woods before you sank a bullet in me?"

The other bowed his head. And a gloomy little silence followed. It was still incredible to the younger man that, in the course of a single day, he could have broken the heart of Rutledge so completely. Perhaps it was sheer bewilderment and despair—the feeling that he was trapped without fairness—that made Rutledge strike out in this fashion. At any rate, the work was done, and here was the hired murderer.

"I've told you everything," said the fellow. "I've laid it all as bare as the palm of my hand. Now what do I get out of it?"

"A hundred dollars," said Glanvil, throwing the money to him. "A hundred dollars and permission to get out of the town and out of this part of the country." He leaned above the other. "I'm a hard man, Lefty. You've seen nothing about me yet that could make you guess how hard I am. But if I come across you again . . . well, my friend, I won't speak to the . . . dogs. I'll let them after you and let them work as fast as they wish. That's all and that's final. Do you understand?"

"I understand."

"So long, then. After all, Lefty, I'm glad to have this nine hundred. I don't know whether to thank you, or Jack Rutledge."

Chapter Twenty-Eight

It was sheer restlessness and the pressure of a savage spirit in his heart that made Glanvil do what followed. It was not time for him to strike back at Rutledge. Neither was it a fitting opportunity, for Rutledge was probably at his home, now, waiting impatiently for the return of his hired man who would give word that Glanvil had fallen.

He would never know what had actually happened. He would never know. If Lefty sneaked back to his master first and told him what had actually happened, then the dangers would be thickening around the head of Glanvil, but, as a matter of fact, there was small danger of that. Lefty would not go back to face the rage of Rutledge. Instead, he would take the advice of Glanvil and fade out of the scene. Besides, he was probably fairly thoroughly frightened by what had happened to him that night as well as what had almost happened. Accordingly he was apt to go as fast and as far as he could to a more pleasant climate, and Rutledge would simply take it for granted that the man had vanished with the money without attempting to attack the quarry.

All of this was perfect for Glanvil. But, in the meantime, he was possessed with a terrible restlessness. So many threads of action lay in his hands, there were so many small and whispering intrigues for him to estimate, that he needed action.

And it was for action, accordingly, that he headed. He hardly knew what he would do. Merely to roam across the country with gray mother and the big black cub was thrilling enough, in the beauty of that wild May night among the mountains. He let them hunt ahead of him, sliding in a weaving road across the country, and coming back to him now and again, as their custom was, to report progress and to keep in touch with him. Once a rabbit chase led them miles away, and they drifted slowly back to him, half exhausted. It was after this that he found himself standing on an open road with a great black mountain lifting up against the moon above him, and, around the corner of the mountain shoulder, there was the *ring* and the *clatter* of the hoofs of horses, trotting horses, not animals at the Western canter.

He heard this clearly. The night was deathly still. There was only the hoarse panting of the two wolves at his heels. And above that he caught the noise of the hoofs—yes, even the stir of voices—young voices singing happily. It was the Glaston stage—this was Croton Mountain, to the side of which he had wandered blindly behind his wolves. And here was Mr. Stage Driver whooping his horses along on the last stretch before they found the barn, and he found the bar. All gay, all singing what could be a better time, for mirth blinds the eyes.

He sent the wolves back into the brush with a word. He himself stepped behind a tall rock at the edge of the road, a black monster that had rolled down from the heights above in some old convulsion of the mountain. There he kneeled, drew out a handkerchief, and tied it over the bridge of his nose. More experienced robbers, perhaps, would not have been satisfied with anything less than a cloth that covered the entire face, but there was no impulse driving toward safety in Glanvil. He trusted to a hat pulled low over the eyes to shade the upper parts of his features enough. But what he wanted was action—danger. He prayed for only one thing, and this was that the men in the coach might be instinctive fighters.

Now they were upon him with a rush of noise, voices of people, the grinding wheels of the coach, the hoofs and the harness of the horses, the *rattling* of the doubletrees, the *jingling* of the chains—and in the face of this he stepped out.

They were almost upon him—more like a moving city than a wagon. For the coach was a loft, cumbersome, old-fashioned affair drawn by eight sweating horses over whose backs the long-lashed whip was ever curling. And he a single man to stop this charge. The thrill of it passed like music through the blood of Glanvil. He was content.

He fired a bullet into the air and shouted.

That was enough for a driver who had been on the Western roads even half as long as this veteran. He dropped the reins and yelled—*"Whoa!"*—at the top of his lungs. Then both hands thrust back on the long handle of the brake. They screamed, locking the wheels, which slid slowly forward and then halted. The team was thrown into confusion, twisting in a broken mass across the road, throwing heads, champing bits, snorting and pawing, and not even glad of the halt—so close to home as this.

The driver, totally occupied in stopping the stage according to the command, then thrust up his hands, but, from the first moment, Glanvil had no eye for him. He saw the guard, however, tilt up a shotgun with sawed-off barrels, and enough slugs within to wipe out half a company of soldiers, no doubt. He saw that, and snapped his revolver shoulder high and fired.

The shotgun exploded with a roar, but the pellets whistled harmlessly away overhead, and the guard, with a yell of pain, dropped the gun and clutched his shoulder. At the same time there was a wild chorus of screams from feminine voices, and the robber heard a loud voice protesting.

"Let me go! Get away from my arm, for heaven's sake!"

"Put up your gun, Mister Conklin!" some hysterical lady answered him. "You'll get yourself murdered! You'll get yourself murdered!"

Glanvil ran up and found a tall man of middle age, his hat fallen from his head, struggling to get his gun hand free from two clinging women; two more girls huddled in corners of the coach, shrieking.

But like a stroke of magic all was silence when Glanvil spoke; there was only the groaning of the wounded guard.

"Put up your hands, my friends," he said. "Put them high up over your head."

"I'll see you go to the devil first!" shouted the other, struggling to get free.

"Your blood on your own head," said Glanvil, steadying his gun.

At that, the other dropped his weapon. It fell, *clattering* on the side of the coach and thence to the ground.

"If I had had free hands," he growled out at Glanvil as he obeyed the order, "you never would have got the money."

"I haven't it yet," said Glanvil. "But I want it . . . and now. You there, my dear young ladies, go to the guard on the driver's box and see what you can do for him. He's wounded, but not badly. Men don't yell when they're badly hurt. Tie up his cut. Now, sir, I'll thank you for the money."

"Find it, then," said the other, still surly and

defiant. "You have no right to ask me to help."

"You fool," said Glanvil, "I can hear the horses coming up from behind quite as well as you do. Do you think that I'll stand by and give you reasons? Tumble out the money . . . and be quick about it."

In fact, from up the road came the rush of two horses or three, hard ridden by spurring riders who, beyond a doubt, had heard the shots, perhaps had heard the screaming voices of the women, and now they were bent on a rescue. Glanvil felt his blood tingling, but to go off without the prize was never in his mind—not, indeed, if the riders were at that moment in sight.

"I've done my best," groaned the messenger. "And if I ever ride in a stage with women again, heaven help me. Here it is." He threw down a small packet, wrapped heavily in brown paper.

Glanvil crushed it under his foot and received, in return, a stiff resistance, very like that of closely packed currency. He stooped and scooped up the packet just as three riders shot around the curve of the road in the moonlight. Aye, and a fourth and a fifth were laboring in the rear, leaning far forward over the necks of their mounts.

"*Adieu*!" cried Glanvil, and leaped backward into the shadows of the forest.

He did not break straight into the woods, but instead he sprinted under the shadow of the trees nearest to the road, heading straight along it. For there the footing was much the best. And, behind him, he heard the rushing hoof beats of the rescuers; he heard the shouts of the people from the coach.

"Straight in there! We saw him go in there! Only one man!"

"One man hold off three?" shouted the scornful voice of one of the riders. "Then you deserve to lose what you've lost. But come on, boys. We're sure to get him. Spread out . . . spread out! Shoot at every shadow that you see! Ride hard!"

Glanvil eased down his gait to a long jog. Many and many a mile through the snow-covered mountains that pace had carried him, while gray mother and the silver cub ranged before him and to the side, hunting.

Then, far up the mountainside behind him, he heard a sudden fusillade of guns—a shouting of many voices—and finally wild yells of triumph. What had they found?

He did not stay to think over that, but jogged on, comfortably within his strength, crossed the road, crossed the valley, and climbed the steeper slope beyond. And so he came again, in good time, to the barn. He paused in the edge of the woods to groom the wolf and himself, wiping away mud and clinging dead leaves. Then he walked about a little until the King had ceased panting and he himself was breathing easily once more. After that, he entered the barn and climbed the stairs to his room.

He remembered the money packet, when he was there, and tore open a corner of it. In that way he could count the contents easily enough. It was all new money, all closely stacked, and it was a haul of ample proportions, and yet it was far and away from the high figures that Mrs. Buxton had assigned. Here he found $12,500 and a little odd, according to his first count. Far from the $40,000 to $50,000 that she had assigned to the messenger who bore the money. Nevertheless, it was eminently worth the trouble he had been through.

He was barely through with that business when there came a hurried knock at the door. He had only time to toss the package under the pillow and recline, busy in the manufacture of a cigarette, when the door was opened and there stood before him Mrs. Martha Buxton, her face filled with anxiety.

"My man Harry has gone out and ain't come back, Mister Glenn," she said. "Have you got any idea what might be keeping him?"

"The broad moonlight, madam," he said, grinning heartlessly at her. "That's dangerous stuff . . . worse than whiskey. You must watch your husband on the moonlight nights, Missus Buxton."

"Ah," she muttered, "if it was only that." She closed the door softly, as one loath to go, and then her faltering step went down the hall.

Chapter Twenty-Nine

The troubled face of Mrs. Martha Buxton was explained eloquently enough the next morning, when it was learned that the five eager horsemen who had plunged into the woods bent on overtaking the robber of the stagecoach had, in fact, actually apprehended Harry Buxton himself, and, although they did not find upon him the package of money, yet they did find on him a revolver and a piece of black silk with two eye holes cut in it, and two strings attached. It was pointed out that if he had had time to hide the money while he was being pursued, he should have had time to hide the black mask, also, but that was overlooked; it was said that he had thought about the most important property only. All the passengers of the stagecoach, and particularly the guard, immediately swore that this was the man, of this same broad build who had held them up, and they were particularly sure about his voice. To this the ladies were eager to testify.

At any rate, there was poor Harry Buxton, equipped for highway robbery and very apparently caught red-handed in the act. He bore himself, it was said, in a very manly fashion, and never complained or begged from the beginning to the end of the affray.

There was only one mystery about the whole affair. That was that the revolver that they found on his person had not been discharged even a single time, whereas it could be proved that the deadly marksman who held up the stage had fired two shots—one into the air as a command to halt, and one through the fleshy part of the shoulder of the guard. However, it was easily pointed out that poor Harry could have thrown away a second revolver and most undoubtedly had done so.

The first duty of Winsor Glanvil was to make a visit to the jail, see Buxton if the sheriff would permit it, and bring the man a basket of fruits and other foods. So Glanvil was equipped with a note from his mistress and another note that the great Jack Rutledge himself had supplied and sent over to the house by messenger. With these and the basket he went to the sheriff.

The latter read the message of the girl and growled out: "There's been the man's wife down here wailin' and weepin' already this mornin'. Am I to do nothin' all of the day but to stand around here and watch folks that are lookin' in on Buxton? If the fool robbed a coach and got caught, it ain't my fault if he served respectable folks before that. Not my fault at all."

But when he read the letter from Jack Rutledge, his tone changed. For here was a man who could elect him or throw him out of office, at will. He scowled still, but he nodded.

"Well," he said, "after all, it's only right that the poor devil should have some comforts while he can . . . and that time won't be long." He added: "Here's Joe Conklin, who will take you in to him, Glenn. Joe, take Glenn and his basket in to Buxton and lay an eye on 'em." He went on more tersely: "Half a minute there, Glenn. I've been hearin' some reports about you in the town. You been walkin' up and down the spines of some of the folks there. You been totin' along a wolf or two and usin' 'em to cut up the dogs of respectable folks. That there has got to stop. Understand? And you been pickin' fights, too. I tell you, that if it hadn't been for the good job that you done on Lightner and Marty Kern . . . which I was glad to get my hands onto them skunks . . . I would've had to call on you, young feller."

It was all to the advantage of Glanvil to listen to this talk and to make no rejoinder, but that he could not do. In spite of himself, the wolfish ferocity that welled up in him had to break out. He turned on the sheriff with a snarl.

"When you've got a case against me," he said, "come and call on me. But until you have, keep your hands clear of me, Sheriff, and keep your tongue clear of me. D'you understand?"

He himself was astonished at the thing he had said. As for the sheriff, he stiffened and stared with amazement, then his face blackened.

"Are you that sort?" he said. "Young man, I

have you wrote down. And not too young to know better. Not by a darned sight. Well, sir, the next time that I got something on you, you can trust me to come and have a mite of a chat with you."

This time, with all of his might, Glanvil fought down the savage impulse in him. It was stupid, useless, undignified, and rowdyish to engage in these broils. And yet there was a wild devil in him, urging him on to the folly. He had turned away behind Joe Conklin when a surge of uncontrollable malice made him whirl again and deliver as a parting shot: "When you come, bring your friends with you. You'll need them, my friend. You'll need them."

The sheriff said not a word, but he brought his lips together in a straight line and glared up from beneath his contracted brows. Then he turned on his heel and walked off as one that dares not let his temper go. Glanvil, in the meantime, had entered the cell at the heels of the jailer. Joe Conklin, like a good-humored man, merely put down his keys into a deep pocket, and then strolled at the farther end of the long room, waiting until the interview had ended.

Poor Buxton maintained himself with perfect equanimity. He sat on the edge of his bunk with one fat knee resting in the cup of his two stodgy hands. So he looked up, unabashed, at his visitor.

"You've stepped into the mud, old-timer," said Glanvil.

"Well, I've done just that."

"I haven't come down to point a finger at you. Here's some chuck that Miss Carney sends along. Also, she wants to know if you have any wishes."

"Only one."

"Let me hear it."

"That they keep Martha away from me. I can't stand her tongue. Keep her away, for heaven's sake." And his face flushed with his emotion.

"Were you . . . hard pressed for coin?" asked Glanvil, deeply curious.

"My brother back in Illinois is a fine, upstanding man. But he's bad in debt. He's got three kids. He's worked hard all his life for them. Now he's going under unless he gets help. He needs four thousand dollars. I intended to take four thousand of that money and send it to him and send the rest back to them that owned it. But the luck didn't run that way. I didn't even get a chance to rob the coach."

"Buxton, are you telling everyone this story?"

"No one but you. I ain't a full fool."

"The point is, did you or didn't you rob the coach?"

"I only seen it done, I tell you. I dunno that my nerve would've lasted to actually hold them up. But I seen the chap that did the work slide out from the trees and hold up the coach. He was pretty slick and pretty cool. Watching him, I decided that I was never cut out for that sort of work. His voice when he sung out was just as steady as mine is now. Well, sir, those are the facts. I ain't whining. I'm telling you the truth."

"It looks black for you, old man."

"I know that. You must thank Miss Carney, but tell her that I'm not putting up a row. I'm taking my medicine. About Martha . . . well, I'm sorry for her, but maybe it'll be good for her. She was gettin' sort of fat."

Glanvil swallowed a grin and left Buxton for the open air. He engaged Joe Conklin in easy conversation as they strolled along together.

"You have a family, Joe?"

"I have," said the jailkeeper, who was, at times when the jail had no one in it, and that was often, the man of all work on the ranch of the sheriff. "I have four kids, a wife, and my wife's little brother. That's about all that I have just now."

"You make out pretty well on your salary?"

"I make out like the devil," said Joe with perfect good nature.

"Well, Joe, sometimes it's not so hard for a man to pick up a little money. Some find it by simply keeping their eyes open."

"Are you telling me how to get rich?" asked Joe, looking sharply at his companion.

"Some," went on Glanvil, disregarding the remark, "make money by closing their eyes."

Joe Conklin stopped short and stared at Glanvil.

"Look here, Glenn," he said. "Are you aiming to get me all excited?"

"Two hundred dollars," said Glanvil in the same speculative tones," is not to be passed up too lightly."

"I see," said Joe. "That's the game, is it? Well, partner, it ain't gonna be that way. I'm an honest man, Glenn. Damned if I'd sell myself."

"I'm not talking about buying you, am I? I'm simply remarking that some people pick up money by keeping their eyes closed. I've known a man to make as much as three hundred dollars in an evening . . . simply by letting a man walk out of a building and go away through a side door. Certainly there can't be any easier money than that."

Joe Conklin was beginning to sweat. "Go on with you, Glenn," he urged huskily. "I wouldn't have my hand in a rotten business like that."

"Of course," said Glanvil more frankly, "it will ruin poor Buxton. I suppose you know that he's a good fellow . . . as level and as fair as they come, I should say. And as I was saying . . . four hundred dollars . . ."

"You could put your price up to the sky," declared the jailer with much heat, "and it would make no difference with me. I'm here to see that Buxton stays inside the jail."

"With five hundred dollars," said Glanvil, "a man could buy a span of horses and harness for them, and a plow. He could work up a bit of plowed ground and sow corn and what not, and do quite a bit for himself. His children might be able to do the plowing while he was away at other work, and so the whole family could build up. . . ."

"They could. They could," sighed Conklin, lost in meditation. "Who told you that I've been breaking my heart to get a span of good workers?"

"One can see what you need. And five hundred dollars would turn the trick handsomely, I suppose."

"Who are you?" asked Conklin suddenly. "Are you the devil?"

"I am not. I am a poor man who works for a living and talks about others who make five hundred dollars by keeping their eyes shut."

Conklin mopped his brow. "Well," he broke out at last, "where would the money come from?"

"From my coat pocket," said Glanvil.

Conklin started. "I can't do it," he said, more to himself than to the other.

"Do you think it would ever get out?" asked Glanvil. "Do you think that I wish to slip into the cell along with Buxton? No, no, Conklin . . . nothing could be safer to play than I am in this little affair."

"I want to believe you," said Conklin. "And I do believe you."

"Take the money."

The hand of Conklin dipped into the pocket and

out again with something crinkling in the clutched palm of his hand. "I've turned myself into a grafter and into a crook," groaned Conklin.

"You've simply shown that you are a man with a heart, and some good sense. Besides, Joe, if you wish to change yourself between now and tonight, nothing I can do can keep you from it, of course. This is only tentative. You can return the money if you decide to change."

"That's it. That's right," said Conklin, delighted to feel that the final decision was put off for the time being, at least.

And straightway the money was dropped into his pocket and left there. Glanvil swallowed a smile. At the door he bade the jailer good bye, and then hurried up the hill. After all, this new business in which he was embarked was more profitable than gambling had been in the old days—more profitable both in cash and in excitement. Here, for $500, he did away with the ill effects of his crime and left for himself over $12,000.

Even the poorest mathematician could understand the meaning of such figures as these. Here at his heels the black wolf was following; the morning was bright in his face; his heart beat happily, and he wondered what in the wide world could cross his path that day to darken his happiness.

He had not long to wait to find out what it was to be.

CHAPTER THIRTY

There was only one reason that kept Louise Carney from going straight to the jail in person to see Buxton, and this was that she had more important work on hand—or what seemed to her more important. She had a brown gelding saddled and rode it down the valley and through the town to the ranch of Jack Rutledge in the hollow beyond. She found him already in the saddle, of course, having come back to the house from an early round of his place.

It seemed to her that he greeted her rather with surprise than with pleasure. There was something almost like fear in the way his eyes widened at her. Fear—or guilt. She wondered at it greatly.

She would not go inside the house to talk with him. For she felt as though the dark, low-built house would act like a blight upon the spirit. This was the house, perhaps, into which she was to go as mistress. And this was the man who was to be her husband. Certainly her heart did not leap at either prospect, on this morning.

"Let's stay out in the open," she said to Rutledge. "Besides, the open goes better with the subject that I have to talk about . . . because it's big and has a sweep to it."

He stood beside her horse, looking up to her

with a faint smile, worshiping her quietly with his eyes.

"And what is that subject?" he asked.

She broke in: "You're very tired, Jack. You look as if you haven't slept. . . ."

"A mite of a touch of insomnia. That's all."

"Nerves, then?"

"Nerves? Of course not. I don't have such foolish things."

She did not believe him, however. If ever she had seen a shaken man, it was he. There was nothing in repose about him. He was full of twitches and of starts, and the smile lived and died by quick turns upon his lips.

"But what is it that's bothering you, Louise?"

"I haven't been able to close my own eyes all night."

"What in the world has happened?"

"The same thing that has happened to you, I suppose."

He frowned suddenly at her. "What's that, Louise?"

"You know, of course. John Glenn."

"John Glenn!" exclaimed the big man. "What the devil has he to do with either of us?"

"Why, Jack, what a way to speak of your friend."

"True," muttered the rancher. "I had forgotten that, for a moment . . . friend. He is my friend."

"You say that almost satirically, Jack."

"I don't mean it that way."

"I could almost imagine," she went on coldly, "that you had forgotten how he saved your life."

"My life? Of course . . . saved my life. I had almost forgotten that. But I shall remember it hereafter."

"You are talking very strangely, Jack."

"I have had a bad night of it, my dear. Forgive me. My head is really spinning."

"You ought to lie down."

He shuddered. "I can't do that. I have to be on the alert now, if I'm ever to expect happiness in the rest of my life."

"Will you still talk riddles at me? Won't you trust me enough to tell me what it's all about?"

"There's nothing, Louise."

"You can't put me off like a child. It's not fair . . . and I don't intend to stand it. Tell me just this . . . is it about Mister . . . Glenn?"

"Your hired man?"

"Yes, my hired man, if you wish to speak of him in that scornful tone."

He made no answer.

She insisted: "Is he the cause of the trouble?"

He looked her fully in the face, and his eyes were big with trouble, but he did not speak.

"Yes, it is he," said the girl. "Of course I knew that or I would never have asked so many questions. But he talked just the same way last night."

"Did you quiz him last night?" asked Rutledge

almost violently, and coming suddenly closer to her.

"Is there anything wrong in that?"

"Of course not, only . . ."

"Only what, Jack?"

"What did he say?"

"About you?"

"Yes."

"Nothing."

"What else did he talk about, then? About himself?"

"Jack, you act as if you were foolishly jealous."

He struck his great hand against his forehead and his voice was almost a groan. "I am in great trouble, my dear."

"Then tell me about it."

"You shall know everything, someday."

"Oh, Jack, that's exactly the way that my father used to talk to me. I can't stand it. I'm not a child any longer."

"No, no . . . not a child. But a woman . . . a true and noble woman, Louise, but just now I can't explain any further. I'm half mad thinking, and . . ."

"Thinking of what, Jack? Let me try to help. It will do no harm to tell me, surely."

"I mustn't breathe it. It makes me sick to think of a soul in the world knowing it."

"You don't trust me, then?"

"It isn't that."

"Isn't it? I suppose I shall go down to my death day and have only one man to remember who would talk to me as an equal, a man to a man or a woman to a woman."

"Will you tell who that was?"

"A gentle, good, and kind man . . . a friend of yours, too, Jack Rutledge . . . a man who you are hating now, for some little cause that is nothing . . . a man to whom you owe your life."

"Glenn!" cried Rutledge.

"Yes. You need not shout at me."

"How can I endure it?" cried the big man. "Is he still with you?"

"Yes. Of course he is still with me."

"And he is talking to you . . . as if you were his equal?"

"You need not sneer, Jack Rutledge. There are qualities in him that any man could be glad to find in himself."

"I suppose so . . . I suppose so. I don't want to quarrel with you, Louise. Particularly I don't want to quarrel with you about him. Will you believe me when I tell you that he's not worth it?"

"That is simply impertinence, Jack. You can't sneer down such a man as he is. I have talked too much with him for that. I know that there is real tenderness, real gentleness and truth in him."

"Do you know that?"

"Heavens, Jack, are you trying to smile me down?"

"I can say only one thing. This fellow is worthless."

"I'll never believe that. It's terribly unfair for you to say such a thing of a man who has saved your life. Jack, a man to whom you are bound for the greatest debt that one man can owe to another . . . and then to call him worthless."

"I'll tell you . . . he's a devil, my dear. Will you believe it? A devil!"

"You sent him to me."

"He forced me to it."

"He forced you?"

At that, realizing that he had gone too far, he groaned bitterly. "You'll want to know how he could have forced me?"

"Certainly. And I must know."

"Well . . . I simply can't tell you."

"Jack, this is very serious."

"I'm not blind. Of course, I understand that it's serious. But I have to tell you the truth. I can't talk any more about him. Only . . . I tell you this . . . with a single word I could make you see the whole truth about him, and I could make you drop him in horror."

"How did you dare, then, to send him to me?"

"I tell you, he had cornered me."

"This is a very strange story, Jack."

"I know it is. And I wish to heaven that I could tell you the whole true story."

"If you wish it, then do it."

"I don't dare. Not even to you, my dear."

She reined her horse back with a jerk. "This is very strange talk."

"Louise, I beg you to have a little patience. . . ."

"Patience? While I hear you slander behind his back the man who saved your life. . . ."

"He lied! He lied!" cried the tormented rancher. "He never saved my life!"

Louise was frozen with indignation. "Before my face he told the story. Before my face and before yours. He told the story and you heard him. As simply and as modestly as any man ever told such a thing. It's incredible, Jack. It really is incredible that you should wish to dodge the thing now and get away from the truth. And so brazenly."

"Do you actually prefer the word of this stranger above mine?"

"Oh, Jack, my heart is bursting. Don't ask me to answer that question. I am going back. I have to be alone for a moment. My head is whirling with all of this. Good bye."

"One single moment more, Louise."

"What can you say?"

"Only this . . . that although this looks very black against me, when the time comes, I can explain everything . . . with a single stroke."

"Jack, that is what criminals say when their backs are against the wall. I had rather have heard you say anything than that."

She drew off her glove and fumbled at a finger on her hand. "After this, Jack . . . ," she began.

Suddenly he clung to the horse's reins and raised up a hand to her. "Don't do that, for heaven's sake, Louise. Don't cut me down. Give me another day . . . or a half day. Let me have a chance to defend myself . . . but now my hands are tied behind my back."

She could not meet his eye. For there was so much weakness and so much despair in it that she was horrified. How different was such a man as John Glenn, who could feel remorse, sorrow, despair, but conquer all those feelings with an exertion of an iron will. Deep shame got hold upon her. She thrust the ring back on her finger; she drew on her glove. "We will have to begin again," she said slowly. "I'm afraid that we shall have to begin again at the beginning."

"I have lost everything, then?"

"With me? Frankly you have. I couldn't believe that these things were possible."

"Then may damnation take him inch by inch!"

"Good heavens, Jack . . . you curse him like a villain in a play."

"I couldn't dream that he would work so fast."

"On me?"

"On you. I thought that there was more discrimination in you. But if I have lost you, I have one sweet consolation, at least. He shall not win you." He showed her a face black and furrowed with grim determination.

"This is simply mad talk, Jack. I am going now. I shall not listen to anything more."

"Good bye! He will hear of this, and, when he does, ah, how he will laugh. It will be a happy moment for him. Good bye, Louise."

So she rushed her horse away from him. She was not in a passion, but, as she pushed the gelding up the hill, she knew that she had come to a decision that would not change. At the rim of the hollow she looked back to the house of Rutledge and to the big man still standing in front of it, just as she had left him.

It all seemed small and dark and tawdry to her now. How she could ever have permitted herself to become engaged to such a man was a sudden mystery. The ring on her finger was a weight—it was lined with an acid that ate into her flesh. So she snatched off her glove once more and pocketed the ring. He should have that the next day.

And as she rode on, some of the words that she had uttered and to which Rutledge had replied rang in her ears like hammer strokes. It had all been the wildest melodrama, and such a scene as she could never have imagined for herself. However, it had been. She had heard one man curse another with a deep and trembling voice. And, last of all, it had been promised that, if he could not have her, at least Glenn never should.

Such a thought, she told herself, had never entered her thoughts before, and now she grew hot of face. Another man she could get from her mind, but not that scarred, hideous face. It ate into her thoughts with a strange persistence—and all the dignity, and the quiet of his mind. Compared with him, the motions of Jack Rutledge were like those of a peevish boy contrasted with a strong man.

Besides, it was all wildly exciting, and she was promised that, if she attempted to take the scar-faced stranger into the place that Rutledge had occupied, John Glenn would be blasted out of her consideration at once.

She began to feel as though an unchained tiger crouched on either side of her, ready to spring at the throats of each other.

Chapter Thirty-One

When she reached the house, she went straight to Kate Preston. For nothing happened in her life that Kate Preston did not hear first of all. She had been the lifelong confidante of Louise Carney. So she stormed in now to Kate.

"It is all over!" she exclaimed.

"With Jack Rutledge?" asked the blind girl.

"How did you guess that?"

"I knew that trouble was coming."

"From what?"

"From Glenn."

"Kate!" cried the other, bewildered again by the strange foreknowledge of the blind girl.

"Is it true, then?"

"That I have broken with Jack? Yes."

"But Glenn?"

"What do you mean?"

"Was it on account of him?"

"On account of Jack's strange attitude toward him. It was maddening. He tried to treat me like a little child. And he spoke of Glenn as if he were a devil, not a man. I was shamed for him. I have never heard such words. And yet Glenn had saved his life."

"Then mustn't there be some reason?"

"I don't know."

"Even jealousy, Louise?"

"How can you say such a thing? A hired man . . . and I've only known him a day or so."

"How long did you know Glanvil?"

"Is that fair, Louise?"

"I know it is unkind. But isn't it necessary? Glanvil was strange . . . very unlike other men . . . stronger, more subtle. But Glanvil was a child compared with this new man."

"Do you think so?"

"I know it."

"Why? Have you talked with him?"

"Enough to be afraid of him."

"Afraid? You, Kate?"

"Yes."

"But what has he said or done?"

"He has turned a wild wolf into a dog to follow him around at his heels. That is something."

"Not a wolf!"

"I think it is. It never barks. You say yourself that it never wags its tail even for its master. It's a wolf, Louise. And what sort of a man is this Glenn, then? He talks like an educated person. Yet he seems to want to play the part of a hired man. Is that reasonable?"

"But what could he gain?"

"I don't know. When he talks with you . . ."

"Well?"

"Is he ever . . . just a little . . . sentimental?"

"Not the slightest trace in the world."

"I don't understand, then."

"You are wrong, Kate."

"Perhaps."

"You are very, very wrong!"

But the blind girl shook her head, and Louise, feeling her anger at this stubbornness grow, left her in haste, fearful of the words that were rising to her teeth.

She sent for Glenn at once, and, when he came, he stood before her with hat in his hand, and the sun streaming over that wrecked, disfigured face of his. And her heart was touched. And when she remembered what Jack Rutledge had said, her anger raged again.

"Mister Glenn," she said, "I have come to let you know that you are in a grave danger, I'm afraid."

"I?"

"Yes."

"Can you tell me from what?"

"From a man."

He frowned in a bewildered fashion.

"Have you no enemies?" she asked.

"I hope not."

"No one you have offended?"

"I am a little impulsive, sometimes," he said. "I may have made enemies in that way."

"But no one you have wronged?"

"I think not."

"Then I intend to tell you the name of your enemy. It is Jack Rutledge."

He fell back a step with an exclamation of dismay. "Jack Rutledge! But that's impossible!"

"Do you think so? So did I, but there is the fact. And if I were you, I should leave this part of the country . . . for a time."

"Miss Carney," he answered, "I never hunt danger, but I don't feel that I can start avoiding it. Why Rutledge should wish to harm me I cannot tell. Would he talk with you this morning?"

"He would not."

The face of Glanvil expressed the greatest solicitude. "May I ask if he has been through some great mental strain recently?"

"I think not. Why do you ask?"

"He seems very much changed."

"It is true. I thought it was on account of you, Mister Glenn."

"I hardly see how that can be . . . when we are such old friends, Miss Carney."

"Then I can't understand."

"Nor I."

"What do you intend doing?"

"Living quietly and peaceably as I have been doing before. And hoping that no trouble comes my way. But if it comes, I shall have to be ready to meet it."

After that, he left her and went back to his work, for, since Buxton was away, he had the horses to care for. But work lay light on his hands this day. There was an inner music in his brain, for he knew from the words of the girl that she must have broken with Rutledge, or at least that she had come close to it.

An hour later a shadow fell across him from the window of the barn where he was brushing down a restless colt. He whirled, with his gun gliding out brightly into his hand and covered—Rutledge himself.

The big fellow did not so much as blink at the sight of the gun. He came in slowly, and sat down on top of the grain bin. He pushed back his hat and revealed a gloomy, drawn face. He did not beat about the bush. He simply said: "I suppose you know why I've come?"

"I suppose that I know."

"You've beat me, Glanvil."

"Steady with that name. People may hear it."

"What if they do? That's a small matter to me. I'm already ruined in the eyes of the girl."

"Would you risk having her know that, too?"

"Not if I can avoid it. But I'm afraid that I'm lost. I've seen her, and then I've come to see Kate Preston."

"Ah?"

"You're interested in Kate, I see."

"Of course. What did she have to say?"

"She says that Louise is about finished with me."

"Very well, but what did she have to say about me?"

"Does that worry you?"

"No matter whether it does or not. Will you tell me?"

"I won't. The important point is Louise."

"She . . . why, you fool, she's nothing."

"What do you mean by that?"

"A dull-wit like you, dear Jack, can't be expected to understand that there's only one brain in that house, and that's the blind girl's. She does the thinking. What smashed me before? You? No, Kate Preston. I give you this as a hint. If you want to win back Louise, work at Kate. But she's too clever for you, dear Jack. I fear that you would make no progress with her. Even me she turns into a small boy."

Rutledge waved this lighter talk away. "The point is that Louise is finished with me. Your cunning lies . . . your simple, cunning lies . . . have torn me to bits, in her estimation."

"Not at all. I never criticized you. I merely put up a stone wall. You, like a jackass, dear Jack, smashed your head considerately against it. That is all that there is to it."

Rutledge flushed. "Very well," he said. "I don't intend to start a quarrel."

"You are wise in that."

"I have simply come to tell you that you have won and find out what your price is."

"I have no price, Rutledge."

The big man sighed and shook his head. "It's no

use bargaining," he said. "I know that your price will be pretty high. Well, man, I have a ranch that's free from all debt. I'm not any millionaire, but I have enough to live on. I can put on a mortgage for two thirds of the entire property. That is the limit of what I can raise, and that is the amount of money that you can have out of me. I tell you that in the first place, because I want to cut the deal short. Leave the country at once and stay away. I'll give you a series of notes. They'll be paid as they come due . . . so long as you are away."

"You discover then, dear Jack, that you cannot win while I'm at hand?"

"I cannot win. I told you that before."

"And when I give up her, what about you? Do you think that I have forgotten this?" And he ran the tip of his finger slowly over his scar.

"Money will heal that and put a mask over it."

"*Tush,* Rutledge. I intend to look at your dead body, man."

"Will you stick at that?"

"With all my might. Besides, there is Lefty Hewitt. . . ."

Rutledge grew suddenly pale. "What of him?" he asked.

"He and I have had a little talk. That is all. Is it enough?"

Apparently it was quite enough. For Rutledge rose from the grain bin and stepped back toward the door—stepped with a tense face and his hand gripping the butt of a gun that he seemed about to draw. He reached the open air, leaped sideways, and was gone. But Glanvil did not so much as follow to the door to see what was happening or whether his foe was stealing back toward him. He turned his back and went calmly on grooming the horse.

CHAPTER THIRTY-TWO

So far as Glanvil could see, there was nothing for him to do, now, but to remain quiet and let the engines, which he had started, continue to work for him. He had so far undermined the position of big Jack Rutledge with the girl that there appeared to be little left in him. More than that, the stage was perfectly set, so that when he fought and killed Rutledge, the entire community, and principally the girl herself, would be prepared to swear that it was self-defense.

This was perfection, and he decided to wait quietly through that day and allow the situation to come to a head. He spent some time comforting Mrs. Buxton before night, but, after the darkness closed down, he could hear her weeping in her room and the sound annoyed him. She was such a simple creature that, when he heard her grief, he felt as though he had misused his strength to hurt a helpless child.

He left the place and went down to the jail. There he paused to speak to Joe Conklin, and found that worthy much disturbed.

"I've left everything open for the fool," he said with great anxiety. "And now I want him to get out. It's dark now as it will be at midnight. There ain't no reason why he shouldn't slide out right away."

"What does he say?"

"He says that he doesn't understand, when I give him a hint. What more can I do?"

"He's a dull fellow," said Glanvil. "Let me go in and have a talk with him."

"If you can make sense out of him, you're a better man than me."

In the cell he found Buxton as stolidly composed as ever.

"Look here," said Glanvil briskly, "your troubles are over."

"Are they?" asked Buxton without emotion, looking gravely up at the other.

"Certainly. We have found a way of opening the doors of the jail to you, man. All you have to do is walk out."

Buxton shook his head. "Conklin has been tellin' me that," he said.

"Don't you believe him?"

"I believe him, fast enough."

"Then why don't you walk out?"

"To what?"

"To freedom . . . what else?"

"What's freedom to me?"

"Good heavens, man, what do you mean? Do you prefer to spend twenty years in prison?"

"They got beds and chuck and regular hours in a prison. I dunno that a prison would bother me much. But if I got loose, what good would it do to Martha?"

"Why, you could take care of her. For that matter, Miss Carney will see to her."

"So she would if I was in prison. Besides, if I go to prison, it won't be more'n fifteen years, they say. I'm forty-five now. That'd let me out at sixty. And my family are long livers. I'd still have ten or a dozen years left. But if I get out now, they'll chase me, most likely . . . they'll catch me. I ain't fast on my feet. I don't know the country very well, and I ain't a good enough shot to live off what I'd hunt down. Nope, I'm going to stay right here. Besides, I'm not the man who held up the stage."

"Facts don't matter. Prison does. And they have you as good as in prison now."

"I'm innocent," persisted Buxton.

"Don't be a fool! Do you think that the real crook will confess to save you?"

"I hadn't thought of that. Maybe he will . . . maybe he won't. But I'll get off in the end."

"How, man?"

"Being right is a pretty strong way to be. This here being in jail is my punishment because I started out intending to rob the stage. But they'll never keep me long in prison for something that I didn't do. There's a sort of a justice in the world, I guess."

"You guess what I don't know. You're a lost man, Buxton, unless you walk out tonight."

"I'm a lost man if I do walk out. I ain't cut out

for sleeping cold in the hills the rest of my life . . . till I'm caught again. I'll see this through. When I was a kid, I used to see that when I was right, no matter what the old man accused me of, they found out I'd been telling the truth, and that made me stronger than ever. It'll turn out that same way now."

Glanvil wondered at him. After all, there was a quiet force about this stupid fellow that bewildered him. It was a rock that he could not budge.

"Are you fixed in your mind?"

"Pretty solid, Glenn. I'm thankin' you just the same."

Glanvil left him and went to Conklin.

"The fool won't budge. He's afraid to take the chance of being hunted down."

A long silence followed this remark. Then: "That money . . . Glenn. I got it put away. I'll bring it down to you tomorrow, I guess."

"You had the right intentions," said Glanvil. "So keep the money and get that plow team. Good night." He left Conklin gaping after him and went off into the night—went with fury in his heart against Buxton, against the entire world, and chiefly against himself.

He had done worse things than this in his life, and there was no real reason why the imprisonment of Buxton for a crime that he had not committed should have weighed so heavily upon him. And yet the weight was there in spite of all his arguing with himself. And he found it a crushing burden. To smash a Rutledge was one thing; to break a Buxton was quite another. And the words of Buxton still rang at his ears: *There's a sort of justice in the world.*

After all, the man was right. There is a sort of justice in the world. Of all the brainy men who he had known, fellows of infinite experience in wrongdoing, how many had ever escaped from the penalties of their crimes? There were years of gay prosperity, to be sure, but, in the end, they were caught. Usually it was some accomplice who betrayed them. But very often the most trifling slip in the most trifling manner turned into the weapon that struck them down.

There is a sort of justice in the world.

Here was Jack Rutledge, most honest among the law-abiding. A clean-hearted man. He had committed one crime, and that was his brutal treatment of Glanvil himself. And what was his reward? The loss of the woman he loved, a broken spirit, a soul so disintegrated and cowed that the fellow hired a murderer to work for him. And that was the working out of a single taint.

He looked back upon his own life. There were a thousand clever wrongs that he had done to society. But what had been his profit from them? In the end, he had been fleeing into the mountains, whipped, beaten, pursued, outcast from mankind. And in those mountains he had found the fruit of the first really good act in his existence—his kindness to the she-wolf and to the cub.

Here was the reward of that kindness. The King slid along at his heels. And, somewhere before them, the gray mother was lurking in the woods, keeping her eyes upon them both, ready to defend them from all assailants, as she had defended them once before on the very night preceding. And more than that—for the thing that he had done to the King was that, also, which seemed to have disarmed Kate Preston against him. It was this that she could not understand. It was this that had made her say that she felt a secret beauty in his life and in his soul.

And he felt, after all, that to have won her esteem even in a partial measure was the greatest achievement of his life. As for Louise Carney, she was a light thing. She had loved him one year; the next she was ready to marry the man who had struck him down, and now, again, she had turned from her second man toward the first. There would be other turns in her life, perhaps. But the blind girl was a soul of iron, true always to herself.

All of these things poured through the thoughts of Glanvil as he strode up the slope toward the Carney place. And still, wherever he looked with sharp eyes into his past, he found the truth of what Buxton had said. There was a deep justice in the world that found out the doers of good and crushed the doers of evil. He had felt the sting of the whip once before; it never cut so deeply as these silent thoughts of his.

When he reached the barn, he went at once to the room of Mrs. Buxton and tapped at the door. She opened it presently and looked out on him with a red, swollen face.

"Well, Mister Glenn?" she said. "There ain't any news? You ain't been down to see my Harry?"

"I have been down to see him."

Her eyes lighted dimly. "What did he have to say?"

"He said a good many things. His spirits are not low."

"He's brave. But what good'll bravery do him, Mister Glenn? What good when they land him in prison?"

"They'll never land him there," said Glanvil out of a sudden conviction. "He's innocent."

"Ah, but can they be provin' that?"

"There'll be some way found."

She shook her head. "You're tryin' to cheer me up, Mister Glenn. That's kind, but it ain't true. My Harry's bound for the penitentiary."

"You must not think so. I am so sure that I'll give you my word he will be set free and all the disgrace wiped away from him."

She had begun to blubber again, the tears running fast down her face, but now she wiped away her tears. She peered out at him in wonder and happiness, saying: "Do you mean that?"

"I do," he said, "and the reason is very plain. There is a sort of justice in the world, although it often seems to be working blindly, to us."

"God bless you," she said. "I feel a mighty lot comforted, Mister Glenn."

"Trust it to me," he said. "Harry will be brought safely through."

Chapter Thirty-Three

It was still a young night, and, since he had the thought swelling in him, he decided that he would act now, because he was in a sort of terror that, by the time the morning came, the heat of the first good impulse might leave him.

He turned about, called the King to him, and started off again down the steep hill toward the town, and, as he went, he was singing lightly, happily, and hardly aware of his song.

He passed the garden, and, as he went, the King growled softly at his heels, and then ran from his side. He followed, and just beyond the garden fence he found the King, standing high, with his great forepaws on the shoulders of Kate Preston, that same strange duo that he had surprised once before. He stopped to wonder at it.

The moon had been up for sometime now, and its slant radiance fell fully on the face of the blind girl, and on her dark eyes, and on her faint smile.

He said out of a sudden strong impulse: "When I go, I must leave the King behind me, with you, Miss Preston."

She pushed the King away and came slowly to the fence. "Why would you do that?" she asked.

"Because the best half of life is lost to you, now."

"What is the best half?"

"What dogs and horses will give us, Miss Preston."

"Do you put them above people?"

"Yes, because they are all we can be sure of. Even our brothers and sisters may have secret impulses behind what they say and do for us. But when a dog licks your hand, you know what is in his heart, and when he wags his tail for you, it means only one thing."

"Yes," she said.

"And what else is there in the world that will love you simply because it serves you? Here is King Silver, who has known you only a day or so, but he would lay down his life for you. That is love, Miss Preston."

"It is, indeed. So you would leave him?"

"Yes."

"You would miss him, though?"

"I can find another."

"Like him?"

"Not exactly."

"That is the cruel thing about men," she said. "One thing will do them about as well as another. If they miss one dog, they can take another. And if they miss one woman, they can find another. They will be only a little less happy with her. Isn't that true?"

"Perhaps it is. Are women different?"

"Oh, very!"

"Tell me how."

"There are no duplications with them, you see. Perhaps it's because they don't own things . . . they are owned, instead. A man puts his wife down in the midst of a list . . . his work, his dogs, his horses, his house, his land, his friends . . . and the wife may have a high place in the list. She may even come at the head of it. But, after all, she is not all of it."

"Is that otherwise with women?"

"I think you are laughing at me. You know just as much about these matters as I do."

"I know nothing about them . . . on my word of honor. I know nothing at all about women. It is you, Miss Preston, who convinces me of that fact. But tell me honestly . . . do you think that a woman's husband can be a really engrossing part of her life . . . after the first year or so of romance . . . after the newness is worn from the polish? After the mornings are found to be as blue as ever? Doesn't the same time come for them?"

"I don't think so."

"Is a man really first in their eyes, then?"

She paused. "No," she said at last.

"You admit it after all, honestly."

"His children come first with her, I suppose. No, I'm not even sure of that." She added with her faint smile: "We are talking very intimately."

"I suppose we are. However, you shall have the King."

"I could never take him."

"Will you refuse him, then?"

"Of course."

"Why do you say of course? I could not take it for granted."

"Think a moment and you will. If I had King Silver for mine, he would be mine in name only. There cannot be two masters. He is single-hearted. He may like me well enough, but that is because he knows that he has you in the background. He can turn to you. But if he were alone with me, half the time he would have his head raised, and he would be watching the horizon to see you come back. He would be listening for your voice through the sound of mine. Oh, I am very sure of that."

"I am not. However, it shall be the way you wish."

"I could never be happy with him unless he were all mine."

"Will you use that same rule for everything?"

"Yes."

"That's rather a hard line to draw. Will you let me ask you a very blunt question?"

"I suppose blunt questions are in order."

"Tell me, Miss Preston, if you have ever cared for any man . . . in this wholehearted way?"

She paused, at that.

"You don't have to answer, of course," he hastened to qualify.

“Well,” she said, “I know you are not a chatterer. And I suppose that I may tell you. Yes!”

He gaped at her in a deep bewilderment. She had always seemed to him like a standing water, clear and calm, with all her inner nature so perfectly protected that never a breeze could have ruffled the surface.

“I should never have guessed it,” he said. “According to that, you have found the one man who can ever enter your life?”

“Yes, and lost him.”

“Ah?” he said, not a little moved. “I should like to ask you a hundred questions.”

She made another of her serious pauses. Then she astonished him more than ever by saying quietly: “I should like you to. I have never talked of this to a human soul before. And a little talk is good for one, I suppose.”

“You have never talked of it even to Miss Carney?”

“Not even to her. But there is a little poetry in men that makes them capable of understanding by imagination, I think. Then I know that what I say to you will be forgotten forever.”

“It shall be exactly as you wish, of course. Tell me one thing. The man . . .”

“Oh,” she said with perfect frankness, “you may speak right out.”

“He cared for you, of course, as you cared for him?”

"No, he detested me, I suppose."

"What a strange story!"

"Is it?"

"He never spoke to you of love?"

"He did not address more than a hundred words to me in all the time I knew him. That was only a few days."

"I can hardly understand."

"I suppose it sounds rather odd. But he came over me with a wonderful clearness the first time I met him . . . like something I could see. Yes, I seemed to have eyes, and I could see him. He had a beautiful face. I knew that before people told me about it. His voice was music. It seemed to me, always, that, when I was near him, I could look down into every crevice of his soul and see his keenness, his clever ways, his clear mind, his perfect evil."

"Evil?" cried Glanvil, once again taken back.

"Yes, his evil. There was no good in him, I think. He was one of those unspeakable creatures who go about the world preying on women."

A chill struck through the very soul of Glanvil. He had not dreamed it until this moment, but now he found himself listening to a confession that she had loved him—Glanvil himself. She who had struck him down. He grew a little dizzy at the thought. And staring at her again, the darkness seemed to leave her eyes, and the pallor left her face. She was like a white blossom, delicately touched with dawn colors, fragrant under the cold moon.

"He was all evil," she went on. "He was selfish, cruel, mean of thought, but he was also strong. And, somehow, I could see him so clearly . . . I could understand him so perfectly. I knew even what was in his mind before he spoke. I could always feel his hatred of me."

"It could not have been hatred. It might have been awe and a little fear, but not hatred. And . . . he never knew?"

"Oh, no. After all, I sent him to his death, you see. And the last he could know of me was to feel that I had loathed him and hunted him down."

"But did you do it?"

"Yes. He had tangled my dearest friend in that artful net of his. He was drawing her down. And I, seeing what he was, had to strike at him."

"He was killed, then?"

"Yes. They caught him and beat him . . . like a dog." She flushed, and her breath came hard.

"You didn't expect that, of course?"

"I thought that they would kill him . . . not humiliate him. Besides, there was something else in him that I had never dreamed of."

"And that?"

"Oh, it was the virtue of all. I said that he was perfectly evil. But I don't mean that. Because he had one saving grace that makes us almost respect the devil himself. He had courage! He had a quiet, still, perfect courage . . . like yours, Mister Glenn."

It was as though she had stabbed him with a blade of ice.

And she went on, before he could speak in answer to her: "In the end, he out-faced them all. I have heard that they flogged him until the blood leaped out from his back. But he did not murmur. He stood it until he collapsed. Afterward, while he was reeling with weakness, he took a gun and went into the house and faced them . . . and shot down the strongest of them all. Then he fled away."

"But you said that he died?"

"One of their bullets must have reached him. His horse came back to the village, after a while, and, a day or two later, they found his body more than half destroyed. He was buried decently, however. I persuaded Louise. And I had her put the right epitaph over his grave."

"And this is the man, then, whom you chose to love? This sneaking heart stealer? I can't believe it!"

"No, I suppose that you cannot. Oh, I haven't told you all of it. After you have been near us a little longer, other people will tell you more. He was a gambler and a cheat. He had a thousand vices. Why I cared for him, I cannot tell. But I did . . . with all my heart, with all my heart."

"Not a soul has guessed it, then?"

"Not a soul. I don't know what has made me talk

to you tonight. Except that from the first moment I met you, you reminded me of his dead voice and something of his ways, too. Except that you are stronger and quieter and simpler. Do you know that at first a wild, wild thought came over me?"

"And what was that?"

"That you were he. But then I found the King Silver, and I knew that I was wrong. Besides, I heard that you had gray hair and a fearfully scarred face. You see that I still am talking frankly? But it was the King who convinced me. He would never have wasted his time over a dumb beast. Never. Well, Mister Glenn, I have told you a long story and an odd one. It will be very safe with you, I know."

"On my honor."

"I do believe you."

She had spoken all this time with a perfectly controlled voice, never raised so much as a half tone above her usual calm manner; now her voice trembled a little.

"I am going inside. It is a little cold, Mister Glenn. Good night."

She turned and hurried away. It was almost, indeed, as though she were fleeing away from him, but he knew better. For it was the memory of that other man, dead to her, from which she was fleeing, and from which she would flee as long as she lived. Glanvil turned about with his brain spinning, and went slowly down the hill.

CHAPTER THIRTY-FOUR

He could not walk steadily on. Every score of steps he had to pause while a thrust of something like cold dread entered his heart and took his breath. She of all women had loved him. She of all women.

Aye, and might she not love him still? Might not one word waken that love in her once more? If he were to say Glanvil in her ear, might not all the living emotion in her rush out to him? If she had loved him once, she could love him still. Aye, perhaps she was loving this new Glanvil even now, only kept back by the feeling that her other dream was dead and buried and that half of her heart was buried with his body.

He stopped and put his hand against a slender young poplar that trembled through all its delicate body at the weight he put against it. He who loved experiments in emotion—what could he find in the world that would mean as much as to see this girl flush into life and vividness, and lift her face to him?

It was to Glanvil like the golddigger's dream of ripping the surface away from the mother lode where the wealth of a thousand kingdoms is stored in yellow gold. It was more than that. For what was gold compared with her? What was any other creature? So, breathing deep, half smiling to himself through the darkness of the night, he stumbled on, and lovely Louise Carney and her millions, now drawn so close to him, began to seem like any common creature, and all of her treasure was less than dirt to him.

For what was there in the world to compare with Kate?

So, half drunkenly, he went on. And he said to himself that already an influence was shining from her and striking across his path—striking in a gleaming radiance across his path.

For it had seemed very hard, very hard indeed, to do this thing that was before him. But now it was simplicity itself, and what he was to give away was nothing—nothing at all of value.

The sheriff's house stood at the farthest end of the street, and straight toward it he went. All the lower floor was dark except for one window, and through that window he saw the sheriff himself seated. Good fortune made him be alone. There he was a prepared prey.

He would have paused to consider, at any other time, but now with this ecstasy in him, all seemed simplicity itself. He knotted a handkerchief around the lower part of his face, again, and he dragged his hat lower across his eyes. Then he took hold on the sill of the window and worked himself up—worked himself up until with a flick of his lithe body he was through and stood in the room with his revolver covering the startled face of the sheriff. The latter had only had time to drop his newspaper, which was still fluttering away across the floor, borne on a gentle draft.

"What in heaven's name are you?" asked the sheriff.

"I'll tell you after a while," said Glanvil, and, backing across the room, he reached the door and closed it gently behind him, then turned the key in the lock.

"It's Red Wainwright," said the sheriff, leaning forward suddenly in his chair. "Well, Red, I know what you've come for."

"What have I come for, then?"

"You've come to threaten to blow my head off if I don't turn Tom loose. Is that it?"

"What if I have?"

"I know your voice, now. I wasn't sure before. Well, Red, I'll tell you what about it. If that there was a cannon instead of a Colt that you got in your hand, and if it was loaded with soup and steel instead of powder and lead, I'd tell you to blaze away and send me to hell or heaven, whichever way I'm bound to go, but I'd never bring Tom one step nearer to bein' loose!"

Glanvil nodded. He had not liked the sheriff before. He had felt that the fellow was a wholly disagreeable law hound and taker of the erring. But he changed his mind willingly now. And still it seemed to him that the sweetness and the light from Kate swept across the world and changed all men and brought out of them strange, bright deeds, like flowers on a desert.

"You're a dead man, then, Sheriff," he said with all the grimness that he could put into his voice.

"Then God help my soul . . . and God help yours, for a sneakin', murderin' skunk, Red Wainwright."

"I'll take my chances on Him."

"You're a gent that boasts about how fast you pull a gun and how straight you shoot. Gimme half of an even break and we'll try you out, Red."

"I'm not a fool, Sheriff. But suppose we switch the subject a little bit. Suppose that we turn around and take a look at something else. You won't let Tom go. Well, would you let anybody else go?"

"Not if I was to get a million dollars the next minute. I've lived square, and I'll die square. I took an oath when I landed in this here office, and I'll stick by that oath until hell freezes."

"Hell will freeze, too," said Glanvil, filled with wonder and with admiration, "when it hears that there's an honest man on earth. Hell will freeze solid to the bottom of the pit."

"You're kidding me a mite now, I suppose, Red. Well, kid away."

"Have you got prayers to say, Sheriff?"

"I ain't a prayin' man. Lemme light a cigarette. There I am. Now turn loose the lead, Wainwright. I'm finished with talkin'."

"It's about Harry Buxton."

The sheriff started. "Him? What you got to do with a simple old gent like him? What's he to you, Wainwright?"

"I was sort of tickled by the yarn he told."

"Him standin' by and seein' another gent rob the stage? That was sort of weak lyin'. And him caught with a gun and a mask on him. Well, what about it?"

"The mask that they found on him was black. The mask that the crook used that held up the stage, Sheriff, was white."

"White? White? Who ever said anything about a white mask? I don't remember that in the testimony."

"No one ever asked the question about the mask. Everyone is too happy to have a goat for this affair . . . a lamb to slaughter, you might say."

"You've picked up a fancy lingo, lately, Red. Darned if you ain't talkin' high and pretty."

"Because I'm not Red Wainwright, Sheriff."

"You ain't? By the heavens, I begin to sort of have my doubts about it, too."

"But about Buxton. You yourself, Sheriff, must have felt that it was an odd thing that a man like Buxton should commit a crime like that . . . as cool and as professional a crime as that?"

"It was smooth work. I admit that. I've laid awake and thought about it. It sure don't seem like Harry's work. I admit all of that."

"And then there is the matter of the masks?"

"Maybe . . . maybe. How come you to know what sort of a mask the crook was wearin'?"

"Very simply. I am the man who robbed the coach, you see."

"Hell and fire," muttered the sheriff. "What's happening here? Are you tryin' to make a saint out of yourself? Tryin' to beg Buxton off from jail? Tryin' to fix me on your trail?"

"I smile at that, Sheriff. The lame and the blind and the crippled like Harry Buxton are for you, but not the fellow who really steps about and uses the devil . . . as I do."

"Young feller, who might you be?"

"*Tush, tush,* Sheriff. You mustn't skip to the end of the book like that. You must read the story all the way through. What I want to know first of all is . . . are you set on sending poor fat little Harry Buxton to prison for the rest of his life while his wife dies of a broken heart . . . the little fool?"

"Martha is a pretty good woman and a darned good cook," said the sheriff reminiscently.

"Are you set on that?"

"I can't say that I'm set on nothin'. Except that I'd like to see the mask offen your face for about a second."

"Would you? It would do you no good, because you'll never have a glimpse of that face again. However, let us come back to the point of our argument. Will you tell me, finally, what I am to expect? You have plenty of influence. You could go to the people who are pressing the charges against Buxton. They have scattered, all of them. There is only the messenger who remains to be a witness against him. Suppose that you could go to the men who employed that messenger and say to them . . . 'I can give you back your money, if you will drop all of the charges against Buxton.' "

"Give back twelve thousand dollars?"

"I said that."

"By the heavens, stranger, how can little Buxton be worth that much to you or to any other man?"

"I tell you, Sheriff, I am a man to whom money is dirt."

"You're crazy, stranger."

"Not crazy, but happy . . . happy . . . happy, Sheriff." And he laughed, but all his laughter did not shake the revolver he held an iota.

The sheriff took heed of this and bit his lip.

"There would still be other little difficulties," went on Glanvil. "There would be the judge. But you know that judge very well. It would be a popular case, Sheriff. You have only to let this whole story be known . . . of how a man came to you and confessed that he committed the robbery, and that you want Buxton set free. Let that be known, and it will make you a popular man. You and the judge can have Buxton out of jail before tomorrow noon."

"Well, I suppose that we could. But that money would have to talk pretty plain first."

A packet came into the free hand of Glanvil and was dropped on the floor. "Count it," he said.

The sheriff raised it with reverence.

"If they's twelve thousand dollars in here," he said, "I don't open it even a crack without witness. And if they ain't twelve thousand dollars in here, Buxton don't get no good out of it." He added, peering at Glanvil: "That's a pretty white thing you are aimin' to do, young stranger. Pretty white, I'd tell a man."

"Thanks, Sheriff. It's amusing, anyway."

"Only . . . by the heavens, I'd like to see how you can get twelve thousand dollars' worth of use out of Harry Buxton!"

"I want to see justice done to him, Sheriff. Justice is worth more than that, eh? Just now, for instance, you wouldn't sell justice for the sake of your life."

"Well," said the sheriff, "for a crook and a stage robber, you got me beat."

"But after all," said Glanvil, "you have to admit that there is a sort of justice in the world."

"There is, son, there is. The quitters and the yaller skunks in the world is the ones that are always hollerin' about the raw deals they're gettin'. But the men are the ones that stand up and admit that they get what's comin' to 'em. Now, young feller, I'd give a good deal to know who you might be."

"You'd give a good deal to see me behind bars, old-timer, but you'll never have that privilege. Good night."

He reached the door, unlocked it, and bowed himself out.

The sheriff, for his part, did not make the slightest attempt to pursue. He sat still, rigid, like one in a trance, seeing strange things beyond this world.

"He talked slick and pretty," said the sheriff. "He talked smooth and easy. He didn't have no trouble with his words." He closed his eyes and contracted his brows. "He talked," said the sheriff in a whisper to himself, "mighty like somebody that I've heard talk before. Who might that've been? Who might that've been? Oh," groaned the sheriff, rising and pacing the floor back and forth, "what a blind fool I am. Why can't I see? I know his voice easy and plain as I know my own."

Up and down that floor he paced, and up and down it, through a long hour. He heard the voice of his wife, but he paced on.

"Are you comin' upstairs to bed this here minute?"

Who could think with such a wail in one's ears? The sheriff rushed to the door and cast it open in a frenzy of rage. "Darn it!" he shouted. "Leave a man be! You'd hang an innocent man for the sake of five minutes of sleep. Lemme be! Lemme be!"

There began a jangling torrent of words in

answer, but the sheriff strode back into the room, breathing hard, triumphant. About once a month he raised his voice in that house, and about once a month he was heard. Those days were set apart from all the rest—strenuous but joyful.

And now, in the midst of his anger, the memory for which he had been struggling came sweetly and suddenly back upon him. There was another man in the town who spoke good English, English as fine as that of Jack Rutledge, even. And this man was of the size of him who wore the mask. It was, in fact, none other than that mysterious new hired man on the Carney place, he who had dared to cross the sheriff's potent self not long before. He, then, was the real robber of the stage!

The sheriff stretched out his long arms and smote his hands together. Not the joy of Glanvil hurrying down the mountain was greater than the joy of the sheriff on the man trail. Much was still to be learned, and much was still to be kept secret. But the certainty of victory was big in the sheriff's heart.

CHAPTER THIRTY-FIVE

The sun was halfway up the sky of the next morning when Jack Rutledge stood before the lady of his love at the end of his last appeal.

"What I've come to ask you, Louise," he said, "is whether or not I can hope for anything. Not because of what I said in the last interview we had together, but because of everything that went before."

"It's everything that went before that makes this last talk so bad," she answered coldly. "Because it looks, Jack, as though you could keep on for many years playing the part of the virtuous man, and not being one. And, in fact, I'm afraid of you. I thought you were a simple person . . . like me. But I've found that you are not. I've found that you are very far from simple. There's malice and hate under that bluff exterior of yours."

"Is that all?" he said.

"I've wanted to speak calmly and quietly," said the girl. "But I can't. I'm sorry . . . but I can't. Oh, Jack, when you rushed in between me and the man I loved, I thought you came like a selfless hero. Not like this thing that I find you are."

"You will never forgive me?" he asked.

"Never!"

"If there were ever any love for me in your heart . . ."

“Oh, there was never a great deal. But I was sorry for you and I thought . . .”

“Well,” he said sadly, “after all, he was right. He was always right.”

“Who was right?”

“Glanvil.”

“You promised me that I should never hear that name again.”

“Did I promise that?” he asked her without heat. “Why, my dear, I might as well have promised that you would not hear the wind or the rain. However, that was what he said . . . that you only pitied me. First it made me rage . . . then it made me sad . . . and I began to guess that he might have seen the truth more clearly than I.”

“I don’t understand all of this. When could you have talked to Winsor Glanvil about such a thing?”

“My dear, that is what I am about to explain. This precious fellow of yours . . . this noble heart . . . this life saver . . . this John Glenn . . .”

“I shall not stay to hear you talk any longer!” she exclaimed with dignity. “I have not come to listen to scandal-mongering.”

“That becomes you,” he said dispassionately. “I like to see you stand so stiff and so straight.”

She could only wonder at him. He stood before her with a lean, haggard face, his eyes pouched beneath with purple, his head sunk between his shoulders. He had aged; he had grown feeble, and his big hands hung loosely at his sides.

"If my love for you has died," said the girl, "it is not hard to see that yours went out at the same time."

He shook his head, watching her with a sick smile. "My love for you will last till I am dead," he answered her. "But just now, I'm sick of living. I'm ready to die. And I think that I shall die before the day is ended . . . unless John Glenn shoots slower and less straight than I think he does. However, I simply see what a hopeless mess I am in. There is no use in struggling. I'm beaten. I'm down and smashed. Well . . . there's an end of that. I don't whine. I thought, three days ago, that I was just around the corner from heaven, and then Glenn came. I suppose you and he will probably be married, after I'm gone?"

She flushed and set her teeth. "Married?" she said. "With my serving man? How else will you be able to insult me, Jack, before you have decided to leave me?"

"Don't you see?" he explained in his heavy, dull voice. "It isn't Glenn. That's not the name."

"What do you mean?"

"All the rot about the saving of my life . . . surely you must have guessed that there was something wrong in that. Or did you really think that I could be such an ungrateful cur? No, no, Louise, it's not Glenn. That's not the name, but one very like it."

"What do you mean, Jack?" she asked him,

panting with something between horror and hope and fear.

"Oh, yes, you've guessed it at last. Glanvil . . . it's Glanvil again, Louise. Come back from the dead in the most romantic fashion imaginable."

"It's Winsor Glanvil come back?" she gasped out. "No, I can't believe it!"

"Send for him. Bring him up here."

"You want him because you want to spring on him with your strength, Jack. . . ."

"I'll not touch him. My word for that. I'll do him no harm."

She ran into the house and sent the cook scurrying down the hill to the barn. Then she came back and walked up and down in the garden with Rutledge. Still she was not satisfied. She sent for Kate Preston, and the blind girl hurried out to her.

"We have just heard a strange rumor," said Louise Carney, "about my new man . . . Glenn."

"It's something wrong? It is something bad?" asked Kate.

"You've guessed that, then?"

"I don't know," she said, and she clasped her hands together.

"Kate, you look sick."

"I . . . I have had a bad headache. I'm quite all right."

"I want you to watch his words while I confront him with an unspeakable thing that I have just heard."

"I shall watch."

"You, Jack, stand there, if you please. Oh, if this is true."

"I thought," said Rutledge, "that you would be glad."

"Glad?" she said, and she flashed a furious glance at him. "A man who tried to . . . to marry my money?"

"What are you talking of? What are you talking of, Louise?"

"It's too strange, too horrible . . . wait a moment, and then you'll hear. Now he's coming. And taking his time. There is something about his walk that is the same, now that I look at him more closely. There is something about the way he carried his head that is the same."

The blind girl pressed closer. "The same as who?" she asked huskily.

"I mustn't say . . . yet. Wait until he comes."

So Glanvil came into the garden and looked at the stern, quivering face of Louise Carney and the gloomy frown of Rutledge and the great, staring eyes of the blind girl. He knew at once what sort of a crisis was before him.

"It is about you . . . Jack Rutledge has been here to talk to me about you, this morning . . . Mister Glenn."

Glenn bowed to them both. "Mister Rutledge is very kind," he said.

"And he tells me a strange thing that cannot be

believed unless you confirm it with your own lips."

"Indeed?"

"Mister Glenn, I want to tell you that nearly a year ago a creature came to this house . . . a typical fortune hunter . . . a smooth-tongued liar . . . a deceiver . . . a practiced love-maker. And he made a fool of me. I thought I loved him and I promised to marry him. At the last minute it was discovered that the creature was a fraud of the rankest kind. I had eloped with him . . . they only stopped us at the minister's. And since that time I have been living in a perfect hell of criticism. Oh, I have been sick with it all. Do you know what else I have to say?"

"I begin to guess."

"Then it is true. You are Winsor Glanvil?"

There was a little gasping cry, but no one turned.

"It is true," said Glanvil. "I only wished to keep the false name until I saw that I had broken matters between you and Rutledge. But now that that's done . . . why, I wash my hands of you, my dear."

"You are Glanvil?" cried the girl.

"I am Winsor Terence Glanvil, very much at your service. You owe equal thanks to Rutledge and to me. He kept you from marrying a rascal. I kept you from marrying a fool, which would have been a much worse fate. Kate!"

He leaped to her and caught her as she swayed.

Then Rutledge brushed him aside, picked the slender body out of his arms, and carried the girl into the house.

"What have you done to her?" asked Louise Carney. "Dear God, if you have been tampering with *her* soul, I'll have you. . . ."

He raised his hand. "At present," he said, "I feel hardly fit to take her name in my mouth. Are you more qualified?"

"This, at least," said the girl, "is the last time that you and I need to lay eyes upon one another. It is the very last day."

"The very last, indeed. I shall be off your place in an hour."

In place of answering, she turned her back on him and hurried into the house, head down. At the door she met big Rutledge coming out. She hesitated, then laid a hand on his arm. "I wronged you a great deal, Jack," she said. "I accused you. . . ."

"Hush," he said. "All that you thought was less than the truth. Let me tell you the rest of that, so that you can truly despise me. Louise, I went so far as to hire a murderer to take the life of that demi-devil."

"Jack!"

"That is the truth. My man failed. Everyone, I suppose, fails when they stand before him. However . . ." He did not complete the sentence but left the house at once and went to his horse.

Louise Carney, having disappeared into the

house, changed her mind and jerked the door open again. But as she did so, and, even as she called his name again, she saw him spur his horse, a towering black charger, down the hill. And her call was lost in the rush and roar of the hoof beats.

Down the hill he swept and reached the hotel with its broad, time-yellowed verandah that had once been shining with white paint. He called a boy to him, who stood by wiggling his toes in the hot dust and looking up the heaving sides of the great black horse.

"Here's fifty cents for you, young one," said Rutledge. "Go up the hill to the Carney place. Do you know the stranger?"

"John Glenn? Sure, we all know him, all right."

"Tell him that I'm waiting for him, here, with plenty of men around to watch the two of us."

The boy stared a moment, as though drinking in the full significance behind these words. Then he whirled and bolted up the street and up the hill.

Chapter Thirty-Six

Harry Buxton sat enthroned. The stove radiated heat nearby. His wife was bustling eagerly around him. And at the window leaned the graceful form and the hideous face of Glanvil.

"How it happened," said Buxton, "I dunno. All I know is that the sheriff himself come to me in my cell.

" 'Harry,' says he, 'are you feeling fit to walk around this morning?'

" 'Fit to walk around this here cell, anyway,' says I.

" 'Old son,' says he, 'you're free. You're fixed up with the judge and the gent that says that he done the robbery. He come in and turned in all the money that was lost. The judge says that you can vamoose so long as we have you handy to put our hands on. And I guess that you ain't a very roving nacher.'

" 'Sheriff,' says I, 'I hate travel.'

"And here I am. That's all that I know. They say that the gent come down with a mask on and stuck up the sheriff and give up the money and made him promise to get me out of the jail. And there you are. There's a sort of justice in this little old world. They don't take innocent men. Not nowadays."

There was a tap at the door. Mrs. Buxton opened it.

"Mister Glenn here?" asked a boy's voice.

"I'm here, son."

"There's big Jack Rutledge down in town on the hotel porch. He say that he's waitin' for you. And he says that there's plenty of folks standing by to watch the two of you . . . and I dunno what he means, but that's what he says for me to tell you."

"What did he give you?"

"Fifty cents, mister. I didn't ask for it."

"Here's a dollar. Go back and tell him that I'm coming. In five minutes I'll be there."

So the youngster fled, and Glanvil left the room. He left a heavy silence behind him.

"What does that mean, Martha?" asked Harry Buxton, his little eyes shining wide.

"Trouble," she whispered, "and terrible trouble if it's between Rutledge and him."

"I wonder does the sheriff know?"

"Harry, Harry, you keep out of it!"

"There's some sort of justice . . . and the sheriff had ought to know about this here message. I'm gonna beat across the lot and tell him."

He leaped up and dashed from the barn, hatless, and raced away as fast as his short legs could carry him. He found the sheriff behind his house, busy saddling a horse in front of his barn.

"Hey!" he called.

"Are you hurryin' back to jail?" asked the sheriff, grinning.

"There's hell a-popping. Rutledge has sent for John Glenn and told him that they's plenty of folks standing by to watch the two of them. Watch them do what, I'd like to know. Fight, I'd say. And fight about what? I dunno."

The sheriff turned and gave the other one an eloquent glance. Then he leaped into the saddle without a word and raced off up the street at the full speed of his horse.

But in the meantime, Glanvil had long since left the barn and strode down the hill with King Silver at his heels. Straight down the street he went, and not a dog dared appear to snarl at the black monster or the monster's master.

He went shyly, lightly. Yonder, standing before the verandah of the hotel, which was littered with idlers, stood the great form of Jack Rutledge. He remembered how, on a day, he had sat at a window at that same hotel and looked down and across the street at the monstrous form of the man with Paul Santelle at his shoulder, telling the formidable story of a formidable man. Things had changed since then. The dimensions of Rutledge had shrunk. And Glanvil himself had grown.

In the shadow beside him, it seemed that the great form of Hector Glanvil, that fearless man, was striding. But the life of Hector had been pure and free from blame. What could be said of his own existence?

He hardly knew what to think of himself. At least, he would tell himself no comforting lies. He had been like a fox, at the first, a sneaking thief of things he did not work for. Then he had turned into a wolf, furious and strong and eager to prey on others.

There was something new in him, now. Here he had before him the completion of his work. He had wrecked one part of the life of this Jack Rutledge. The taking of the life itself remained for the making of a full and a perfect revenge. And yet, as he drew nearer to the big man, he felt no surge of fury in his heart, no lust to destroy.

Now he was close. He paused, with the sun slanting across his face and the dreadful scar glinting like polished silver.

"Rutledge," he said, "I'm willing to call quits if you say the word."

"Call quits?" cried Rutledge. "Man, there's nothing left me worth living for. Perhaps there'll be something worth dying for. Defend yourself, Glanvil!" And he snatched at his gun.

As well might the house dog fat with lazy life attempt to outspeed the leap of the wolf. The gun of Glanvil spoke before that of the mountaineer was clear of the holster. He sagged at the knees. From his hand his Colt dropped and was buried in the deep dust. Then he himself fell face forward.

A thin white cloud puffed up around him. But he did not stir.

There was a sudden shouting. And men leaped from the verandah and ran toward the prostrate figure. But Glanvil was calmly mounting the big black horse and galloping away toward safety down the street.

Behind him came the sheriff with a rush. But the horseflesh that the sheriff bestrode would never overtake Rutledge's big black, and the sheriff knew it. He paused, therefore, to make out the extent of the damage done to Rutledge. It was far less than had seemed. The head of Rutledge had swayed back because the bullet had glanced across his forehead, turned halfway from his foe as he jerked at his own gun to fire. The pellet had furrowed the bone deep, but Jack Rutledge was both breathing and groaning when the sheriff leaned above him.

He waited to learn no more. After all, it was not a murderer or a gunfighter who he was to pursue, but only a thief, and that took half of the charm from his work. A thief, and one who had voluntarily given back his gains.

Altogether, it was not nearly so important a trail as he had expected. Moreover, the very proof of the theft was still dim and distant. He could say only one thing—that he thought he had recognized in the voice of the masked man who had held him up the night before, the voice of

Glenn—or Glanvil. Both names seemed to be on the tongues of people now. That would be most shadowy stuff to put before a judge and a jury.

However he rode on, and picked up two able assistants to help him in the trailing. That trail led deep into the woods, and through the mountains, at first. Shortly after noon they lost it altogether. The afternoon was half worn away when they picked it up again after much cutting for sign, and then they found to their surprise that the tracks headed back for the town.

Straight back they went, with the sheriff following in wonder and disbelief. Straight back, and through the gathering dusk he and his men followed the sign—easily legible in the wet dirt—across the outskirts of the town, and then up the hill toward the Carney house.

A scant hundred yards away the sheriff and the others dismounted, threw their reins, and stole forward.

"For he's sure to be here," said the sheriff. "There ain't a chance that he got here more'n a half hour ahead of us. Maybe he's come back for money. A gent that's wanderin' needs the coin."

They were nearly at the house when the sound of voices led them around to the garden hedge. The sheriff walked first, lightly, for it was a man's voice that he heard. And when he came in view of the garden he saw Kate Preston in the arms of the man with the scarred face, her blind eyes lifted to him, and such perfect happiness written in her face that the sheriff marveled.

He heard the fugitive say: "I remembered what Buxton said . . . there's some justice in the world. And I decided to take my medicine. And besides, to have one sight of you, dear, was worth all of the danger."

Her voice trembled in such a way that the sheriff's weak heart trembled, also.

"But if they take you, Winsor?"

"I intend that they shall. And, besides, I have some debts to pay, some money that's got to be returned to various parties in order to square my account with the world. I've seen the worst that they can do to a man, and I'm not afraid of it. I carry with me the sign of their strength. Put up your hand, dear."

She raised her hand, and he forced the soft fingertips over the ragged scar that ran down his face—until she shuddered and shrank from it.

"It's as though I could feel my own flesh torn. Oh, horrible," she said. "Why did you make me do it?"

"Because, after all, we must both remember. It is a sign. . . ."

"Of horrible brutality!"

"Of justice, Kate," he said.

And just then the King Silver came to join the happy pair.

Acknowledgments

"Mountain Made" by George Owen Baxter first appeared as a six-part serial in Street & Smith's *Western Story Magazine* (12/13/24–1/17/25). Acknowledgment is made to Condé Nast Publications, Inc., for their co-operation.

About the Author

Max Brand is the best-known pen name of Frederick Faust, creator of Dr. Kildare, Destry, and many other fictional characters popular with readers and viewers worldwide. Faust wrote for a variety of audiences in many genres. His enormous output, totaling approximately thirty million words or the equivalent of five hundred thirty ordinary books, covered nearly every field: crime, fantasy, historical romance, espionage, Westerns, science fiction, adventure, animal stories, love, war, and fashionable society, big business and big medicine. Eighty motion pictures have been based on his work along with many radio and television programs. For good measure he also published four volumes of poetry. Perhaps no other author has reached more people in more different ways.

Born in Seattle in 1892, orphaned early, Faust grew up in the rural San Joaquin Valley of California. At Berkeley he became a student rebel and one-man literary movement, contributing prodigiously to all campus publications. Denied a degree because of unconventional conduct, he embarked on a series of adventures culminating in New York City where, after a period of near starvation, he received simultaneous recognition as a serious poet and successful author of fiction. Later, he traveled widely, making his home in New York, then in Florence, and finally in Los Angeles.

Once the United States entered the Second World War, Faust abandoned his lucrative writing career and his work as a screenwriter to serve as a war correspondent with the infantry in Italy, despite his fifty-one years and a bad heart. He was killed during a night attack on a hilltop village held by the German army. New books based on magazine serials or unpublished manuscripts or restored versions continue to appear so that, alive or dead, he has averaged a new book every four months for seventy-five years. Beyond this, some work by him is newly reprinted every week of every year in one or another format somewhere in the world. A great deal more about this author and his work can be found in *The Max Brand Companion* (Greenwood Press, 1997) edited by Jon Tuska and Vicki Piekarski. His Website is www.MaxBrandOnline.com.

Center Point Large Print
600 Brooks Road / PO Box 1
Thorndike, ME 04986-0001 USA

(207) 568-3717

US & Canada:
1 800 929-9108
www.centerpointlargeprint.com